Dave Hill is an author and journalist who has written books on football, pop music and politics, and who has contributed to many national newspapers, in particular the *Guardian*. His debut novel, *Dad's Life*, was a bestseller. He lives in east London with his wife and his six children.

# man alive

## DAVE HILL

review

First published in 2004
by REVIEW

An imprint of Headline Book Publishing

10 9 8 7 6 5 4 3 2 1

ISBN 0 7553 0190 0

Typeset in Baskerville by Avon DataSet Ltd,
Bidford-on-Avon, Warwickshire

Printed and bound in Great Britain by
Clays Ltd, St Ives plc

HEADLINE BOOK PUBLISHING
A division of Hodder Headline
338 Euston Road
London NW1 3BH

www.headline.co.uk
www.hodderheadline.com

For Laura, Frankie, Nat, Dolores, Conall and Orla.

# ACKNOWLEDGEMENTS

Sincere thanks to . . .

My editor, Martin Fletcher, especially for his merciful attitude to deadline surfing.

Martin's assistant, Catherine Cobain, and everyone else at Headline who has worked on *Man Alive*.

Lucy Ramsey, award-winning publicist.

The charity Bliss (www.bliss.org.uk) for insights into certain neonatal matters.

Brook Advisory which gave its blessing for me to reproduce passages from its website (www.brook.org.uk)

Maria Gatward, executive development consultant to The *Guardian* among others, who introduced me to the fascinating world of Myers-Briggs.

My agent Sara Fisher, brilliant as ever.

Sheila Fitzsimons, dearest *bean an tí*.

part one: spring

# chapter 1

'Time to move on,' said Derek Hawker as he plucked the mangled body of a dead wasp from his dashboard. He used a Flash antibacterial wet wipe, a pack of which was in his glove compartment at all times. Derek wasn't speaking to the dead wasp – things hadn't got to that stage yet. He was speaking to himself as had become his habit lately: plotting his way forward to a new life.

Cradling the ex-wasp in its fragrance-free damp shroud, Derek eased through the door of his Lexus – the excellent RX300 SE–L in Stafford Blue – and strove to prick some unfamiliar bubbles of self-doubt. It was a bright spring morning: a Monday morning, the last before Easter. On his way to work, driving from his home in the nearby village of Brayston with *The Best of Blondie* a-bopping on the 6 CD music system, Derek had felt sun-kissed and serene, a high flier on freedom highway. But then he'd rolled the sun-roof open and the wasp had wafted in to buzz around his ears with such demented rage that by the time Derek had made it to his reserved parking bay his man-of-destiny vibrations were disturbed. He had been briefly fortified by then smearing the invader – one precision strike with his rolled-up *Daily Mail* and the beast had buzzed no more – but that had only got him thinking about his daughter Charlotte and what she would have said if she'd been there.

'You enjoyed that, didn't you?'

'What do you mean, "enjoyed"?'

'Don't go all defensive. Why be ashamed of a bit of casual killing?'

'I'm not ashamed, Charlotte. And I don't do defensive.'

'You ought to be ashamed. At this time of year that was probably a queen wasp, preparing for nest building. But don't let it worry you.'

'Wasps are unpleasant creatures, Charlotte. They're pointless and erratic and they sting.'

'So?'

'So I don't like getting stung!'

'They only sting if they're attacked – you told me that yourself when I was little. It's the other things about them you don't like.'

'And what's that supposed to mean?'

'It means you get all stressed by things you can't control.'

'Where do you pick up this rubbish?'

'I've got a brain, you know. And many years' experience of you.'

'And I haven't got a brain, right?'

'Let's just say I'd rather be a wasp than a sheep – like those dopey shoppers in your lovely mall.'

'It's not a mall, Charlotte darling. It's an eco-friendly leisure destination.'

'Oh, exc-use me.'

'The difference is significant, you know.'

'Of course it is, dear Daddy. Silly me.'

Derek shook his head as if to banish Charlotte from it – her voice, cool and appraising, her manner ever questioning – and began walking towards the rubbish bin that stood close by. He'd only gone three paces when from the front seat of the car his mobile summoned him. Derek decided to ignore it – this was just the sort of moment Matthew would call. He could imagine their exchange only too well.

'Hi, Dad! How's Hertfordshire?'

'Hello, Matthew. It's to the north of London, as usual. And full of bloody wasps.'

'Hey! And still not even Easter!'

'I just killed one, actually. Nasty little sod.'

'That's fine. I'm sure it was in self-defence. And a preemptive purge of surplus aggression is no bad way to start the week!'

'Yep, well . . .'

'And let's face it, Dad, wasps are unpleasant creatures. They're pointless and erratic and they sting.'

'Matthew, I know this. What do you want?'

'Well, Dad, it's Monday evening here in Sydney . . .'

'I know this too. Cut to the chase, Matthew, please!'

'. . . and I was thinking, Dad, about your Myers-Briggs type . . .'

'*Oh, Matthew, give me a break . . .*'

'*I'm pretty sure you're ENTJ. Your energy comes from interaction with others, you're a big picture dude, losing control and sloppy attitudes in others piss you off.*'

'*Probably, Matthew, yes.*'

'*Dad, I wish you'd do the questionnaire I sent you. You might learn something useful. More and more executives recognise psychometric testing as a valuable personal development tool.*'

'*Yeah, maybe, Matthew. How's, ah, Hayley?*'

'*Hayley's cool. Erogenous Tableware is the coming thing!*'

'*It would be.*'

'*That's not very original, Dad.*'

'*It was the best I could come up with. Send her my best wishes.*'

'*I will. I'd like you to meet her, Dad. We're thinking of coming over maybe later this year. What do you think?*'

'*Matthew, I'd love to see you both, but, you know . . .*'

'*Dad? I have something to say to you.*'

'*You can try . . .*'

'*You sound more tense than usual lately – lacking your usual wit and energy . . .*'

'*Oh?*'

'*Dad, are you succumbing to emotional outbursts? Or getting too caught up in detail? These are typical signs that your type is under stress . . .*'

'*Sorry, Matthew. Didn't catch that. You're breaking up a bit . . .*'

'*This is a difficult time for you, Dad, I understand . . .*'

*'Matthew, I'm all right . . .'*

*'. . . what with the Mum thing and the time of life you're at.'*

*'Static's terrible this end, Matthew. Go to go now. Bye.'*

Derek disposed of wasp and wet wipe with a shiver that wasn't triggered by the deceptively crisp breeze. Why wouldn't Matthew leave 'the Mum thing' alone? Denise was away for a few months, that was all. It happened. Life goes on.

Returning to his car Derek checked his mobile and found Matthew hadn't called but he had been left a message by his colleague Geoff.

R U REVVED?

'Cheeky git,' Derek said. He switched the mobile off and placed it in his briefcase with the death-soiled *Daily Mail*. He refiled *The Best of Blondie* in its allotted space between *Abba: Greatest Hits* and Elton's *Goodbye Yellow Brick Road*. Finally, he got out of the Lexus again and stood gazing for a minute at the magnificent vista to his right. It *was* more than a shopping mall, of course. It was the realisation of a dream Derek had had back when he'd been nearer forty than fifty, a dream in which the joys of shopping and tranquillity of nature could be seamlessly and stylishly combined. Derek had envisaged this peerless aggregation of quality retail outlets set among orna-mental ponds and miniature jetties, cascading water features and exotic glasshoused plants. It was Derek who had imagined the great atrium entrance with its glimmering arced masthead. *Welcome To Harboreta*, it announced. It was the towering achievement of his career so far.

At last, Derek turned away. He checked his Omega Constellation. It told him it was 8.20 a.m. 'Time to move on,' Derek repeated to a small flowering shrub and paced vigorously towards the low-level hi-tech building to his left that housed the Head Office suite of Quintessential Futures plc.

'Hi, Sophie.'

'Hi, Derek.'

'Boss is expecting me.'

'She'll be a few minutes, Derek. Shall I buzz you when she's free?'

'Yes please. You're looking nice today.'

'Thank you!'

She chirruped the word 'you' with the pert mock-primness she always affected for their flirtation ritual. When Sophie had first become Amelia Hardwick's PA, Derek had partaken cheerfully in these set pieces. Today, though – and not for the first time lately – he and Sophie's exchange – his mock-confidentiality, her *faux* flushing response – deflated him vaguely. He felt trapped in the relationship, the prisoner of a convention that now struck him as slightly foolish for a man of his status and age. It was not a situation that appealed.

Sophie took a call – 'Quintessential Futures! Sophie speaking!' – and Derek hurried to his office, hoping Geoff had not come in early too. He liked Geoff – liked him a lot in a competitive sort of way – but he wasn't in the mood for any rakish repartee about weekend motoring adventures or new novelty ties; especially as Derek knew it would only be a cover for further truffling by Geoff after what Derek's meeting with Amelia was for. To 'take stock' was all Derek had revealed; though God knows why he'd even mentioned it. To taunt Geoff and tantalise him? Probably. To make it harder to back out? Possibly that too.

Passing the office of 'Geoffrey Lunt – Property Resources' Derek glanced through its glass door and was relieved to see that no one was inside. Once within his own office he checked his appearance in the full-length mirror he'd had fitted to the wall when he'd moved in: the white shirt he'd ironed first thing that morning; his tie, a glimmering light grey that picked out matching flecks on his dark worsted trousers; a navy Boden blazer with jetted side pockets and a centre vent. The blazer worried Derek, slightly. He wasn't sure what signals it sent. Was it too snappy or too staid? On a man of fifty-one, did it suggest a sorry case of mutton dressed as lamb?

'Marshal your resources,' he murmured under his breath, and from an 'at ease' stance deliberately assessed his strengths: his height, five feet eleven, which could pass for six on a good day; his well-cut hair, now nearly as silver as it was dark but still bristle thick; blue eyes that could get by without the long-sight glasses he'd had to purchase three years back; a firm, determined mouth; a fairly handsome face; a nose that had never once made people laugh. True, there was no more concealing the spread of flesh round his middle. But Derek was reconciled to this, seeing it now as an expansion to be managed rather than a crisis to be fought. He was confident he had gone past that stage.

Derek took pride in believing that the same robust realism informed everything he thought and did. After some days of cogitation he believed he saw his situation clearly. Despite being of an age when an executive's stock can begin to fall, he knew he was too highly valued to be quietly moved aside or kicked upstairs. Derek's trademark talent, though, was for seeing what lay ahead and driving projects towards it and that was why he'd asked to meet Amelia today. His hunger for innovation, his appetite for change . . . since he'd stepped back from Harboreta these urges had gone unsatisfied. Derek no longer felt energised – no longer truly alive.

From his desk drawer Derek took a set of nail clippers and cut short the rogue ambitions of a lurking nostril hair. Then his intercom buzzed and Sophie's voice came to him in tinny upsong. 'Derek? Amelia can see you now?'

'OK. On my way.'

Retracing his earlier steps he returned to Sophie's desk. Amelia waited at her elbow. 'Come in, Derek,' she said neutrally and swivelled towards her lair. Derek followed and as he did so was ambushed by awful thoughts. What if I break wind loudly? What if I sneeze all·over her?

What if my trouser button pops off suddenly? His horror at the prospect of such embarrassments – *Jesus Christ, what if?* – drew a low cry of pain, causing Amelia to look over her shoulder.

'Are you all right?' she asked.

'Pardon me,' said Derek, pressing a hand to his chest. 'Touch of heartburn. Don't know why.'

Amelia poked in her handbag, which squatted bulbous on her desk. She tossed him a pack of Rennies. 'So, Derek,' she said as he bent to pick them off the floor. 'About your future . . .'

She left a silence there, the type Derek usually filled with concise evaluations, can-do conclusions and flashes of comedy. This time, though, his mind ran slightly wild. How old was Amelia, he wondered? A bit older or a bit younger than he was? She was unmarried, he knew that, and lived alone; not a handsome woman, but clever, charismatic and, as Geoff often ruefully said, always a step ahead. Her eyebrows arched in expectation. At last, Derek said, 'Amelia, I've decided to resign.'

There was a moment's silence. 'I see,' Amelia said. Derek tensed for an expansion of this response but none came. Instead, Amelia nodded towards a corner of her office where a new soft-seating niche had been installed, a deep floret of upholstery in dusky pink. 'Let's get a bit more comfortable, shall we?'

She rose and click-clacked over to it on heavy heels. Again, Derek followed her, popping a Rennie pointlessly into his mouth. Amelia sat and he took his place across from her. Engulfed by billowing folds he was struck by how inhibiting intimacy could be.

'How are things with Denise?' Amelia asked.

'They're fine,' Derek lied.

'How long has she been in China now? Two months? Three?'

'A little over two.'

'Teaching English, yes?'

'That's right. And travelling.'

Derek maintained a level tone but juddered inwardly. Amelia wasn't meant to know about this. Geoff must have been blabbing: not to Amelia directly, but probably to Sophie who would have done the rest.

'Your children are grown up now, aren't they, Derek?'

'So they tell me.' It was a poor bid for empathy. Amelia had no kids; no family of any kind as far as anybody knew.

'And they've left home?' Amelia continued.

'Well, Charlotte is at university in London – her second year. She's got a place in ... it's, ah, near Clapham.'

'Very nice,' Amelia said. 'Can't be cheap round there.'

'It's in a shared house, so that helps.'

'What's she studying?'

'Biology and psychology – cutting edge stuff, apparently. She's nineteen now; twenty in August.'

'Impressive. And how about your son?'

'Matthew? He's twenty-two and in Australia – Sydney.'

'Doing?'

'Working for a firm of management consultants; specialising in executive development, would you believe.'

'Two high flyers, then!' Amelia's tone was admiring. With a tilt of her head she invited Derek to express paternal pride.

'You could say that,' he replied.

Derek respected Amelia: she was smart and straight-forward and had always allowed him the leeway he needed to thrive. He also liked her – she knew how to take a joke. But this was foreign to him, the two of them discussing personal matters in this way. She smiled and Derek saw that a speck of lipstick had strayed on to one of her front teeth. He tried not to stare at it as she said, 'Derek, you must know that QF doesn't want to lose you. You've done so much outstanding work – especially, of course, with Harboreta. You don't need me to tell you how well respected you are or how badly we need your sort of insights, going forward. There aren't many like you around, you know: executives with your drive, your passion; your experience; your knack for reading the runes.'

She sat a little straighter, letting her eulogy sink in.

'That's very flattering, Amelia.'

'So what's behind this, Derek? Have you had a better offer? Is that the problem here?'

'There is no problem, really. It's simply that I need a change.'

'Of company? Of career? Forgive me, I shouldn't pry.'

'I'm going to set up my own business.'

'Oh, I *see*,' Amelia said. 'That's very bold.'

'For a man of my age, you mean?'

'No, Derek, that isn't what I meant!'

They both laughed: time's remorseless passage was their common ground for joshing.

'What sort of business?' Amelia enquired.

'Oh, consultant, fixer, adviser, predictor. You know the sort of thing. High street chains needing a tweak, independents stretching the envelope. And there's the international dimension, of course – all those global wide boys building plazas and gallerias in Bucharest and Bangkok. I've put out a few feelers. But I'm going to set out slowly. To start with it'll be just me, based at home.'

He felt a little calmer now, finding asylum in jargon.

'Would more money help?' Amelia asked. 'Help persuade you to stay, I mean?'

'It's not about money,' Derek replied. 'It's about needing a new challenge. Since Harboreta got up and running, well . . . I feel my work here is done . . .' He dried up. It felt strange. Even to him his explanation suddenly lacked conviction, as if one key ingredient had inexplicably gone missing. Amelia waited. Derek said, 'The point is, when I came here, eight years or so ago, the company lacked direction. It was sound enough but it was tired and had no vision . . .'

'True, very true,' Amelia said. She'd been brought in a year or two after Derek's arrival and quickly identified him as a major QF strength.

'I like to think,' said Derek, 'that I turned my side of

the operation round. I made a few mistakes but I was bold and energetic and it worked.'

'True again,' Amelia said.

'But this last year or so...' Derek faltered again. Speaking off the cuff was one thing, but this was speaking from the heart. 'I sort of feel... I've lost the will to go for it. The hunger's gone – the *passion*. It's not that I'm not interested. It's not that I don't care. But somehow it doesn't *matter* to me in the same way any more and ... and to me that just feels wrong.'

This time Amelia said nothing. She nodded, though, and Derek struggled on. 'I need something different,' he said, a little helplessly. 'Something I can build with my own hands. I'm not explaining very well. Do you know what I mean?'

Amelia looked him over. 'Yes, yes,' she said reflectively. 'I think I do. It's such a big thing, isn't it? Getting our priorities in order, deciding what it is we really want. So many of us never find the answers.'

'And some of us find we need new ones,' Derek replied.

Back in his parking bay Derek punched in a stored number in his mobile and mentally composed the message he presumed he'd have to leave. When Charlotte's voice said 'Hello, Dad' he was surprised – she hardly ever had the bloody thing switched on.

'Hello, Charlotte. Just wondered how you were.'

'I'm very well, thank you.'

'I'd like to come and see you.'

'Oh. All right.' There was a pause. 'When?'

'This evening. I'll buy you dinner . . .'

'I'm a bit busy, actually . . .'

'Oh, well, I wouldn't want to ruin your elaborate social plans.'

'They aren't *social* plans.'

'Whatever. You have to eat sometime, don't you?'

'OK, OK, OK . . .'

It hurt, having to squeeze blood from the stone. But Derek wanted to tell someone what he'd done – preferably someone who loved him. He wondered whether Charlotte qualified.

# chapter 2

The tapas bar in which he waited was a compromise location: just clean enough for Derek, just scruffy enough for his daughter. He ordered a second beer from a cheerful young waitress. She was young, black and braided and smiled at him indulgently, making Derek feel aged, white and dull. He checked his watch again – 18.25 – and squinted at the semi-bearded wannabe banditos gathering at nearby tables. For the second time that day he was unsure of his appearance. At home he'd sifted endlessly through his wardrobe and opted for a timeless look – black turtleneck, short brown leather jacket, brown brogues and easy fit jeans. It had seemed like a riskless choice. But now Derek felt as if he had 'easy fit' written all over him.

'Your beer, sir.' The waitress placed the open San Miguel before him. 'Are you ready to order food?'

'I'm still waiting for my fellow diner, I'm afraid.'

'No worries!'

'Nor me!'

She laughed a bit more loudly than the comment merited and spun away. Derek wondered if the Lexus was OK. He'd left it in a side road parallel to the one where Charlotte lived. It was 'near Clapham', he'd told Amelia that morning; well, three hundred yards nearer Clapham than the half-trendy Brixton side street where he was sitting now. With self-conscious bravado Derek grasped the frosted bottle and was taking a long swig when he saw Charlotte walk in. Her dark brown hair was double-plaited and she clutched a stack of cardboard folders to her chest. She wore flared jeans and a duffel coat: retro hippie fashions whose invasion of the high street mortified her dad. Warily she scanned his face. 'Oh, God,' she groaned. 'Something tells me I'm late.'

'Just the usual half hour.'

'I got held up.'

'I believe you. Thousands wouldn't.'

Charlotte ignored him and commented instead, 'Don't look so nervous. They won't eat you, you know.' She meant their fellow patrons.

'Nervous?' protested Derek, just a bit too much. 'Don't be daft. I was hanging out in tapas bars before half this lot were born.'

Charlotte slapped herself lightly on the wrist. 'Sorry. Silly me. I forgot you were a trendsetter. Have you ordered?'

'Of course not. I was waiting for you.'

'I'm not hungry.'

'But that's why we're here – to eat!'

'Don't get stressed with me, Dad.'

'I'm *not* stressed!'

'Yes you are.'

He was, too: stressed because his daughter exasperated him, and because he was on edge. She was cross with him, of course. She was always cross with him. But she'd become even crosser since he and Denise had told her about China and the way things were and how they might have to change. Matthew's reaction had been different – one of non-stop overpowering concern. Charlotte, though, had simply taken a big step back and embarked on a never-ending fume. She took the large card menu from her father without asking and perused it dutifully. 'Laurent's coming in a minute,' she said, not looking up.

'That's fine,' Derek said.

'I know it's fine.'

'I know you know.'

'I know you know I know . . .'

Remain calm, Derek thought. She's maddening, but she's mine. He spied on Charlotte's face. She looked healthy enough and very pretty with her hair like that. He thought of saying so, but opted for a dreary little pleasantry instead. 'How's Laurent?'

'He's OK.' Disdainfully, Charlotte let the menu fall back to the table.

'Listen,' Derek said. 'Please order *something*. I've been waiting for you. And I've come all this bloody way.'

'Only because you *wanted* to.'

She made proper eye contact for the first time. It was

all icy blue but Derek preferred that to being blanked. He looked squarely back at her. 'I don't remember you turning me down.'

'Hmm.'

The waitress hovered once again. For her, Charlotte smiled. 'Just a mixed side salad for me, please, and some bread.'

'OK. And for you, sir?'

His daughter's asceticism felt like a challenge. Derek rose to it with a selection of meat dishes plus another San Miguel. He looked across at Charlotte. 'Don't you want a beer?'

'No thanks. I might have a sip of yours.'

Derek turned back to the waitress. 'Better bring one more, anyway.'

Charlotte frowned. The waitress jotted without comment. Derek said, blandly, 'Have you heard from Mum at all?'

'Yes,' Charlotte replied, too lightly.

'How nice. What did she send?'

'A video diary.'

'When did that arrive, then?'

'Dunno. Two weeks ago.'

'Two *weeks*? Were you ever planning to tell me?'

'What's the panic, Dad? Don't tell me you're *missing* her, or something.'

'That isn't the point.'

'What *is* the point, then, Dad?'

The point, for Derek, was fair play. He'd forwarded to

Charlotte all the perfunctory e-mails Denise had sent him since she'd left.

+ arrived safely in shanghai, moving on soon.

+ in my lodgings in chongqing.

+ visited school today, children obedient and sweet.

It didn't surprise him that Denise would send a more personal and elaborate communiqué to Charlotte. Still, not knowing about it bugged him.

'I'd like to see it,' he said bluntly. 'Is that OK? Or is it a private thing?'

'Well, it might be, mightn't it?' teased Charlotte. 'Mum might be telling me all sorts of things about you, mightn't she? And, of course, she might be getting up to all sorts of things on the other side of the world that she doesn't want you to know about.'

Weariness fell across Derek like a heavy cloak: first his meeting with Amelia, now this. 'Charlotte, I haven't got the energy to quarrel.'

'Really? That's unusual. You're not having a crisis, are you?'

'No, I'm not having a crisis, thanks.'

'An affair, maybe . . . ?'

'Well, that's a nice thing to say. Your mother and I have very sensibly agreed to spend a few months apart – a few months after being married for twenty-four years. It was a difficult and very serious decision, not some scam on my part to run round chasing skirt.'

Charlotte snorted at this point although it wasn't clear to Derek why. Was the snort in reaction to his righteous indignation or to the idea of his getting a woman into bed? Things weren't going very well and he hadn't even told her about leaving QF yet. Throughout his drive down from Brayston he'd tortured himself speculating about how she might react.

*'About time too – all those gormless consumers waving their credit cards.'*

Or: *'Didn't you even discuss this with Mum? What happens if you end up bankrupt? Is that what you want her to come back to?'*

Or maybe both. The prospect had daunted him but he hadn't let it put him off. Now, though, he couldn't bear the thought of Charlotte's being both scornful and upset. To hell with it, he thought. I'll keep my little bombshell to myself.

'Forget the video,' he said. 'It doesn't matter.'

'Don't sulk! I'll get it for you if you want.'

'Always supposing you can remember where you live.'

He thought Charlotte would thump the table then and shout. Instead, she laughed tipsily at the ceiling. 'You just can't stand it, can you? Charlotte the fluffhead who's always late? Whatever happened to the Hawker efficiency genes? Looks like Matthew took the lot!'

'It was only a joke.' Derek was unnerved, not because of his daughter's delighted accusation but by the jarring realisation that Matthew was so right: not being in control and sloppy attitudes in others pissed him off.

Charlotte laughed a bit longer, then looked round as

Derek nodded to someone approaching from behind her. 'Oh, hi, Laurent,' she said.

Laurent stood next to her, indecision oozing from every pore. His black greatcoat hung open and a grubby canvas bag dangled shapelessly from his shoulder. A straw mop of sun-bleached hair fell across his face. 'Ah, hi,' he said finally, though whom he said it to was not entirely clear. Although he had been born and mostly brought up in Kensington, Laurent's mother was French and he spent a lot of time in an apartment in Pigalle, the famous bohemian district of Paris. On the few occasions he and Derek had met – occasions much like this, though previously with Denise there to jolly things along – Derek had pondered whether alternating between two different cultures accounted for Laurent's permanent aura of confusion. Still, he was glad to see him now, even though he thought him daft. At least his vacant presence might melt the ice a bit. 'Why don't you sit down?' he said, indicating the bench space next to Charlotte. 'You can help me eat.'

'Ah, I'm not hungry,' mumbled the newcomer. He was rooting in his bag, his hallmark nervous habit. Rolls of film and battered flashguns appeared briefly from its bowels only to be stuffed straight back.

'Oh, come on,' Derek urged him. 'Here's the food now.'

The waitress distributed earthenware vessels of pseudo-Spanish titbits round the table. Laurent viewed the spread with grave suspicion. Derek pushed a plate of complimentary cheese-spattered tortilla chips his way. 'There you go, Laurent: this one's vegetarian. Get stuck in!'

Laurent gloomily pushed one into his mouth.

'How's the salad?' Derek asked Charlotte.

'Better than what you're eating, I expect.'

Derek sighed and kept his counsel then affected insouciance while Charlotte and Laurent talked in lowered tones between themselves. Charlotte's contemptuous nibbling was nothing new. She'd ceased eating lustily when she'd entered her teens, prompting Denise to root regularly in her bedroom for hoarded Wispa bars or concealed swing-bin liners full of sick. Yet neither bulimia nor anorexia or any other eating disorder had been to blame. It seemed the adolescent Charlotte simply didn't have a lot of time for food. Or, for that matter, clothes, boy bands, shopping or any of the things that obsessed most girls of her age. To Derek's hidden disappointment she was far more interested in unpleasant insects and primordial wriggling creatures dredged from the bottoms of ponds. The building blocks of life enthralled her. A stack of high-grade GCSEs was followed by straight-A A levels in biology, physics, chemistry and psychology. At the time the last of these had seemed curious in combination with the others. Now, though, exploring the science of behaviour looked like becoming his daughter's career.

'We've got to go, Dad,' Charlotte announced suddenly.

'Go where? You've only just got here.'

'I told you – I had plans already. Laurent's going to Africa tomorrow – to Cameroon, to shoot an ape conservation project – and he wants me to help him pack.'

'Congratulations, Laurent,' said Derek drily. He'd never heard sex described that way before. 'Don't worry about me. I'll just become a fat pig on my own.'

He was on to the fourth beer now; well, no one else had wanted it. Maybe after they'd gone he'd treat himself to a cigar. Then he saw Charlotte reaching in her duffel coat pocket. 'Look, Dad,' she said, as she and Laurent rose to leave. 'Here are my house keys. I'd like to keep the video, but if you want to see it you can watch it round at mine.'

Derek was astonished, and then suspicious. Charlotte had moved into the student house she shared the previous summer, yet only Denise had visited her there. Now she was offering him her key fob, one of those plastic trolls with long pink hair.

'You remember the address, don't you?'

'Yes, thanks.'

In fact, he had it punched into his palm pilot, but chose not to risk disclosing this shocking evidence of his paternal love.

'I've told the others about you,' Charlotte added ominously. 'Just let yourself in. OK?'

Derek checked the Lexus first. Dusk had been and gone so he settled for establishing it hadn't yet been stolen or relieved of all its wheels. He would comb the bodywork for signs of passing vandalism the next day. He then set off round the block to Charlotte's place, clutching her keys inside his jacket pocket as he counted down the sporadic door numbers in the ill-lit terraced street – 36, 34, must be 32 and so on – until he came to number 12. There, he paused for a few seconds taking in the spindly privet and overflowing bins and what looked like an old blanket hung in the front window where a curtain ought to have been. Yellow bulb light formed its intermittent border and when Derek pricked his ears he made out the sound of laughter, some of it human, some of it coming from a TV. 'What a dump,' he breathed.

Quietly, Derek let himself in. But having eased the door shut behind him and tiptoed past the bicycles that lined the barren hall he heard the TV noise loom louder and found he was confronted by a girl of Charlotte's age with three nose rings, a snake tattoo and blue hair.

'Hi,' said Derek, falsely cheery.

The girl said nothing.

'I'm Charlotte's dad,' continued Derek, dangling the troll fob before the girl's impassive gaze much as Bugs Bunny might offer a bulldog a bone.

'Oh, yeah,' the girl said finally. 'Her room's upstairs.'

'You're very charming,' Derek said.

' 'S all right,' the girl replied doubtfully. She inhaled a mucous logjam and was gone.

Derek climbed the stairs, bushwhacked in the dimness by memories of a student house he'd had the misfortune to visit sometime in the late Sixties: the mustiness and stale body odour; the undeclared half-promise of casual sex. He hadn't been to university and took a macho pleasure in the fact – unlike some execs he could mention he'd worked his way up from the shop floor. On the upstairs landing he was blankly propositioned by three closed bedroom doors. One bore no decoration, another was distinguished by a peeling Slipknot sticker and the third carried a poster attacking GM food. Confident that this was the portal he sought, Derek took heart from the poster's deference to the perpendicular, turned the Bakelite doorknob and stepped into his daughter's private world.

The first thing that struck him was the rustling: small, furtive noises that reached him through the darkness from the far side of the room. The ceiling light wasn't working so he groped for a wooden lamp whose outline he made out beside the bed. Thanks to its pale illumination – Charlotte was committed to low-energy bulbs – he was able to take in the scene of blithe disorder before him: an Aztec print double duvet left twisted into a mound; books, papers and dog-eared cardboard files covering half the floor in subsiding heaps which Derek yearned to straighten; a lopsided clothing rail across which skirts, jeans and jackets slumped as if in mourning for the hangers they so obviously craved. In the corner at right angles to the room's only window an improvised stack of shoeboxes, birdcages and glass tanks stood on a low table. It was from these that the rustling came and they were the final confirmation to Charlotte Hawker's father that he was in his daughter's room.

Derek peered into each of the accommodation units,

but saw only piles of curling vegetation and little card-board cartons with doorways cut in the sides. The rustling sounds continued, but the patients making them had taken fright. He exhaled his disapproval, then, looking around, spotted the video diary on top of the television; the one he had bought for Charlotte when she'd left home. Its matt black casing was now lavishly festooned with artificial ivy in whose plastic fronds a postcard had been wedged. Its picture was of a small, anonymous hotel. Derek turned the card over and read.

*18 January*
*Shanghai*

*Darling Charlotte,*
*Here I am in the land of bicycles and noodles! This is the place I'm staying in until they move me to the barren wastes of the south-west. Still can't believe I'm doing this! It's a long, long way from home! But what a great adventure! And who knows – I might meet the man of my dreams!*
*Love and kisses, Mum*

Derek slotted the cassette into the VCR (he had bought Charlotte that as well) then sighed with the realisation that even if he could locate the two remote controllers they'd be broken or the batteries would be flat. He took the manual route instead and soon there was Denise with her blonde highlighted bob cut and her big smile and her hands shoved into the pockets of her jeans. She offered a cheery greeting in what she then revealed was beginner's Mandarin before continuing in English: 'Well, Charlotte, here I am! Hard to imagine, isn't it . . . ?'

It was hard for Derek to imagine too; hard to take in solid evidence of the deal he and his wife had made. There'd be a trial separation lasting almost a year – a *real* separation, something that would put their marriage to the test. After months of rows and silences the details had been easily agreed. Derek would stay in Brayston and simply carry on at QF – which was all he'd thought he'd wanted at the time. Denise, in contrast, would fulfil her long-held ambition of travelling to some far-flung corner of the world. There she would channel her neglected skills and frustrated energies into a good cause and track down some exotic wildlife too. Sometimes they'd discussed this calmly, other times less so. Derek remembered one remark from Denise vividly: 'I'll have more fun with the pandas than with you!' Whatever, she'd be back in time for Christmas but not in time for their silver wedding anniversary, though neither of them dwelled on that uncomfortable fact.

The video diary lasted for twenty minutes.

'. . . Well, Charlotte. It's time to say goodbye. Give my love to Laurent and I'll be in touch again soon! By-eeee!'

Derek watched impassively as his wife's image leaned towards him blowing ostentatious kisses from both hands. Then the screen turned blue. Derek rewound the cassette, switched off the TV and rose to leave. First, though, he took his BlackBerry Wireless Handheld from his inside pocket and checked his e-mails. He'd received only one since leaving the tapas bar. It looked very promising; more promising than he'd dared to hope.

Hello Derek Hawker. I wonder if you're the man I'm looking for. Please call. Yours, Libby Ford.

There was a number at the bottom and Derek was tempted to ring it straight away. He decided, though, that such matters were better handled from home – and definitely not from the rebuking gloom of Charlotte's room. He placed her keys on top of the TV as she'd requested – 'someone else will let me in, or I'll just break in,' she'd said – and was soon back in the Lexus, nosing through the London traffic, heading north. His mood had improved enormously. 'I'm in business,' he declared, taking one hand off the wheel to punch the air.

# chapter 3

The next day Derek hoovered in the bedroom: his and Denise's bedroom as he presumed it remained until one or both of them decided otherwise. When, if ever, that decision would be taken was unclear to Derek, as was so much else about his possibly doomed marriage to the woman he didn't know if he still loved.

Derek's vacuum cleaner was a Dyson DC07. He gazed approvingly upon the stylish *über*upright with its distinctive clip-on Clear Bin™ and reversible cleaning wand. He unspooled the power flex and bent to press the plug into the socket next to Denise's dressing table, an ornate *nouveau*-ish piece passed down to her by her late mother as a wedding gift. As such it held piquant memories for Derek too. These now caught him unawares as his mind's eye turned back to him and Denise together in the first home they'd shared, an interwar Edmonton maisonette. He saw her perched on the button-studded stool between the dresser's angled mirrors, sometimes wearing the frothy French underwear she'd favoured at that time, sometimes steaming gently beneath a knotted towel. He saw himself stretched on their bed, gazing at his new wife's bare shoulders and reflected face while luxuriously fingering his credit card collection or fondling a Habitat brochure.

'Derek,' Denise would say, not turning round. 'Are you getting ideas?'

'What sort of ideas?'

'Any sort of ideas.'

'Marketing strategy ideas, you mean?'

'Derek, you know what I mean.'

'Store development ideas?'

'Derek!'

And then Denise would be beside him, tickling and teasing and flinging the cards and brochure into a corner of the room. Had those times been happy? Had that feeling been love? Resting his thigh against the Dyson Derek struggled to recall. 'But that's all history now,' he said. Why, that very morning he'd given Libby Ford a call and arranged to meet her the next day.

With vigour and precision he put the Dyson to work, leaving no square centimetre of powder blue wool twist pile ungroomed. In truth, the carpet required no such attention but Derek didn't care. He was suddenly euphoric, almost on fire. The hoovering completed, he went down to the kitchen where he constructed a diagonally symmetrical ham and watercress sandwich and poured a Grolsch into a glass that was precisely the right size to accommodate the contents of the can. This and the sandwich he consumed neatly at the table before placing his soiled crockery in the Bosch dishwasher and heading back upstairs to savour the emptiness of his new office.

This was to be his engine room, his relaunch hub. The only furniture inside it was a lightweight swivel chair and a glass-topped desk on which lay a pristine slab of iBook. The beige carpet, newly laid, gave pleasantly beneath Derek's slipper-socked feet. The walls were bare, clean and cream, still smelling of fresh paint where the decorator had been. 'Perfect,' Derek said, although that wasn't strictly true because a metal plate bearing the legend *Matthew's Room* was still fixed to the outside of the door. Derek could have unscrewed it but that risked leaving an unpleasant indentation which might prove even harder to ignore. Would Matthew be upset when he found out he'd been evicted? Of course not, Derek thought. He was a grown-up now. He didn't live here any more.

The Grolsch began to take effect and a novel state of vacancy settled in Derek's head. He wandered on to the landing and into Charlotte's room. This too had been transformed from how it used to be though not by Derek and not in the same way. After Charlotte had gone up to university the autumn before last Denise had retouched the paintwork, dusted down the many books, had the curtains dry-cleaned and given the procession of porcelain elephants pride of place on the staggered ornament shelves. A light dustsheet shielded clean bedlinen. The idea was to always be prepared for weekend visits, although so pointed and complete had Charlotte's absences become that the room now seemed to Derek like a shrine.

He looked out of Charlotte's window at the back garden, a wide swath of sculpted lawn stretching beyond his sight line from the patio and elegant conservatory, with daffodils and bluebells blooming in the bordering flower beds. It occurred to him that with Denise not around he'd have to find a gardener from somewhere. Feeling sleepy he sat down on Charlotte's bed. A large, shabby panda was propped expectantly against the pillow. It was one of Charlotte's oldest cuddly toys. Derek pushed it to one side, lay down and closed his eyes.

He was woken three hours later by the doorbell. Derek plodded blearily downstairs to the front door. In the porch stood the little girl who lived next door. She beamed at him winningly, displaying jagged spaces where her front baby teeth had been. 'Hello, Derek,' she said.

'Hello, er . . .'

'Nessie, remember? Well, I'm not Nessie *egg-zackly*, I'm really Natalie, but Nessie is what I'm called.'

'Right,' said Derek fuzzily. 'I think I already knew that, didn't I?'

'You should do. I've been your next-door neighbour for two years.'

'Fair comment,' Derek said. 'So how can I help you, ah, Nessie?'

'I like your panda,' she said.

Derek looked down to find Charlotte's old friend

dangling from his right hand by a threadbare paw. Nessie asked, 'What's its name?'

'Um. Mr Heath.'

'That's unusual,' the child said sweetly and skipped quickly from foot to foot. Her tousled curls bounced brightly. A row of tiny red lights flashed in the soles of her trainers.

'Yes,' agreed Derek, 'I suppose it is. Anyway . . .'

'Anyway, Sam wanted to know if you could pop round for a moment. He's got a favour.'

'I'm a bit busy,' Derek hedged. He wasn't keen on Sam, who was a life coach for a living and did yoga. The whole idea of him made Derek's toenails curl. He wasn't sure of Sam's wife either, a steely, limber woman by the peculiar name of Moz who was a personal trainer to several City types and ran an expensive gym. She and Denise had become friendly and Derek often wondered what unflattering things about him she'd been told.

'You don't *look* busy, egg-zackly,' Nessie said. 'You look as if you've just got out of bed.'

'Well I haven't,' said Derek. 'Why does your daddy want to see me?'

'He says it's about retail therapy.'

'I see . . .' Pain in the ass, Derek thought. Still, best to get it over, he supposed. 'OK, Nessie,' he said briskly, 'I'll come now.'

'Could I hold Mr Heath?'

Derek hesitated. 'Well, OK then, just this once. Be careful with him, though. He's very old.'

Nessie skipped off with Mr Heath under her arm. Derek followed, glancing around the sweeping arc of Willow Close where he'd be spending much more time. It contained only two other houses, both of them large, modern and built in traditional rural styles like his own. Like his, too, they had wide front lawn aprons, elegant chain-bordered forecourts and double garages, although each of the three houses was of a different design. The estate agents had dubbed them collectively 'a luxury new frontier community in a historic sylvan setting', which delicately signalled their social separation from the rest of Brayston village, with its abandoned school and church and its post-war council prefabs with their grimy net curtains and gardens littered with motorbike entrails.

Hawker House was the first on the right as you entered the close. Sam and Moz's garden adjoined Derek's and completing the trio was the erstwhile country retreat of a TV executive and her actor husband. Their sporadic appearances had generally comprised a Friday night arrival from London and a departure the following Monday at dawn. Sightings of them had been wordless and fleeting. What were their names again? Helena, perhaps? And Ben? They had now been replaced by the close's newest arrivals, Lorcan and Galina O'Neill who'd moved in a few days after Denise left for China and swiftly announced their presence by installing on the front lawn an ornamental wishing well and a small army of garden gnomes – or leprechauns, possibly – and a nameplate proclaiming *Emerald Isle* on the door. Derek had been careful to avoid the newcomers – both the O'Neills and their plaster of Paris pals. Although he was lively and gregarious at work, neighbourliness struck him as both time-wasteful and dull. But one morning Lorcan had caught him putting out his wheelie bin. 'I positively *insist* youse come and have a drink with us one evening,' he'd enthused.

Lorcan was a short, quite tubby man of roughly Derek's age with very little hair but the surprising rosy cheeks of a small boy. Derek had been struck by the bizarre combination of a mildly officer class English accent with the sprinkling of Irish idiom. He'd stalled for a minute but then thought what the hell. Result? He'd be joining the O'Neills that evening. 'Six o'clock then,' he'd agreed. 'Absolutely, Derek,' Lorcan had replied. 'To be sure.'

Nessie excitedly pushed open her front door. 'Come on in,' she said. Derek had been in Sam and Moz's house before, though only once or twice. The hall was all orange orchard shades and the floor was made of aged hardwood boards. A tropical plant soared lewdly from a terracotta pot and a hand-tinted rear-view photo of a naked man hung in welcome on a wall. Derek disliked this picture: not for itself but because he was convinced that visitors were meant to think the perfect ass belonged to Sam.

'He's upstairs, I think,' Nessie announced.

'Talking to a client?' Derek asked.

'Oh, no,' Nessie replied. 'Sam doesn't do business calls after we're home from school.' She looked at Derek knowingly. 'He's in the bedroom with Moz.'

'I see.' How old was this child again? Seven going on seventeen Denise had once remarked.

Nessie bellowed – 'SAM! DEREK'S HERE!' – then beckoned Derek through to the kitchen. 'Norton's doing multiplication,' she announced over her shoulder, 'so don't say the wrong thing.'

'What's the wrong thing?' Derek asked, but Nessie didn't answer and soon Derek was faced with a small, blond blob of heavy concentration sitting at a circular table in the centre of the room. It was smaller than its sister and had a pencil clutched in its left fist. The tip of its tongue peeped from the corner of its mouth. On its head was a blue tea cosy hat worn low over the eyes, with a single word stuck on the front – MATHS.

'Norton!' said Nessie loudly. 'Say hello to our guest!'

The blond blob appeared hostile. It didn't speak.

'Hello, Norton!' said Derek in a cheery half-bellow then felt a tremor of discomfort as Norton's brow furrowed by way of a reply. At that point Sam walked in.

'Hi, Derek!'

Sam held out a hand. He was tall and lean and handsome in a slate grey T-shirt and jeans. Only the crinkles round his eyes and a shake of salt and pepper in his dark curls signalled that he'd seen the back of his thirties. His blue eyes were as bright as his smile. As Derek returned the handshake he noticed that Sam's feet were bare.

'Hi, Sam. So, your daughter tells me . . .'

'Sam!' Norton spoke for the first time. 'What is three times three?'

'Eight,' Sam replied.

'*Ach-ully* it's nine.'

'*Ach-ully*, you're right,' conceded Sam. Norton bent over his pad again. Sam turned to Derek. 'Cup of tea?'

'No thanks, I can't stop.'

'Or a biscuit? Haven't you offered him one, Ness?'

'Maybe Derek doesn't do biscuits,' said an older female voice. 'After all, even men have to watch their figures these days, don't they?' Moz – for it was she – walked up to Derek, eyebrows arched. She wore a red silk kimono decorated with exotic coiling flowers. She brushed a strand of raven hair out of an eye. 'What a surprise to see you,' she went on. 'Have you come to borrow something? A cup of sugar, maybe? A set of jump leads? Isn't that what neighbours are for?'

Derek caught her smell: all yeasty and warm. 'I'm not here to borrow anything,' he replied evenly. 'I'm here to enlighten your husband.'

'Best of luck,' Moz replied. She turned her attention to her children. 'And hello to my *babies* . . .'

Norton didn't seem to hear her – he and his hat were deep in numeracy – but Nessie said, 'Hello, Mummy. Are you feeling better now?'

'*Much* better, thank you. Sam has taken care of all my needs. And who's this?' she went on, spotting Charlotte's panda, whom Nessie had laid gently on the table.

'It's Mr Heath,' said Nessie.

'Ha ha!' exploded Sam. 'Brilliant name! Who thought of that?'

'My father,' said Derek. 'Big Common Market man. He gave it to my daughter when she was born.'

'Ted Heath's pandas,' said Sam in nostalgic wonder. 'Remember those dark days of the early Seventies, Derek? The three-day week, the coal strikes, power cuts and all that?'

Derek did remember them. He'd been in his early twenties and already bossing the menswear section of Keeble's department store in Kingston sporting a Kevin Keegan haircut and a turquoise kipper tie. He wondered what Sam had been doing at that time. Smoking dope in some public school dormitory, probably.

'Those pandas never did get it on, did they?' Sam observed wistfully.

'I'm not an expert,' Derek replied.

'At what?' asked Moz. 'Pandas or procreation?'

'Moz!' scolded Sam. 'What sort of a question is that?'

'Oh, don't be a prude, Sam,' growled Moz playfully. 'Derek's a man of the world. His wife told me so.'

'What's this about pandas?' Nessie asked.

'They were the Prime Minister's gift from the Chinese government,' Sam explained. 'Imagine getting two real live pandas for a present!'

'Wicked!' Nessie said.

'And speaking of China, Derek,' Moz continued. 'How is Denise getting on?'

'Pretty good,' said Derek, flinching inwardly.

'You're missing her, I expect.'

'Oh, yes.'

'Are you still in love with her, Derek?' Nessie enquired.

'What?'

'Nessie!' said Sam sharply. 'Of course Derek still loves her. I'm sure he can hardly wait till she gets home.' He spoke again to Derek. 'She's called Nessie 'cos she's a monster,' he explained indulgently. 'She takes after her mother.'

'I'll remember that,' said Derek.

Moz chuckled mysteriously. 'Well,' she said, 'I can't stand round gossiping with you girls all day. I have a hot bath to get into. See you, Derek.' She sashayed smartly away.

'Anyway,' Sam said. 'The reason I asked you over was, I was wondering if maybe you could give me a bit of background on the state of play in retailing these days. I've got a new client, you see – in that line of work, but it's a first for me. Fellow called Arthur. I don't need a lot of detail, just the basic lie of the land.'

'Sure,' Derek said. 'No harm in that.'

'Could I pop round? One early evening, maybe?' asked Sam. 'After Moz gets back from work.' He raised an eyebrow in the direction of Norton. 'We'd have company, otherwise. You know what I mean, Derek. You're an old hand at being a dad!'

'Fine. Right,' Derek replied, with sinking heart.

From underneath his maths hat Norton asked, 'Sam? How many minutes are there in a year?'

'I'll get back to you on that one, Nor,' said Sam.

'I'd better be going,' Derek said, and headed for the door. Nessie rushed to open it for him.

'How old is Charlotte?' she asked.

'She's nineteen.'

'Is she married?'

'No.'

'Does she have any babies?'

'Er, no.'

Derek edged past her and struck out for home. He thought he had escaped when Nessie called after him. 'Derek! You've forgotten Mr Heath!'

He toyed with feigning deafness. But his feelings for the panda were too strong. 'Thank you, ah, Nessie. I'd better take him home.'

The little girl disappeared then hurried back. Softly, she kissed Mr Heath goodbye. 'Can I play with him again?' she asked.

'I expect so,' Derek said. 'The next time Charlotte comes home.'

'When will that be, *egg-zackly*?' Nessie asked.

'I wish I knew.'


'Now, Derek, yer man. Try this.'

Lorcan's face had the blush of a spring radish. He took one of the heavy tumblers from the tray Galina held. Derek took the other.

'*Sláinte*,' announced Lorcan, 'as me dear Aunt Mary used to say.'

'Is Irish word,' explained Galina, looking to her husband for approval. 'Is meaning "cheers", I believe.'

Lorcan threw back his head and downed his inch of

liquor in one go. Derek did the same then composed an expression of intrigued appreciation.

'What do you think?' Lorcan asked. His hopeful face left room for only one reply.

'It's good stuff,' Derek declared, his urge to heave firmly concealed. 'What is it?'

'Kilkenny Kicker – a traditional mead from the county of my birth. I've brought fifty bottles over; be fascinating seeing how it goes.'

'Goes where?' Derek asked.

'Oh, sorry, didn't I say? At my pub, Doonican's in Stevenage. It's a traditional Irish family pub, the first of a chain I hope. We're having a big show on Good Friday. Youse ought to come, old bean, so's you should.'

'I'll think about it,' Derek said. His heart went out to the Doonican's patrons. Kilkenny Kicker? Kilkenny Killer, more like. 'What do you think of it, Galina?' he asked.

'It is a man's drink, I believe,' Galina said. She made a deferential hum and clasped the empty tray against the soft swell of her belly like a shield.

'One sniff of this stuff and you'd be flat on your back, wouldn't you, love?' Lorcan said. He gave Derek a sly wink. Derek wasn't sure how to respond. Happily, though, the background croon of the Bachelors' 'Diane' was drowned out at that moment by a burst of canine yelps from the garden. Galina dropped the tray on to a rustic-mood occasional table. 'Excuse me,' she said, rushing off. 'It is possibility.'

Lorcan watched her disappear and pulled an embroidered footstool towards him with his toes. 'She's only thirty-six, youse know,' he said. 'I'm old enough to be her father.'

'Good for you, then,' Derek said. By now the yelps from the garden were interspersed with high-pitched eastern European urgings. Lorcan chuckled knowingly.

'Ah . . . what's happening with the dogs?' Derek asked.

'Rumpy-pumpy, I'll be hoping,' Lorcan said. 'Sometimes Favour needs a bit of help. You know, with climbing on board. We've all been there, I suppose!'

'Speak for yourself,' said Derek, returning the verbal embrace. 'So, how long have you two been together?'

'Only six months. It was a miracle we found each other. She'd only been here a few weeks from Minsk, fleeing persecution. You know, it's virtually still Communism there. Like Boris Karloff never happened. She was desperate for the freedoms of the West.'

Lorcan heaved himself sideways, tummy quivering amicably beneath a Riverdance sweatshirt. He took a confidential grip of Derek's wrist. 'She was working as a waitress in a restaurant in Sittingbourne: so fragile, so obviously in need. At first it seemed plain wrong to try to pick her up, although of course it crossed my mind. She's an attractive woman, after all.'

Derek nodded politely. Galina was shapely with a pleasant, florid face that smiled often and breathlessly. Everything about her spoke of eagerness to please. She wasn't Derek's type, but she appeared to be meeting Lorcan's needs.

'It was a whirlwind romance,' Lorcan enthused. 'I took her out a few times. Then I showed her the seaside: Dover, so I did. You couldn't get more English, could you? Anyway, I saw the love light in her eye and proposed to her on the beach. We got married straight away. I was still caring for Aunt Mary at the time, God rest her . . .' Lorcan broke off to make a quick sign of the cross, 'but when she passed away Galina and I decided we would look for our dream home.' He released Derek's arm and flourished an open palm towards the dark green velvet curtains and heavy farmhouse-style furnishings that distinguished his lounge. It was the gesture of a game show compère triggering audience applause. 'And here we are today. She looks after me and I look after her – to be sure.'

'That's fantastic,' Derek said.

'You know, Derek,' Lorcan went on. 'There's so much to be said for settling down. I never thought I'd feel that way. But as we say in the Republic, "there's no bigger heifer than a one-legged nun".'

'I'm sure you're right,' said Derek gravely.

Galina reappeared and Derek noted that her fair hair was dishevelled. Panting lightly, she reached for the bottle of Kilkenny Kicker and refreshed first his glass then her husband's.

'Any luck, turtledove?' Lorcan asked.

'Puh! Favour is wanting to,' Galina snapped, 'but is too much excitement as usual. Puts it everywhere but up.

Grace is get cross and run away.' She let her raised hands fall to slap against her skirted thighs. 'If those puppies ever happening, they better be worth it, I believe.' With that she stomped out to the kitchen from which rich cooking vapours flowed.

'It's a lot of stress, dog husbandry,' Lorcan sighed. 'It wears me out.'

'I can see that,' Derek replied. As it happened, the animals perturbed him slightly. He didn't mind dogs as such, but preferred the types whose tails concealed their vents and gonads. This was not the case with Grace and Favour whose private parts were very frankly on display and had been rubbed disturbingly against his leg when he'd arrived.

'The thing about the shar-pei,' Lorcan said, expertly, 'is they are basically lazy even though in the past they've been trained as fighting dogs. They're from China. Did youse know?' Derek's insides contracted sharply. 'Isn't that where yer man Mrs Hawker is?' asked Lorcan cheerfully.

Five hours later Derek stared hard at the light fitting above his head. Like the ceiling it hung from, the Palamino five-arm chandelier – £85 from John Lewis, he recalled – had stopped going round and round, but only just. He'd stayed to eat with the O'Neills: Irish stew, à la Belarus. He'd also had more drinks. The two opening shots of Kilkenny Kicker had been followed during the meal by several large glasses of what Lorcan had described as 'Doonican's house rosé' and several fat fingers of Jamesons after dessert. After dodging Lorcan's questions about Denise and reassuring Galina that he was coping OK without 'a woman's touchings' as she put it so charmingly, he'd sat back and soaked up their flattery. When he'd revealed his midwife role in the birth of Harboreta, Galina had nearly kissed him and Lorcan had spluttered, 'Holy Pope!' He'd decided not to mention he'd resigned. Well, it had seemed a shame to break the spell. And tomorrow he'd be meeting Libby Ford. 'You're a free man, Derek Hawker,' he said in a loud voice, as if trying to convince the silent walls.

# chapter 4

He talked with confidence and passion, sometimes
making chopping motions with his hands. He had a good
face, she thought – strong and fairly handsome, determined yet quite kind, even when he was speaking of his
wife.

'We've been mature about it,' he explained.

'That's a good thing,' Libby said.

'Nothing's decided yet, but we've agreed in principle.'

'It'll be nice and friendly, will it? Not your typical
divorce?'

'Let's say it will be civilised. It's obvious to me that our
marriage has run its course and I'm sure she thinks so
too.'

Libby dragged on the Silk Cut wedged between her
scissored fingers, stubbed it out and said, 'Will you excuse
me, Derek? I need to powder my nose.'

'Of course. I'll order coffee.'

'Lovely. Black for me.'

She smiled her gratitude and headed for the Ladies,

noticing en route that she and Derek looked like being the last lunchtime diners to leave. He liked her, she could tell, and she rather liked him too. As when they'd spoken on the phone he'd been positive and droll, especially about what he called 'my lifetime of adventures in the shopping game'. She'd loved his stories about Keeble's circa 1969: cutting lengths of net curtain for suspicious housewives; cultivating the pester power of small, unpleasant children; assisting a flamboyant window-dresser called Clive. 'It started as a Christmas job,' he'd said. 'By New Year they were begging me to stay.' Then he'd made her giggle with his tales of Vegard Jonsson, called the Veg for short, a 'half mad futon mogul from Norway' for whom he'd worked as 'store manager, chief buyer, grape peeler, whatever', until the firm had been bought out by a larger German company and the Veg had disappeared to hunt elk.

'Stop me if I'm boring,' he'd insisted.

'No, no,' she'd said, 'please carry on.'

And so he had. He'd credited his 'Veg phase' with completing his 'street wisdom', his 'nose for evolving tastes'. He'd described taking a string of senior management positions – with music shops, a pizza franchise, an accessory outlet, the list went on – as the 1980s consumer revolution had taken hold. 'Then came QF,' he'd said, 'a real opportunity to put all my creativity to work.' There had been little malls at first, then larger ones and, finally, the mighty Harboreta. 'I was the one with the vision,' he'd explained. 'I hand-picked the instruments and then

I made the orchestra play – if that doesn't sound too vain!'

Well, it had a bit. But Libby had just smiled. 'If only my story was half as interesting,' she'd said. It was, very simply, that she'd opened a children's clothing shop in downtown St Albans five years ago and now she was looking to expand. Perhaps to new premises. Or maybe she could make better use of what she had. She wasn't too sure what to do and when she'd spotted Derek's listing on the Chambers of Commerce website – Vision Thing Consultants – she'd thought she might give him a try. She'd been frank with Derek at that point. Although she'd loved talking to him and was quite certain he could help, hiring a consultant was a luxury a small-time shopkeeper like her could not really afford. And that was when she'd made her proposition. He was still thinking it over . . .

Libby stood before a sunk-in basin and a mirror lit from above by tiny bulbs. These were unforgiving but she confronted them levelly, dusted her face lightly and dismissed a passing impulse to suck in her cheeks. She faced herself squarely. She was, objectively, a petite, 42-year-old not bad-looking brunette who had a pretty good body and about the standard quantity of creases round her eyes for a hard-working divorcee who'd brought up her daughter on her own. She was strong, independent and well past caring what some people thought of her. Libby applied a dab of lipstick, thoughtfully. She had believed Derek's account of his career. She wasn't so convinced, though, by what he'd said about his personal life. Not that he was deliberately lying; more likely he was deceiving himself. Oh, there had been fights and furies: she could tell that by the clouds that had gathered behind his eyes. But whatever his future held she doubted it was as clear as he pretended. What he needed was her intimate attention. He could think of it as being paid in kind.

Derek watched Libby discreetly as she returned to their table. She was beguiling, certainly; dark eyes, red mouth and matching fingernails. She looked the part without being remotely obvious about it; in fact, he'd never have guessed. She was a good listener too, as such women often were – or so he'd read. Indeed, he'd been amazed by how candid he'd been with her, how much he'd said. He'd intended only to give her his personal sales pitch to convince her he was both genuine and not to be messed with. Next thing he knew he was speaking openly about how things were with Denise, the children, his character, his state of mind . . .

'You're quite an idealist, aren't you, Derek?' she'd said.

'Maybe. But not a dreamer.'

'Not a dreamer, no. How do your children feel about the separation?'

'Oh, they're fine about it. They're smart kids. They understand.'

He really trusted her. It was bizarre. Then she'd sprung her surprise on him . . .

She rejoined him at the table. 'So, Derek, what do you think?'

'About your proposition? To be honest, I'm not sure.'

He sipped his caffè latte and watched her eyes. She looked straight back into his. 'I'm a class act, I promise. I have a string of satisfied clients.'

'Oh, I'm sure you do.'

'It's only natural to be nervous. I'm offering you something you've never tried before.'

'Oh, I'm not nervous.' Derek chuckled, then fell silent as a waiter cleared their table. When he'd gone, Derek lowered his voice. 'OK, let's be blunt. I've never thought I was the type to go in for . . . what you're suggesting. I've never felt the need.'

'But . . .'

'But, having said that, circumstances change; *my* circumstances have changed. And I've enjoyed meeting you – and talking to you – very much. So what the heck? I'm in Welwyn Garden City on a Wednesday afternoon and there's no one waiting at home . . .'

Libby smiled knowingly. Derek called for the bill.

# chapter 5

Derek looked out at Willow Close through Matthew's former bedroom window feeling positive and clean. It was half past one on Thursday afternoon. Derek had woken pleasantly late and lain in, thinking of Libby. What a girl she was! He'd be visiting her shop on Saturday. At noon he'd risen, showered, shaved and invited the absent Pierce Brosnan to kiss his ass. Returning, naked, to his bed he'd propped his shoulders on a pillow, the better to survey the carnal assets spread below.

Derek had found since his late thirties that assessments of this nature were best undertaken supine: a full view of your feet was more likely to be afforded and not only your feet, ho ho ho. Derek had decided he quite liked what he could see. His ribcage mole was shorn, his toenails were rasped and his dry skin problem areas had been soused in Fabulous Fruits Body Whip. Pity the distance round his middle now stretched to nearly a yard. But never mind, Derek had thought – only the last three inches were lard. Upon completing this inspection he had donned his candy striped bathrobe and hip-swayed across the landing to commune with his iBook and check the close for signs of human life.

Across the way a car door slammed and Derek peeked between the slats of the handmade hardwood blind at Lorcan's silver Audi pulling away. Somewhat to his surprise he then submerged fleetingly in a blue reverie in which he dropped in on Galina on some ludicrous pretext – to borrow clothes pegs maybe, or to seek composting advice – and commanded her to bend over the sofa. Then came the sound of another car, this time heading into the close. It was Sam and Moz's blue Toyota Previa and as it halted on their forecourt Derek snooped shamelessly. Three occupants emerged. The weather was still, so their conversation reached him quite clearly.

'Sam?'

'Yes, Norton. What now?'

'What is four times four?'

'Fifteen, Norton, I think.'

'No it isn't, Sam. It's sixteen. And five times four is twenty, and six times four is . . .'

'Sam?'

'Yes, Nessie.'

'Why is Moz cross with you?'

'She isn't feeling very well.'

'She wasn't *egg-zackly* feeling well on Tuesday either, was she?'

'No. That's why she couldn't take today off too.'

'Is she having her period?'

'Ness!'

'I'm only asking.'

'Just get in the house, please, both of you. Bring your art folders and your book bags and don't fight . . .'

Derek wondered vaguely why the children were back from school so early then guessed it must be the last day of term. Mostly, though, he revelled in seeing Sam under stress. 'Wanker,' he said brightly and walked back to his bedroom where he eased open his pants drawer using only his big toe, relishing the smooth action of a top-of-the-range ball-bearing silder system. Derek knew about these things. He knew about pants as well. His were displayed in three immaculate ranks, each item folded and positioned by his own discerning hand. From left to right: boxers, trunks and briefs. Derek internally reviewed their differing specifications.

+ *Briefs: good for profile, though not ideal for keeping tackle fresh.*

+ *Trunks: figure-hugging and snug on winter mornings. Downside: tendency to crush as well as cling.*

+ *Boxers: cause congestion in tighter trousers, but freer than the rest.*

Derek took off his bathrobe and tossed it on to the bed, but was unhappy with the shape it took on landing. He picked it up and tossed it down seventeen times more until the garment took on the leisured drape alignments Derek would have demanded of a strong window display. Then he returned his full attention to his smalls. He pondered them pleasurably, enjoying his personal freshness, his fragrant nudity. He made his pick, pushed the drawer shut with a deft flick of his heel and stepped into the midnight bluest pair of pure silk boxers he possessed. He hoisted the waistband into the pugilist position and strode across the room scowling and rolling his shoulders, then stopped and dropped a hip like he'd seen Trinny and Susannah do. Finally, he hit an imaginary nine iron to within six inches of an imaginary pin. 'Born to birdie, baby,' he growled.

The rest of Derek's outfit fell effortlessly into place – green classic chinos and a compatible Ralph Lauren polo shirt that he'd rarely worn when Denise had been around because when he had she'd told him he should change his name to Sheldon Milksop Vanderbilt III. His Black-Berry was, as ever, close by. He sent a swift e-mail to g.lunt@quintessence.com. It read: Geoffrey! Still good for eighteen? Del.

Downstairs in the kitchen Derek peeled an orange and was just tossing it into his Samson Ultra juicer when his landline rang.

'Hello.'

'Derek! I say, you old bastard!'

'Hello, Geoff. Nice to hear your voice.'

'I say, you dark horse!'

'Not really,' Derek replied.

'I say, snake in the grass! Made your first million yet?'

'Working on it, Geoff. Have we still got a date?'

'Do you want me naked?'

'There's no danger of that.'

'Clubhouse at two-thirty?'

'Two-thirty it is.'

Derek envied Geoff's uncomplicated method: a hitch of the wrists, a waggle of the hips, a smooth swish of a swing. Geoff held his follow-through position for a second, the seven iron a teaspoon in his hands, and Derek shared his bell jar of golfer's satisfied silence as Geoff's ball soared, dropped and thumped into the distant green. It stopped about five yards beyond the flag.

'Great shot, Geoff,' Derek said.

'Thanks, mate. Keeps me in with a shout.'

'More than a shout, I think.'

'I say it isn't over till the fat lady sings. Or in my case the fat git.'

The two men set off again, striding along the fair- way tugging their trolleys behind them. The weather was delightful, in sweater terms a single Pringle day. Derek looked certain to lose this hole to Geoff, yet his mood remained bullish. It had been his idea to make a contest of the round: match play, a tenner a hole. Geoff was the better player but Derek had stayed level with his ex-colleague so far. This was his day. He just knew.

'Missing the missus, Del?'

Derek was more than ready for this line of questioning. He'd already given Geoff his explanation for his de- parture from QF, together with a sniff of his dynamic business plan. With work talk out of the way, the next

topic of conversation was always going to be women –
meaning sex.

'Missing her? Yes and no,' Derek replied.

'I say more no than yes.'

'Do you, now?'

'Who is she, then, Del?'

'I never mentioned any "she".'

'I say you didn't have to mention one. I say it's written
all over you.'

Derek laughed but didn't look at Geoff. 'OK, I'm seeing
one.'

'*Seeing* one, eh?' said Geoff. 'Not seeing *to* one,
perchance?'

They were approaching Derek's ball. It lay pristine in
the greenness aching for his pitching iron's kiss. Geoff
headed off towards his own ball, putter already hoisted
from his bag. 'I say dark horse,' he called over his
shoulder. 'I say Romeo. I say ram.'

Derek laughed obligingly. He was back at Libby's
house, a neat three-bedroom house on a small private
estate. When they'd arrived there from the restaurant
she'd rummaged for her keys and noticed Derek glance
at neighbours' windows. 'Don't worry about them,' she'd
said. 'They're used to me by now.' She'd eased the front
door open and ushered Derek inside. 'Here,' she'd said,
'I'll take your coat. Then we go straight upstairs . . .'

Derek prepared for his third shot, picturing it in his
head. Then he played it for real. There was a sweet click
and the ball was on its way.

'Handsome!' called Geoff as it bounced towards the hole.

The ball hit the flagpole hard and disappeared below ground.

'Nice one, Tiger,' applauded Geoff. He removed the flag and threw Derek his ball. Then he lined up his five-foot putt. He had to knock it in to stay level with Derek, but the ball hit the edge of the hole and skewed off. 'Puts you ahead, I think,' grinned Geoff.

'Sorry, partner,' fibbed Derek. 'Stroke of luck.'

'Luck?' retorted Geoff. 'I say you *deserve* your luck. I say you *made* your luck. I say *enjoy* it, mate.'

Derek, though, could not enjoy it yet. This, he reflected, was the difference between him and Geoff. At QF he had respected Geoff's no nonsense energy but sometimes found him slapdash, especially when bored. Restlessness affected both men, though in very different ways. In Derek, it triggered fevered thoughts of groundbreaking new projects and strategic overhauls. In Geoff, it led to sarcasm and shortfalls on delivery that others were expected to make up. This had once or twice hacked Derek off.

'Your honour, Tiger,' said Geoff, and made way for Derek with a bow.

'Don't take the piss. You know as well as I do that I'm good for fifty quid.'

'Bollocks, you are.'

'Bollocks I am too.'

The two men belly-laughed together. This was

convenient for Derek, for it concealed how desperate he was to win.

The next five holes were contested with quiet ferocity. The larger man was joking less and Derek sensed his closer concentration but it wasn't enough to get him ahead. Then Geoff won the fourteenth. He won the fifteenth, too. He was suddenly two up with three to play. As they went to the sixteenth tee Derek prepared to put a brave face on defeat.

'You'll have more time to practise now.'

Geoff's voice came from behind a wooden screen. He was having a very long, very audible pee.

'How do you mean?'

Geoff reappeared, searching under his stomach for his fly. 'No missus, no kids, nobody to answer to but you.'

Derek grinned, a little stiffly. 'You've never had that problem, have you? Commitment?'

'True. Very true.'

He said it rather smugly. Derek was reminded of a chat they'd had way back. Project Harboreta was progressing well and Derek had been talking about relocating the Hawkers to the country, as rising executives did. He'd showboated a bit. 'So when are you going to settle down, Geoff? Nice little wife? Couple of kids?'

The answer had been succinct. 'Well, Derek, it goes like this. Say I'm seeing this girl – whatever girl. And say she is a lovely girl. I ask myself, what now? I weigh all the options. Do I stick or twist? Do I get out while I'm ahead or plan a life of wedded bliss? I have a good long think about it. From all angles I stalk the beast. Then I come to a conclusion. I say, "Worse than death, Geoff. Worse than death."'

Derek had laughed at this, of course, as married blokes were meant to do. The truth, though, was he'd felt a little hurt. Was Geoff implying he was boring? Was Geoff calling him a girl? Like everyone else at QF he had conspired in furnishing Geoff's colourful reputation as a man who kept a bachelor pad in the Barbican and hit on giggly blondes in hospitality tents. He begrudged it, though, a bit.

'Right then.' Geoff took up his easy stance and swung his driver, mightily. The ball hurtled into the distance and then hooked. It kept on hooking and slammed into the rugged left-hand rough. 'Sod it,' Geoff announced, though his tone spoke less of anger than of indifference, as if he had the match already won.

Slapdash when bored, thought Derek. Failure to complete . . .

He sent his own drive down the middle.

Geoff looked for his ball.

Derek hit an immaculate second to the centre of the green.

'Bastard thing's disappeared,' called Geoff from the undergrowth.

Derek picked up his ball. He was back to all square now and heading for the last.

In golf, as in life, destiny beckons now and then. Even at club level players whose handicaps will always remain in the high teens may occasionally stumble into a state of perfect certainty, one where they know exactly how much strength to put into each chip shot, and detect precisely the subtle slopes and pace of every green. Derek now fell into such a state. And from this plane of Zen he flew a five iron into the sky like a questing osprey and watched it fall upon its prey, the compact, elevated green of the brutal closing par three.

'Mr Kipling,' Geoff intoned, 'really does make exceedingly good cakes.'

His own tee shot finished on the green as well, but only just. His first putt was steady but left a difficult four-footer for a three.

'Pick it up, Geoff,' Derek said.

'I say you're not serious.' For once, Geoff's tone had no trace of Clarkson-casual.

'No, seriously,' breezed Derek. 'I'll give you that one. I'm sure you'd knock it in.'

Geoff didn't move, perhaps suspecting a jape. So Derek picked the ball up for him. 'Go on,' he said, tossing it Geoff's way. 'It's only a game.' Then Derek walked over to his own ball. Six feet lay between himself and victory and he knew he'd already conquered every inch. He hit the putt with no preliminaries. The ball rattled into the plastic cup. Derek was serene. What clearer vindication of his renewed optimism? What better metaphor for the relaunch of his life?

'You win, one up,' Geoff confirmed. He pumped Derek's hand sizeably, then pulled from his trouser pocket a crumpled ten-pound note. 'It's yours, Tiger,' he said. 'Don't spend it all at once.'

\* \* \*

Derek motored home in triumph.

Haircut 100 sang 'Favourite Shirts'.

Back at the house Derek took another shower and put on more clean clothes. He turned back the cuffs of his best Jeremy Hackett to just short of his elbows and went to his desk in Matthew's clutter-free ex-bedroom where he switched on his iBook, selected a screen saver of a fleet of flying saucers and created a file called Vision Thing – Website Homepage Draft. He said, 'Now to conquer the world.' Four bullet points followed in quick time.

+ My Experience: thirty-three years in retail at all levels.

+ My Commitment: total and undimmed.

+ My Strength: foreseeing evolving trends.

+ My Pledge:

He thought hard about this last one, pacing round in circles and pinching his top lip. Nothing happened so he decided to eat. By the time he'd cleared up two portions of microwaved lasagne darkness had settled on Willow Close. Derek sat in the lounge to rest. His legs ached. He became aware, as always after eight o'clock, of how quiet the house was – how large and how empty. It was awful the way loneliness got to him, even after two such splendid days. He was tempted to ring Libby, but resisted – it wasn't that sort of relationship. He couldn't ring Geoff either: ditto, albeit in a different way. Out of habit he went through each member of his family.

Matthew? No.

Charlotte? Double no.

Denise? Don't think so!

Derek walked to the front of the lounge and through a crack in the curtains peered round the close. One option was eliminated quickly: Derek shuddered at the thought of being life coached by Sam. The O'Neills' lights were on, though, and the silver Audi was back on the forecourt. In his wallet he had Lorcan's business card. He picked up the landline cordless and punched in the number.

'Hello,' said a distinctly English voice.

'Hi, Lorcan. It's Derek, your neighbour. About your Good Friday special. If it's still OK, I'd love to come.'

Lorcan sounded delighted. 'Oh, it'll be great *craic*, oh yes to be sure.'

Derek hung up and went back upstairs. In Matthew's former bedroom he switched on the iBook and opened his Vision Thing file again. Next to the bullet point *My Pledge* he typed: *to feel alive until the day I die*.

# chapter 6

Derek's first impression of Doonican's was good. The front was painted green, it said *Fáilte* over the door and a chalkboard announced that Batty Power and the Shamrocks would be performing live that night. Lorcan showed him round the music lounge which had a small wooden stage and interior decor that Lorcan emphasised had 'a strong authentic feel': ploughshares dangling from the ceiling, sepia photographs of large, careworn families digging turf out of the ground, vintage Guinness adverts everywhere. True, the illuminated Virgins that lit the alcove tables were a bit over the top but the basic vibe felt right and for Derek this was key – he couldn't bear a pub that wasn't competently themed.

The music lounge clientele appealed to him as well: smart-but-casual groups and couples in their thirties and above. They contrasted sharply, though, with the younger, more male crowd in the sports bar on the opposite side of the building where Lorcan took him next. Here, the *bricolage* Gaelic decor was less conspicuous, Top 40 music thumped from corner-mounted speakers and the dominating feature was a massive television screen on which a football match took place between two Nationwide League teams nobody present cared about.

Lorcan squeezed towards the bar exchanging nods and winks with customers as he went by; clearly, he possessed a flexible social style. Putting an arm round Derek's shoulder he hailed the nearest barman – 'Pint of Guinness for my man here!' – then asked to be excused for a moment. Derek feigned fascination with the gradual formation of the Guinness's creamy head while monitoring Lorcan on the sly. He was heads down in a huddle with three younger men but spoke to only one of them, an unsmiling crophead who was lovingly accessorised with tattoos. Lorcan became animated, stressing his words with sharp arm movements and tapping his wristwatch several times. He concluded by slapping Tattoo Man on the shoulder. The gesture was not returned. Finally, he rejoined Derek.

'I like to maintain a personal approach with the patrons,' Lorcan explained. 'It's good *craic*, as we say.'

'And with great success, I see,' Derek replied.

Lorcan acknowledged this plaudit. Yet he seemed a tad distracted, fidgeting with his King of Ceilidh tie.

'What time is Batty Power on?' Derek enquired, keen to get back to the music lounge.

'Soon,' Lorcan replied. 'But I've something else to show you first.' He beckoned Derek to follow him down a corridor, which swung right and right again before leading on to an L-shaped dining room. The Celtic ambience rose to a climax again, with condiments cradled by pottery leprechauns and Irish tricolour napkins cascading from each wineglass. At the furthest tip of the L Derek saw that a pair of double doors connected the dining room to the music lounge from which came a jaunty rendering of 'When Irish Eyes Are Smiling' as the troubadours hit the stage.

'Sit, Derek, sit,' said Lorcan, leading him to a corner table, his manner verging on the debonair. Derek did as he was bid and while gently sipping his Guinness took in the swirly line sketches of celebrated writers on the walls. Brendan Behan, Edna O'Brien, George Bernard Shaw . . . just like the Dexy's Midnight Runners song. As Lorcan handed him a menu, Derek saw that the same pantheon adorned the place mats too. His was of Oscar Wilde, and it carried a quotation underneath. *We are all in the gutter, but some of us are looking at the stars* . . .

'He went the other way, you know, Wilde,' Lorcan announced knowledgeably.

'I'd heard that,' Derek replied.

'A lot of the great writers did.'

'Is that so?'

'It is a well-known fact. And James Joyce was very interested in faeces.'

'Oh.'

'He wrote the Voyage of Ulysses. It's all set in Dublin and ancient Greece, as you know.'

'Fascinating, isn't it?' Derek said, although the last bit didn't sound quite right.

'Oh, to be sure,' confirmed Lorcan. 'To be sure. Now will you have a look at the menu? Oh, you will, you will, you will, you will, you will! And remember – everything's on the house.'

'That's very generous of you, Lorcan,' Derek said. 'Sounds to me like you're making a few quid.'

'Getting by,' Lorcan replied, 'getting by.'

Dispensing this largesse made his apple cheeks glow as Derek weighed the competing claims of the Prime Oirish Cattle Burger and the Fine Old Oirish Spud Omelette.

'Have you seen the specials blackboard, Derek?' Lorcan asked.

Derek had. It was hanging on a wall two yards away but Lorcan leapt to stand beside it anyway, pointing out each item and providing a commentary. Derek sat back and drained his glass. Lorcan was a big kid, no doubt about it. Yet he had a winning touch of the adventurer about him and Derek could respect that. A waitress appeared and he plumped for the Oirish Cattle Burger followed by Cavan Carrot Cake. And he had another pint of Guinness. Lorcan sat down opposite him. 'So, Derek,' he said, all hopeful expectation. 'What do you think of my little venture so far?'

What did Derek think? It turned out he'd think a lot of things before the night was through, many of them self-loathing and appalled. For the next hour or so, though, he praised the potential of the Doonican's brand and professed himself warmed by the general ambience while Batty Power and the boys belted through their first set, which climaxed with a rousing 'Delaney's Donkey'. Derek provided these and other telling insights with the verve and confidence that had distinguished his career at Quintessential Futures and he was cheered to find the old magic still there. Lorcan was clearly thrilled by Derek's praise. 'Some might call it naff,' he said proudly. 'But what's wrong with a little bit of old-fashioned Irish charm? "No surrender," as we say!'

Once again, Derek wasn't sure that sounded right. He didn't let it bother him, though. The cattle burger arrived and he munched contentedly while Lorcan again left him for a while. 'Forgive me, Derek,' he panted, 'my head barman is off sick and I'm having to help fill in.' Derek didn't mind. He washed down his carrot cake with the second pint of Guinness and then ordered a third, which he carried through to the music lounge. There, he found an empty bar stool and was introduced by Lorcan to an accountant and his wife who was so impressed to learn that he'd invented Harboreta that she kissed him on the mouth.

Derek had a fourth Guinness and a fifth. Then he stopped counting, figuring he'd take a taxi home. Batty Power – a diminutive trouper wearing a Harp lager T-shirt under a green corduroy suit – completed his second set with a tremulous 'Danny Boy' and soon it was closing time. The house lights went up and punters began filing out in an orderly manner. Derek was ready to leave too when Lorcan appeared beside him and whispered urgently. 'Will you stay on a while, Derek? I've lined up a little after hours entertainment. I'd really like you to be here.'

'What sort of entertainment?' Derek asked.

'Traditional,' Lorcan said and rushed off towards the sports bar without another word.

Soon the music lounge was empty and all the staff had left. Derek was just starting to wonder what was going on when a rather agitated Lorcan reappeared. 'Follow me,' he hissed and led a puzzled Derek into the now deserted kitchen.

'Listen, Lorcan,' said Derek, with a slight slur. 'I've a terrific time, but . . .'

Lorcan interrupted. 'Just hold on here for a minute. I want it to be a surprise.'

Puzzled, Derek sat down and burped. He read a set of health and safety regulations. Then he nodded off and only woke again when he heard Lorcan's voice, though this time from a distance and struggling against lurching feedback. 'Gentlemen, I'm glad to say that Mr Plod has done his rounds. And so, at last, it's time to turn this Good Friday night . . . a little bit bad!'

There were cheers – raucous cheers – and from the sound system exploded the bawdy bass line bump of a dance track Derek hadn't heard before. He walked dizzily from the kitchen to find the music lounge transformed. The stage where Batty Power had gone about his work was again the centre of patrons' attention. Now, though, it was adorned with a silver reflective backdrop and a pair of metal poles. As his eyes grew used to the darkness, Derek saw that the room was packed entirely by men, some laughing and applauding, others with their heads bent over their glasses as if already repenting for the sin they were about to commit. Then, from behind the silver backdrop, two young women in stiletto heels emerged, their underwear clearly visible beneath gossamer gowns that reached down to their toes. Derek felt a sudden surge of nerves – he'd never been to a strip show before.

The women stepped on to the stage and coiled themselves around the poles. Derek squinted across the room towards the exit. It seemed to be being guarded by a squat, bulky man with a thick neck and no hair. Derek recognised him: he was one of Tattoo Man's sidekicks from the sports bar; one of the two who didn't speak. He saw the other silent one now; he was behind the bar pulling pints and – lo and behold – pouring shots of Kilkenny Kicker. Tattoo Man himself stood alone and aloof from the main crowd. His interest in the action was something other than erotic, it appeared.

'What do you think, Derek?' Lorcan was back beside him, his MC duties done. He scanned the audience fretfully.

'Is this legal, Lorcan?' Derek asked.

'Well . . . you know . . .'

'I think I'd better go . . .'

'Oh no, Derek, please don't. Stay on for a bit longer. Anyway, I'm sober. I can give you a lift home.'

Derek's inebriation was substantial but he still had some sense left. He realised he was stuck, constrained by drink and a helpless loyalty to his strangely needy neighbour. Half mortified, half grimly fascinated, he watched the strippers flex and taunt then toss aside their tasselled bras before stepping down from the stage to invite closer inspection of their charms. As a finale they returned to the stage, peeled off their G-strings and stood naked for a few seconds before dashing from view. There was a long burst of sweaty-palmed applause.

'Is that it?' Derek asked Lorcan.

'Erm, not quite.'

As the clapping died away a third woman walked onstage. She looked older than the other two and was of more substantial build, although her starting attire was much the same. She carried a cordless microphone, which she raised to her mouth and licked lewdly before she spoke. 'Good evening, gentlemen. I'm wondering if one of you can help me out – out of these knickers, I mean . . .'

At this point Derek's head started to spin: the heat, the darkness, the gallon of Guinness, the pumping expectation of the other men. He half covered his face as the new woman plied her patter and settled her attention on a table close to her where a group of six young men were sitting. Taking the freshest-faced one firmly by the hand the stripper tugged him up on to the stage and as he stood before her she expertly de-bagged him.

'What's your name, love?' she demanded.

'Glenn.'

'Are you sixteen yet, Glenn?'

'Yeah.'

'You don't look it. But you look fit!'

Some of the audience cheered. One howled like a wolf.

'This is a big night for you, I'll bet.'

'It certainly is,' Glenn said.

'So do you think you could rise to the occasion?'

More cheering. Another howl.

'Not really,' Glenn replied and looked round for his mates. His hands clutched at his modesty. A desperate grin twisted his face.

'Why not, love?' the stripper asked.

'I . . . um . . . I'm a police officer,' he said.

At last the taxi came to Brayston. It was not long before dawn. 'Holy Jesus and Mary,' wailed a dismal voice from between its owner's knees. 'I'm a broken man!'

'Shut up, Lorcan,' Derek said. He directed the driver to Willow Close. At the foot of his neighbour's drive he coughed up forty pounds then heaved his hunched companion up to the front door. Galina, in a pink nightie, opened it, distraught.

'Oh, my God!'

'Mother?' Lorcan cried, lifting his face towards the waning moon.

Galina went to embrace him and accidentally kicked him on the knee. 'It is me, Galina! I will be your mother!'

Lorcan's head dropped again. Galina stooped to cradle him. Derek could barely conceal his disgust. Remembering Lorcan's business card he'd called her from outside Doonican's as soon as he'd been allowed to leave. 'There's been an incident,' he'd told her. 'A few punters got a bit rowdy and the cops had to be called. Lorcan's a bit distressed . . .'

Distressed? Lorcan had been so pathetic that Derek had considered telling Galina everything, just to teach him a lesson. But then he'd thought again. It was possible, of course, that Galina had always known what had been planned for late Good Friday night at Doonican's, in which case nothing would be gained from telling her. On the other hand, if – as Derek suspected – she was wholly in the dark about it, Derek had good reason for keeping it that way. He felt tainted by the experience. And who would believe he'd not intended to be there? Best for all concerned to keep it quiet . . .

The porch melodrama continued at Derek's feet.

'Lorcan! Lorcan! Sweet angel . . .'

'Mother? Is that you?'

Derek cleared his throat. 'I'll help you get him in, Galina. Then I think I should go.'

'Oh, Derek!' Galina howled. 'You have been such a friend!'

'Forget it,' Derek snapped. 'Let's just get hold of him.'

He grasped Lorcan under one armpit and Galina tucked in on the other side. Together they heaved him forward, impeded by Grace and Favour who jostled for the pleasure of snuffling at Lorcan's groin. Once in the front room Derek and Galina pulled and dragged Lorcan to his favourite armchair. He fell into it with a moan and instantly started to snore.

'My *bay-bee*!' sobbed Galina. She fell to her knees and pressed one of Lorcan's hands to her cheek.

Derek, sweating heavily, looked on. The adrenalin of the previous three hours had cut through the alcohol. The embarrassment and anger, though, remained. 'Galina,' he asked wearily. 'Will you be all right? Shall I help you get him into bed?'

She turned a tear-streaked face towards him. 'It will be OK, Derek. You go now.'

'Are you sure?'

She nodded and began fumbling with her husband's shoelaces. Pity pricked Derek's heart and he was going to insist on staying to help her when from his jacket pocket his mobile buzzed. He saw that he'd had a message from Charlotte. In the noise and chaos of Doonican's he hadn't heard the call.

*Hello, Dad. I don't know where you are but I've come home for the weekend. Lucky you.*

Derek's first response was panic. Bloody hell! Might she be waiting up across the road? But no, if she'd been worried she'd surely have tried again. With luck she was asleep.

He left as Galina lifted Lorcan's feet on to his footstool. He walked quickly across the close and let himself in quietly. After listening in the hall he tiptoed upstairs and

peeked round Charlotte's open door. There she lay
beneath her duvet, snoring gently in Mr Heath's ear.
Gingerly, Derek examined his emotions. He found a
mixture of annoyance and relief. Too revved to go to bed
he went back downstairs, sat on the lounge sofa and
thought back over the evening's events.

For the three hours that had followed the unveiling of
Glenn, the Law had gone stoutly about its work. First,
Glenn's drinking companions had risen to their feet
and shown their badges. Then, with Glenn himself still
pulling his trousers up, a gaunt, commanding figure
leaning against the bar had told everyone to stay exactly
where they were and ordered the house lights to be
turned on. After speaking briefly into a two-way radio
he'd added, 'And in case anyone's thinking of slipping
quietly away, I should tell you that this building is
surrounded.' To prove this clinching point there'd been
a loud thump on the door. One of the plain-clothed
officers had shot back the bolts and a uniformed
sergeant had stepped in from the car park, waved
cheerfully and said, 'Good evenin' all.'

That was when Tattoo Man had made his move. At
first Derek had thought it was he the punch was aimed
at, not knowing who was hiding behind him. There was
no mistaking, though, whose solar plexus felt the main
force of the blow – as if to double check that he hadn't
been dreaming Derek felt the tender spot there now.
Derek had fallen backwards and landed on the crouching
Lorcan thereby protecting him again, this time from the

ill-directed swings of Tattoo Man's feet. He had lain there helplessly until two of Glenn's fellow officers stepped in and pulled his assailant away.

Derek recovered in an alcove. Half an hour later he was being interviewed by the gaunt commanding officer with only an illuminated Virgin for support. He was told that Tattoo Man had been arrested and might be charged with assault if Derek was interested, but Derek's response to this was anything but gung-ho. He just wanted to go home. Then the policeman asked him about Lorcan.

'So you live in the same street as Mr O'Neill.'

'That's right.'

'A friend of his then, are you?'

'I wouldn't put it quite like that.'

'No? Well, I suppose if I were you I wouldn't put it that way either. Unfortunately, he would. He says you're a very good friend indeed. And some sort of business associate.'

'Well, that's news to me.'

'That's as maybe,' the officer replied. 'Anyway, you can leave now. I expect you'll hear from us again.'

It was five in the morning when Derek fell asleep where he sat and only two hours later when he woke. That was partly owing to his bladder, but also to a terrible retching sound from upstairs.

'Charlotte?'

There was no reply – no verbal one anyway, only further vomit eruptions of an extremely gruelling kind. Derek laboured half-blindly to the bottom of the stairs, a spot which instinct told him squared respect for her indignity with concern for her welfare.

'Charlotte? Are you OK?'

He heard the sound of the flush. Finally, she appeared, pale and puffy in her pyjamas, looking down.

'Have you been drinking?' Derek asked.

'No.'

'Are you ill?'

'No.'

'What's the matter with you, then?'

'I'm pregnant, Dad,' she said.

# chapter 7

It was when Charlotte entered her teens that she became bookish and hard to know – that's how Derek saw it anyway. He had to look back a long way for memories of straightforward affection from his daughter, the holiday rough and tumbles, the pleasure she had taken in the sweets and other treats he'd now and then brought home from work. Her enthusiasm for him had nourished his sense of being a good family man: a faithful husband to Denise and a diligent provider who ring-fenced quality time during weekends. Oh, he'd expected things to be less comfortable with Charlotte once the oestrogen kicked in – that was only natural. Even so, he'd been surprised by the reproachful disapproval of his little princess when she stopped being quite so little any more.

Matthew at that stage had been a simpler proposition. Even during his spotty know-all phase Derek had rubbed along with him playfully as with a promising junior colleague. Matthew had enjoyed a good friendly argument and didn't take it personally if he lost, as was usually the case because Derek couldn't help it if he knew best. The adolescent Charlotte, though, had declined to debate with her father on these terms. Instead she would become stand-offish or else question the very premise of the discussion taking place and keep on questioning until the fun went out of it and Denise had to step in with soothing reminders about natural history programmes soon to start on television or peace-making slices of chocolate cake.

No Denise around right now, though.

*I'm pregnant, Dad . . .*

Head fugged from lack of sleep Derek squinted through a gap in the lounge curtains. There was no sign of activity at the O'Neill house – no light showing, no open curtain. Two pints of milk idled on the front step. Reliving the traumas of the night before seemed almost escapist now, so trivial had they become compared with what Charlotte had just told him. He'd said nothing in reply except for 'Bloody hell', then walked away. She had walked away too. But then Derek had heard her pad quietly downstairs, go through the kitchen and out on to the patio. The swing seat began to squeak. He knew he'd have to join her out there soon.

Derek walked stiffly to the far end of the lounge, pulled back the sliding window and stepped into the morning light. In sharp contrast to him the air was fresh and clean. Derek inhaled deeply and self-consciously, knowing Charlotte knew he was there. The nearest edge of the patio was twenty paces to his left. It was one of the property's most stylish features, decoratively tiled rather than functionally slabbed and with an elegant conservatory at its furthest end. From the corner of his eye Derek could see the swing seat with its orange floral design. He could see Charlotte swaying in it with her legs stretched straight, apparently fixated by her toes. He wandered towards her, squinting affectedly at distant cloud formations. He felt obliged not to signal any firm sense of purpose – which wasn't difficult since he possessed no such thing. Uncertainty was his principal emotion at that moment – that and its unpleasant cousin, fear. Those two strangers were hanging around far too often lately.

As he approached her, Charlotte hugged her knees. Derek unstacked a plastic chair and sat down facing her.

'How did this happen?' he asked gently.

'Well, there was me and this man, see, and . . .'

'Charlotte, I am aware of how babies are made.'

'I might have used a donor and a syringe.'

Derek faltered, slightly shocked. Then he said, 'You might have, yes, but I don't suppose you did.'

There was a hint of annoyance in his voice. Others might have ignored it – but not Charlotte. 'Oh, back off, will you, Dad? I feel like shit.'

Derek did back off. Hearing his daughter use ripe language still jarred him. More softly, he asked, 'Is it Laurent's?'

Still more softly, she replied, 'Oh, it could be anyone's, Dad. Let me see: Bill's, Bob's, Brian's, Bert's . . .'

'I didn't mean that.'

'I'm pleased to hear it!'

'OK, OK. Does Laurent know?'

'No, he doesn't. Nor did I until Tuesday – not for certain anyway.'

'Does your mother know?'

'Not yet.'

'How come?'

'Haven't got round to it,' Charlotte said.

He let that answer lie. A secret piece of him was pleased to be the first to know.

'So . . . what are you going to do?'

She shrugged. 'Get rid of it, I suppose.'

Squeamishness and sympathy conspired to make Derek flinch. He said, 'Will you need money?'

Charlotte bristled: 'Well, thanks a lot for *that*.'

'What?'

'Jesus, Dad . . .'

'Hold on, hold on! I'm trying to help.'

'There might be a bit more to this than bunging me a few quid.'

'What am I meant to say, Charlotte? You turn up in the middle of the night . . .'

'No. I turned up in the evening. It was you who arrived in the middle of the night. I heard you come in, actually. I was too worried about you to sleep. Aren't I good at pretend snoring?'

'All right, *all right* . . .' Derek was back on his feet, hand pressed to his forehead. Had she looked in Matthew's room yet? Good job he was the sort of man who always left doors shut. 'Never mind that now. But here you are, out of the blue, with this . . . surprising news. If you don't want me to help you, why are you here? Why have you told me about this?'

'Maybe I shouldn't have bothered.'

'I wasn't thinking that.'

'Weren't you?' She was sulking now, scowling at the blameless barbecue.

'No, of course not. I *want* to help . . . Look, I'm glad you've told me.'

Charlotte made a fizzing sound by sucking on her bottom lip.

'It's not something you want to go through on your own,' continued Derek. He was thinking about hospitals or clinics – wherever these disturbing things were done. All messiness and mixed feelings, so far as he could tell. While they did it would he be holding Charlotte's hand?

'I've got friends, you know,' Charlotte said. 'They'd look after me.'

'Have you told any of them?'

'Not yet.'

Derek recalled the housemate he'd encountered in Brixton, the one with the runny nose. Then Charlotte smiled at him, too sweetly. 'Don't you want to be a grandad, then?'

'In principle I wouldn't mind.'

'I expect you're a bit young for it yet. How old are you now?'

'Fifty-one. Just.'

'I should have known that, shouldn't I?'

'Not necessarily.'

'Did I send you a card?'

'Yes. Did Mum have to remind you?'

'That's not very nice.'

'Diddums.'

'Diddums yourself.'

She hadn't come to see him, though. That had hurt him, just a bit. 'OK, I'm sorry,' Derek said. 'But look. This is silly. We've got to think about this situation clearly.'

'Not much to think about, really,' Charlotte said.

'There's Mum to consider,' Derek said.

'How touching that you should show such concern for her.'

'What I mean,' Derek persisted, 'is that you might want her advice.'

'And what *I* mean,' Charlotte said, 'is *I've* decided, haven't I? *I'm* not going to worry her. *I'm* not going to spoil her time away.'

'And what about when she gets back? Is this going to be our little secret?'

'I'll have to think about that.'

'She might be very upset.'

'No change there then.'

Charlotte scowled at him. He felt wounded and provoked and – worst of all for Derek – out of his depth. 'Listen,' he said. 'I have to go out. It's a work thing.'

'Off you go, then,' said Charlotte.

'I know it's not ideal . . .'

'Don't worry about me. I'll be all right.'

'But we can talk about it later. Maybe when we've both calmed down.'

'I'm perfectly calm, thank you.'

Aren't you just, thought Derek, letting someone else have the last word for a change.


'Can I help you, sir?'

The sales assistant seemed a bit suspicious. Derek guessed he must look like death. 'I'm here to see Libby. She's expecting me.'

'Oh. Well, she'll be back in five minutes.'

'OK, I'll wait.'

He wandered round the shop affecting a casual air. Even in his frayed condition he saw that it was over-stocked: jammed floor-to-ceiling shelves dominated every wall and you had to shuffle sideways between the rails and carousels. And he couldn't place the market niche. It didn't seem to cater for mainstream tastes at all – the big frocks and flashy waistcoats were too showy for that, though he supposed you would expect that from a shop called Kids Nite Out. Some of the stuff was cheap and flashy but some of it was classy; very good quality with prices to match. The customers were difficult to classify as well: all female, of course, yet running the social gamut from elegant upscale to what some would have called white trash.

Two women stood near him, talking. One reminded

Derek slightly of Denise: it was the pedal pushers and infectious animation. 'This is cute,' she said, holding up a tiny suit. It had black velvet trousers and a top with a body panel of reflective silver quilt. At the neck a ribbon bow tie was stitched to a mock dinner shirt insert. Her friend looked at it doubtfully. 'Age two to three,' she said, inspecting the label. 'He's not even born yet.'

'Vicki will love it, though.'

'Will she? What about her husband?'

'What's it to do with him?'

They laughed and Derek moved quietly on. Instinctively he began tidying a display of toddler shoes: pale blue slip-ons with elasticated sides, tartan canvas lace-ups, powder pink sandals with sewn-on hearts, all displayed in clear plastic boxes. Some had been knocked to the ground and Derek bent to pick them up. A voice above him said, 'I've been watching you, you know. Are you casing the joint or hoping to get a job?'

Derek pulled himself upright, feeling a knee joint crack. 'Hello, Libby.'

'Hello, Derek.' She looked at him closely. 'Are you all right?'

'Not great, as it happens. Could we go out for a coffee or something?'

'Of course.'

'Thanks.'

They went outside into the teeming St Albans shopping street. Derek was feeling faintly sick.

'So what do you think of my shop?' Libby asked, then

added with a wink: 'The more *legitimate* of my business activities.'

'Well, my first impression is you've got something distinctive there.'

'You mean it's a mess?'

'I didn't say that.'

'You didn't have to. I already knew.'

She laughed and turned down a side road. A café called Serenity offered a welcome on the right. Before going in, Libby turned to Derek and said with certainty, 'Family crisis?'

'You could say that. It's Charlotte. She turned up last night. In a bit of a state.'

'Why am I not surprised?'

'Boyfriend trouble,' Derek said, rolling his eyes; a futile stab at levity. 'He's gone abroad, to Cameroon. He's a photographer and his mother's French, so he speaks the language there and . . .'

'She's pregnant, isn't she?'

'How did you guess?'

'Maybe it wasn't a guess.'

'Maybe not.'

'Don't be a cynic, Derek. Call it a mother's intuition, if that helps.'

Charlotte wasn't sure where to look next. She'd started in his bedroom – the obvious place – and searched through his chest of drawers, scoffing at the regimented ranks of underpants and perfectly paired socks. Then she'd been through every pocket in his wardrobe: dull suits, conservative shirts and trousers cut for the comfort of the middle-aged man. She'd even taken a deep breath and opened his briefcase, fingertip searching every pocket and compartment with no clear idea about what she might find. All she knew was that she'd know it when she found it. She hoped it wouldn't be anything too corny, such as kinky little knickers or a smutty lipstick message on the back of a postcard, but with men of her dad's age you had to fear the worst. That's why she was relieved not to have unearthed any porn. The only magazines by his bed were *Golf Monthly* and *Men's Health*, and that wasn't really sleazy – just sad.

Where had he been so late last night? She'd begun rooting around when he was still out at eleven though only superficially: what if he'd come back and caught her at it? So she'd called his mobile to find out where he was and then she'd left a message to scare him. He hadn't called her, though, and then she'd started to get cross – with herself, mainly. She'd got the train up on an impulse, inexplicably seized by a desire to share with him what had happened to her – to somehow make it true. There was no one else she felt an urge to tell: not dear, blue-haired Lindy or any of her other housemates, not yet anyway; not Laurent, no way; and not Mum who would leap on to the next plane home and then all the bloody rows would start again. That left Dad. Did he qualify as someone who would share the burden of her coming loss? Would it feel like a loss at all? Charlotte wasn't sure.

She was bored, now, and decided to go out. She shoved her bare feet into her sandals and tugged on an old cardigan she'd borrowed from Denise ages ago – old clothes were so much fun. She found a set of spare house keys – she'd already managed to mislay her own – and was soon mooching into the main part of Brayston village, arms folded, head down, pondering with interest what an idiot she'd been. She'd known it was risky, doing it without a condom a week before her period, but she'd done it anyway and hadn't thought about a morning after pill. How typical, she reflected, of me.

Coming to a halt beside the scrubby village green Charlotte used her mother's sleeve to mop a tear. Then a voice behind her said, 'Uh. Hi?'

Charlotte turned round. 'Hello.'

The girl looked about seventeen and she was stunning: slim and pretty with milky skin and a rippling cascade of golden hair. She held her hand out and said, 'Bou.'

'Eeek!' Charlotte replied.

The other girl looked confused. 'Excuse me?'

Funny, Charlotte thought, how Americans use 'excuse me' in a completely different way. 'I said "Eeek!"' she repeated, helpfully. The girl's smile was turning nervous. Taking pity, Charlotte explained. 'You said "Boo!" so I went "Eeek!" . . . to show I was surprised. It was a joke.'

The other girl frowned. 'So is Eeek, like, not your name?'

'Ah, no . . .' Now it was Charlotte who felt out of her depth.

'Because, um, Bou is, like, *my* name. It's short for Boudica. You know? British warrior *queen*? Fought, like, the *Romans*?'

Charlotte cut her losses. Abandoning humour, she regrouped under the banner of briskness. 'So, Boudica, how can I help you?'

'I'm looking for . . .' She produced a small address book. 'Willow Close? Number two? The home of Sam Blake and Thomasina Long?'

'And their two children,' Charlotte said.

'Hey!' Bou exclaimed. 'You know them?'

'Very slightly.'

'This is a real village, right? Everyone knows everyone else?'

'Well, up to a point.'

Charlotte gave directions: back down to the church, turn right, two hundred yards. Bou thanked her and walked off. Charlotte watched her thoughtfully – what an interesting weekend this was turning out to be.

Derek drove back to Brayston. Having had to leave the Lexus outside Doonican's he was using Denise's car, a bright blue Subaru Impreza Turbo with zebra-stripe upholstery and a selection of punk rock compilation tapes, which filled Derek's head with distant memories. He'd met Denise for the first time at a New Wave disco in Bexley. She was in the first year of her teaching career and had recently jumped on stage with the Rezillos. He was working for the Veg and a bit too old for punk, although he quite liked the Police. They'd compromised on Blondie. *Parallel Lines* had been the soundtrack to their romance. Now the title seemed fitting for its decline.

As he entered Willow Close Derek scanned the terrain for neighbours. To his relief, he spotted none. He swung the Impreza through the double garage doors and as they closed behind him slumped back and closed his eyes. 'Be systematic, Derek,' he said.

*PROBLEM ONE – WHAT I DID LAST NIGHT*

+ *I went to the Irish theme pub belonging to the clown over the road and I got drunk. Check.*

+ *The clown over the road turns his pub into a strip joint after hours. I wish I hadn't been there. Check.*

+ *The place got busted. Check.*

Derek remembered Glenn's indignity and shuddered. Thank Heaven he'd been hiding at the back.

+ *The bloke with the tattoo took at a swing at Lorcan but hit me instead . . .* Derek touched his stomach. Ouch . . . *Check.*

Those were the facts, now for the evaluation. It boiled down to just one thing:

+ *If Charlotte finds out about last night I'm dead.*

In the darkness Derek shuddered again as he confronted . . .

*PROBLEM TWO – MY MADDENING TEENAGE DAUGHTER'S IN THE CLUB*

Again, Derek set out the key points in his head.

+ *She won't tell her mother.*

+ *I don't want her to tell her mother because her mother will go mad, fly back from China and find out I've left my job. She may decide to kill me and dying would conflict with my strategy for relaunching my life.*

*+ She won't tell Laurent. I know he's a complete dope but it still bothers me somehow.*

*+ She won't tell anyone else either so it's my duty to support her at this difficult time. I know I must do this. I know I must do it without shouting, sulking, moralising or advising her to keep her knees together in future. I must at all times remember Libby's firm advice: 'Be kind to her. She's the one who's scared, so you must be the one who's brave. She may still be wrestling with difficult decisions and needs your help to work them through. For whatever reason she's chosen to rely on you. In the long run you may be glad.'*

Finally, his conclusion.

*+ Help.*

Derek left the garage by the internal door connecting it to the house carrying the bags of shopping he'd hurriedly bought so as to have a cover story if Charlotte asked him where he'd been. He moved through the utility room as quietly as he could, and as he did so wondered why. He realised it was in case Charlotte was resting, something he knew pregnant women did (Denise must have done it, he supposed, although all that was a long, long time ago). But then Charlotte had said she wasn't going to keep the baby so, logically, she wouldn't want to rest. Logic, though, seemed less important than to demonstrate some kind of reverence. And Derek's heart began to swell with unscheduled tenderness as he emerged into the kitchen and cocked a caring ear.

Then he frowned. He put the shopping down. He could hear voices: female voices deep in conversation coming from the lounge. Derek edged closer to the source and was relieved to hear that Charlotte was one of those talking. He quickly identified the two other voices too: Moz's and – oh, shit! – Galina's. Derek kicked himself. He should have known she would come round to thank him for bringing Lorcan home. He should have pre-empted this by going over there first, but what with Charlotte's shocking news and their tiff that morning and the thought of seeing Lorcan . . . He shivered. Galina seemed to have bought his cover story last night, but there was no telling what she might have found out since.

For a few seconds Derek dithered. There'd been no indication his return had been noticed and he thought of sneaking back to the garage and hiding there until the coast was clear. But then he heard another voice, again female, suddenly louder than the rest. Someone had turned up the volume on the TV.

'It's lightweight, but not so lightweight you're going to get your bra showing through. It's quite all right to flash the bra strap, but some of us prefer not to . . .'

The patter was unmistakable. They were watching QVC. Derek's curiosity got the better of his fear and he walked into the room. Charlotte spotted him first. 'And here's the man of the moment!' she announced.

She was smiling widely, though how sincerely was difficult to say. The others were smiling too.

'Well *hello*, Derek,' said Moz. Her stockinged feet were

on the coffee table. She held one of Derek's shallow cocktail glasses in which a maraschino cherry bobbed brazenly. 'Galina has been telling us *all about* what you got up to last night. *Very* alpha, I must say.'

Her shoes lay on the carpet. She wore a short, black, tight-fitting dress. Derek fought for composure. What the hell was happening? Cocktails? Daytime television? Admiring comments and smiles? As suavely as he could he said, 'You shouldn't believe everything you're told.' He shot a look at Charlotte who was curled insouciantly in an upright chair. It *might* have been called resting. It might have been called glee.

Galina was last of the three to speak. 'Oh, Derek,' she enthused. She stood up and advanced, clutching a damp tissue in her hand. Paralysed by uncertainty Derek offered no resistance as she took hold of his head and kissed him wetly on both cheeks. 'How can I thank you, Derek? How can I thank you enough?'

Derek mustered a reply. 'Well . . . you could start by telling me what I've done.'

'Oh, come on, Dad,' goaded Charlotte. 'Take us through it blow by blow. How many of them were there? Two? Five? Ten?'

'How many of who?'

'Violent assailants,' drawled Moz, sipping her drink. Derek was still taking in the detail of the scene. A bottle of his sparkling white wine stood on the table. Two more of his cocktail glasses, too. Yet it was as if he'd walked into the wrong house by mistake.

'Oh . . .' Derek waved his hand, he hoped carelessly. 'It wasn't like that really.'

'Don't be modest, Derek,' scolded Moz.

'Come on, Dad, own up,' said Charlotte. 'All these years we've thought Batman was Bruce Wayne and it turns out to have been you.'

Derek grinned and cleared his throat. Nobody had mentioned strippers yet. 'How is Lorcan today?' he asked Galina.

'He is recovering,' she said, 'but he is very weak.'

Derek was acclimatising slowly; feeling slightly less like a hen night entertainer with stage fright. He fielded a few more questions, batting aside bouquets: oh, it was only a few yobbos and the police arrived quickly; it was pure self-protection, really – what else can you do when some young drunkard takes a swing? And then he said, 'If you'll excuse me, ladies, I'm needed in the kitchen.'

Derek made good his escape and numbly began unpacking his shopping. Faint backdrop talk reached him of sweetheart neck tunic tops in blended acetate and polymide with fluted bottoms and appliqué detail although, unhappily, the size 12 in topaz had already gone.

'You like air fresheners, don't you?' It was Charlotte. Derek jumped: in his fatigued, distracted state he hadn't heard her follow him out. She picked up one of his purchases, inspected it, and quoted from the packaging. '"Glade Plug-ins. Essence of Nature. Forty-five days of freshness." Good heavens! What will happen on the forty-sixth?'

Derek said nothing.

'Don't put one of those in my room, will you?' Charlotte said.

'Why? Are you staying?'

'For the weekend if that's OK.'

'Fine, then.' Derek lowered his voice. 'You haven't told them, have you?'

'About my fall from grace? No.'

'Good.'

'Not yet, anyway. Oh, this is interesting.'

It was a pack of Odor-Eaters. Derek snatched it back. 'What do you mean, "not yet"?'

'Oh, don't worry, I won't shame the family name – unless, of course, you refuse to reveal full details of your heroic bar room brawl.'

'It wasn't like that, really. Not at all.'

'Oh, don't spoil it, Dad! It's going to be the talk of tomorrow's party.'

'Party? What party?'

'The one Moz is throwing. She's invited both of us – that's why she's here.'

'She looks like she's already at a party,' said Derek grumpily. He hoped the cocktail glasses hadn't left any rings.

'Striking, isn't she?' said Charlotte dreamily. 'Like Trinity in *The Matrix*. Anyway, it's an Easter egg party and it's in the afternoon.'

'I don't suppose I'll be there,' Derek said.

'Oh, I think you will.'

'Why?'

' 'Cos I've invited Granny and Grandad. You'd want to keep an eye on those two, wouldn't you?'

# chapter 8

The sounds that Derek's ears were pricked for reached him as he picked lint off the hall rug: the buzz of a Triumph Spitfire alighting on his forecourt; a driver's side door slamming almost before the engine noise had died; Hush Puppy footsteps quick-stepping up the path. Derek opened the door to a small man in a salmon-coloured shirt tucked into white casual slacks. Matching patches of cropped grey hair bookended his head. In his arms he held a cardboard carton. Breathlessly, he said, 'We've brought a few things with us, son. Just to help out.'

Derek's father Lester raised his Ray-Bans and smiled. It was a wide smile but with a hint of caution in it. From the step Derek looked down at a grid of foil-covered corks poking from corrugated housings. 'That's fantastic, Dad,' he said, feeling a faint ache in his heart – an ache of love spiked with foreboding. He looked down the drive and called, 'Are you OK there, Mum?'

His mother, Phyllis, was lifting a cool box from the Spitfire's tiny boot. She said, 'We tried the new superstore yesterday . . .' then tailed off, not looking up. 'It's just some . . .' She set the cool box down again, flipped open the lid and squinted in. 'Eh . . . barbecue chicken wings with tangy, ready-to-cook salsa-style coating. I bought some coleslaw too. And some Easter eggs, of course . . .'

'That's new, isn't it, Phyl?' her husband called. 'The salsa-style coating?'

'It is, yes.'

'It's new, you see.' Lester offered the confirmation to his son.

'Les, give us a hand.' Phyllis had heaved the cool box out of the boot again and was now swaying dangerously on her kitten heels.

'Coming, love,' said Lester and skipped bandily towards her. Derek was impressed by how nimble his father was at seventy-eight. As he had learned to accept his physical decline he had compared himself more often with the man who'd sired him and hoped that enduring sprightliness had been passed down. Derek's looks came from his mother who had decided straight after his extremely tricky birth that she'd bestow this gift just once. 'Never again,' she'd told the midwife as soon as Derek's cord was cut.

The three Hawkers went through to the kitchen. Derek looked on as his parents negotiated stewardship of their gifts, flitting round each other like courting butterflies, each completing the other's train of thought.

'Shall I put these . . .'

'. . . in the fridge? I would.'

'What about the . . .'

'. . . leave it on the table, for a minute.'

This was the way they carried on, looking to Derek for approval now and then. Their need for praise reminded him of the similar hunger he'd felt during childhood: should he, perhaps, reward his parents with a stick of liquorice or a boiled sweet?

'I was wondering,' said Lester, 'where our beautiful granddaughter is.'

'Beautiful *and* brainy, Les.'

'She's already next door,' said Derek, 'helping with the preparations.'

'We got a card from Matthew last week,' said Phyllis, bending over the champagne case.

'Got a lady friend, he says,' added Lester. 'A sculptor, apparently.'

Derek said, 'Do you need a hand with that champagne, Mum?' He didn't want to talk about Matthew, who'd telephoned that morning.

'Hi, Dad! Happy Easter!'

'Thanks, Matthew.'

'Ours is nearly over! Isn't that strange?'

'That's the time difference for you . . .'

'Right! You're OK there, are you, Dad? I spoke to Mum earlier.'

'That's nice.'

'She seems fine. Going well, apparently. Do you have company today? Is Charlotte down?'

'She's here but still asleep.'

(This was untrue: she'd been recovering from her morning pukefest.)

'That's students for you, eh! Dad, I wanted to say something to you . . .'

'As it happens, Matthew, I was just getting in the bath. Could I call you back later? Maybe tomorrow morning your time?'

Lester got the kettle on. Phyllis briskly made some parma ham sandwiches. Derek wondered if his parents had decided not to ask after Denise, a possibility he pondered with both guilt and relief. Once again he wondered if he ought to be more honest with his parents. Once again he let things lie.

Nessie greeted the three Hawkers when they arrived. She showed them her friendship bracelet which, she explained, she'd made that morning with Charlotte and this nearly grown-up girl who was Sam's long-lost relative. 'She's called Bou. Funny name, isn't it? It's short for Boudica who was a queen and a warrior in Olden Times.'

'Would *you* like to be a warrior?' asked Phyllis.

'It's more fun being a monster,' Nessie said.

She led them out to the garden. Half a dozen other adults had already arrived along with their small children; friends of Nessie and Norton, Derek presumed. Moz moved effusively among her guests wearing a short, shocking pink cardigan over a black jumpsuit that clung to her like a skin. Norton was at her elbow, looking stern. There was no sign of Sam.

'Is that the lady of the house?' Lester asked after checking that Phyllis was out of hearing range.

'It is, Dad, yes,' Derek replied.

'How old would she be then? Mid-thirties, maybe?'

'Early forties, I think, Dad.'

'Bit like Madonna, isn't she?'

'Not a lot, Dad, no.'

'Oh, you know what I mean.'

'Yes, probably . . .'

Moz spotted them as they spoke. She rushed across. 'How nice to see you, Derek,' she enthused. She kissed him on the cheek rather more firmly than he expected and offered him her own cheek in return. He pecked it chastely, conscious of his father looking on. Moz kissed him as well. 'You must be Lester,' she informed him as he went on tiptoe with puckered lips.

'A pleasure meeting you, my dear,' beamed Lester and squeezed his hostess's hand. Like Derek, he was breathing in Moz's perfume, which signalled something other than maidenly observance of a big date in the Christian calendar.

'It's a *madhouse* here,' said Moz, with relish. 'Thank goodness for your daughter, Derek. She's a *wonderful* organiser and *brilliant* with children.'

'You can keep her if you like,' Derek replied.

'Oh, she's a talented girl,' said Lester. 'May I ask what that is you're wearing, by the way?'

Moz looked down at her outfit. 'It's just a fun thing, really,' she laughed. 'I call it my *Avengers* rig. As in Diana Rigg.'

'I meant your fragrance, my dear.' He was still holding Moz's hand. 'It's Obsession, isn't it?'

Moz turned to Derek, impressed. 'Your father is a connoisseur! I'm sure Sam wouldn't have known.'

Lester basked. Derek winced. He asked, 'Where is Sam, by the way?'

'Oh, he's in charge of catering – with a little help from Bou. I expect you'll meet her soon; now *there's* something to look forward to.' Her raised eyebrow capped a vaguely pregnant pause. 'Anyway, gentlemen. I must get the egg hunt started.' She pivoted and swept away.

'Shut up, Dad,' said Derek.

'I didn't say anything!'

'I could hear you thinking. She's a married woman, you know.'

Further down the lawn, Moz clapped her hands for silence and began to speak. 'Firstly, thank you everyone for coming,' she said. 'It's so lovely to see you all – friends and neighbours – and so nice of you to join us at such short notice. As you'll be aware this little gathering isn't only about Easter but it's also to welcome a very special guest . . .' She paused and looked around. 'Where is she now . . . ? Sam? Do you know where she is?'

She was looking towards the conservatory, which was where Sam had been. He was hovering over the buffet and taking a closer interest in the humus dip than even humus dips are usually comfortable with. 'I think she's over there,' he answered disconnectedly and pointed to a rhododendron forty yards distant. From behind it, a female voice cried 'Over here!' but it was Charlotte who stood up. Then Derek saw that she had company: another teenage girl whom Charlotte took by the hand and began leading in the direction of the party throng.

Derek could detect, even from a distance, that Charlotte was relishing the absurdity of the scene. Her companion, though, appeared less keen. As the pair drew closer it became increasingly clear that the contrast between them did not end there. Bou – for it was obviously she – was both smaller yet larger than Charlotte at the same time. Where Charlotte made a virtue of appearing to be plain Bou was petite yet busty, and her hair was dazzling. She looked a little lost. Charlotte, on the other hand, was in her element. 'Sorry about that,' she announced. 'We've just been inspecting some early season aphids, haven't we, Bou?'

'We sure have,' Bou agreed, though not exactly as if she'd been waiting to inspect an early aphid all her life. She fiddled with her fingers. 'Well, hi, everybody.' She blushed and waved, self-consciously. Moz picked up the thread.

'Well, Boudica is from Houston, Texas. She is a long-lost relative of Sam's – isn't she, darling?'

Sam did not respond.

'ISN'T SHE, DARLING?' repeated Moz.

Sam jumped as if someone had just turned up his hearing aid. 'She is, darling, yes.'

'Just turned up out of the blue, didn't she?'

'She did. She did. Indeed.'

Derek detected a new angle on the couple's chemistry. Sam and Moz; S&M. Shouldn't their forename initials be reversed?

'Anyway,' concluded Moz, 'we're all *delighted* to see her . . .' Bou smiled again. She was, Derek could see, exceptionally pretty – and terrified. Moz laughed a little wildly, and switched tack. 'Now! Children! Would you all please listen carefully!' The youngsters shoaled like hungry fish. 'Boudica and Charlotte have hidden the eggs all over the garden,' Moz explained. 'When I say "go" you can rush off and try to find them, but . . .' She raised a hand for emphasis. 'But *no one* must start eating an egg yet. The game is to bring them all back here and there will be a prize for the person who finds the most. When all the eggs have been found, we'll share them out equally. That means there won't be any squabbling and no one is left out. Do you understand?'

'Yes,' the children cried. Nessie and her friends were all ready to run, although Norton in his maths hat stood all on his own several yards away.

'Good,' said Moz. 'I ought to say, by the way, that this excellent egg hunt system was all Charlotte's brilliant idea.'

'Well done, Charlotte gal!' shouted Lester, and started clapping. Charlotte performed an extravagant mock curtsey. Phyllis led the others in joining the small ripple of applause. If only, Derek thought, Charlotte's birth control arrangements had been so smoothly organised.

'All right, then!' said Moz. 'When I say "go" . . . GO!'

* * *

For Derek, the next hour passed painlessly enough. He watched in wonder as the egg hunt was won by Norton. When the other kids rushed off he proceeded calmly towards a secluded garden shed. Nobody noticed him go in there or emerge five minutes later pushing a small wheelbarrow. It contained seventeen eggs, which, as Norton pointed out, was just over half the number hidden. That meant he'd already won the prize and was it a new calculator, please?

Moz looked at him suspiciously. 'Norton, did you cheat?'

'No.' He blinked under the maths hat, a human R2D2 without the little wheels.

'OK, Norton, let me put it this way. Did you play a trick?'

'No.'

'Norton? Did. You. Play. A. Trick?'

'Ach-ully, yes.'

The full picture emerged gradually. Earlier in the day, when Charlotte and Bou had been out hiding the eggs, Norton had used his telescope to watch them from an upstairs window. Then, when they'd come in, he'd sneaked out. 'He claims it wasn't cheating,' Moz told Derek. 'He said it was thinking ahead.' She added, enigmatically, 'It's not a trait he inherited from his father.'

Something in the way she said it caused Derek to look at Sam who stood nearby with Bou. An air of absence clung to him as the edgy young visitor explained to Lester and Phyllis how she got her name.

'It's short for Boudica? You know? British warrior *queen*? Fought, like, the *Romans*?'

'Sounds like your British connections go back a very long way,' said Phyllis kindly.

'Well, sort of . . .' Bou made a small, embarrassed bray, perhaps to symbolise the burden of history.

'So how does it all link up with Sam?' Lester asked. 'Has he fought any Romans lately?'

'It's a complicated story,' said Sam, ignoring the joke. 'You know Americans: always trying to dig up family roots. I'm sorry, would you excuse us? We're needed in the kitchen.' He took Bou by the elbow and virtually dragged her away.

'Is she a cheerleader?' asked Lester after they'd gone.

'No, silly,' Phyllis replied. 'Weren't you listening just now? She's a hairdresser in London. Lovely girl, isn't she? And very young to be so far from home.'

'Still, travel broadens the mind, doesn't it, Phyl?'

'It certainly does, Les.'

Derek had to smile. His parents' enthusiasm for all things continental had been a defining feature of his Hounslow childhood. Thanks to it no one alive had been better qualified than he to help the Veg exploit the English discovery of Scandinavian chic. The smorgasbord was part of Derek's culture. Lester and Phyllis had been in the vanguard of the Ryvita revolution and sawn six inches off the legs of their old furniture before anybody else in the A3 corridor knew a sauna from a Saab. When they'd moved down to their elder community in Folkestone three years ago they'd said it was to be nearer the Euro. It was only half a joke.

'Who's the fellow in the wheelchair?' Lester asked.

'Huh?' Derek was deep in thought. Charlotte was pregnant – it was too much to compute.

'Over there. Just arrived with his wife – I presume it's his wife. She's talking to Charlotte. Can you see?'

Derek could. In the wheelchair sat Lorcan wearing an Ireland rugby shirt and a pair of wraparound shades. From her station behind him Galina waved.

'Friend of yours?' asked Lester.

'Neighbour,' Derek groaned. 'Dad, I've got a business call to make. I'll have to nip back home. Is that OK?'

'Don't worry, son,' said Lester as Derek ducked away. Hawker junior would have scarpered at that moment but was detained for several minutes by Moz's introducing him to several other guests. At last he made it to the hall and was giving a parting scowl to the prize ass on the wall when a voice with a familiar foreign accent called his name.

'Derek! You're not going? Please! Lorcan needs you desperately.'

He turned in near-exasperation. 'Does he, Galina? What for?'

'Is about Doonican's; and the police. Is very serious, Derek, please.'

Derek's shoulders slumped. She had her helpless face on and he reluctantly caved in.

'All right, Galina. Where is he?'

'In here.' She was standing near the doorway to a room Derek hadn't been in before. 'Too much sunshine outside,' she explained. 'Go in, please. I will come back later.'

She dashed away. The door stood slightly ajar. Derek pushed it open and walked in on a scene from a surrealistic dream. Lorcan had settled his pink portliness into an oyster-shaped armchair that set the standard for the rest of the decor. A pair of life-size china tigers lounged on either side of an elaborate fireplace. A thick, mocktiger rug was spread across the floor. Derek recognised the aspiration: chic bordello; love nest; sexual libertines live here – and who knows what they get up to amid these soft furnishings. Lorcan's presence there did not enhance the effect although he'd clearly made himself at home. A wooden walking stick rested against one of his knees. He was still wearing the shades. Derek wondered where the wheelchair had gone.

'Hello, Derek,' said Lorcan sombrely. 'I owe you an explanation, to be sure.'

Derek said nothing. He sat down in another chair, straightened a wayward antimacassar and said, 'Come on, let's hear it then.'

Lorcan cleared his throat. 'I'm deeply embarrassed by what happened on Friday night,' he said. 'And deeply damaged too. I'm not only speaking here about my reputation as a businessman but also about my health. As you can see,' he went on, touching the walking stick, 'the trauma has had a cruel effect on me.'

'I didn't realise,' Derek said, 'that putting on a strip show can make such an impact on your legs.'

'Oh yes,' said Lorcan with a bitter laugh; the laugh of one who knows. 'In my case, yes. You see, I didn't want any part in it. It was forced on me.'

'*Forced* on you? How?'

'By Hooper.'

'Who's Hooper?'

'The one with the tattoos who tried to hit me.'

'Right. And hit me instead.'

'You saved me, Derek. I'll always be grateful.'

'Yes.' Derek scowled. 'I've heard all about my heroic exploits from your wife.'

'Certainly, by St Paul. It was a frightful business and not cricket at all.'

No, Derek thought. Not cricket. Pretty scary, actually. And this was getting pretty scary too. Had Lorcan lost his mind? Derek said, 'Get to the point, will you – what is this about?'

Lorcan shifted in his oyster. 'Derek,' he said, 'I need your help.'

'You'll be lucky,' Derek said.

'Please, Derek, hear me out. I've been charged by the police with licensing offences and I want to call you as a witness in my defence.'

'What defence?'

'Like I said, Derek, I didn't want those . . .' He hesitated then continued, slipping into his heritage accent. 'I didn't want that parcel of whores in my pub. It was all Hooper's doing. He organised the whole thing and he took all the money. He said if I didn't agree to having his girls in his boys would trash the place. Derek, what could I do?'

Derek thought his answer over. He settled on 'Bullshit'.

'Derek, it's not! I promise on St Jove.'

'Don't make me laugh, Lorcan. And what about Hooper anyway?'

'He's disappeared,' said Lorcan. 'Left the country probably – and his boys. But the police don't care about him, Derek. They're just out to get me!'

'Oh, come on.'

'Oh, so they are! They're always out to get us Irish! Remember the Godalming Four?'

'It was the Guildford Four.'

Lorcan chuckled mirthlessly. 'Not for my people, Derek. Not for *my* people. Oh no.'

Derek had had enough. Lorcan was a lunatic. Must be.

He had to get away. 'I want no part of this,' he said and rose to leave.

Then Lorcan said, incongruously, 'Galina still knows nothing about it, by the way.'

Derek halted. 'Why do you mention that?' He stared at Lorcan hard. But he remembered something, too: keeping Galina in the dark was also important for him.

'Oh, no reason,' said Lorcan lightly, then added: 'Your daughter's very clever, isn't she?'

'What are you saying, Lorcan?'

'I'm only saying, ahem . . .' He was suddenly tentative,

a twittish Englishman again. 'I'm only saying that clever people tend to . . . well, they work things out.'

'Are you threatening me?'

'Em, sorry, how do you mean?'

'Are you hinting that if I don't help you get off the hook in court you'll tell Charlotte what really went on at Doonican's?'

Lorcan appeared flustered suddenly. 'Good heavens, my dear old chap! I never meant any such thing. But you see, you see . . . if I'm found guilty then it'll be in all the papers. And then, well, there'll be no keeping it a secret after that . . .'

Derek's face was thunderous. Yet Lorcan's logic could not be faulted. He was stuck with this idiot, bound to him in this insane complicity.

'. . . and Galina might see it and what might happen when your wife comes home?' Lorcan shrugged helplessly. 'You know how it is, Derek – women do love gossiping, don't they?'

# chapter 9

In the Animal Hospital small hearts fluttered in wood shaving nests as Charlotte thought about the thing growing inside her, the thing she didn't yet know what to call. Bud? Seed? Alien Invader? Embryonic Harbinger of Doom? She was back in her room in Brixton seated on the floor with her back against the wall and her wildlife sanatorium at eye level on her right. She listened to the rustling of a recovering blackbird that had slammed into her window. She returned the whiskery stare of a wounded mouse she'd rescued from a cat. She was thinking hard. 'What next?'

Nobody answered, for Charlotte had no immediate company. Lindy and the other girls were watching the final night of *Easter Bunny Big Brother*. Their outraged shrieks, and groans of derision, reached Charlotte from downstairs.

'Bimbo!'

'Slapper!'

'Tart!'

'Can you believe it's still engaged?'

Lindy was the most outraged. She was conducting a frantic phone vote vendetta against a contestant called Alice, a blonde, flirty girl from Barnsley with a jewel in her navel and manicured hands that either hung limply from daintily cocked wrists or were thumb-hitched in the plunging waistband of her tiny shorts.

In Lindy's fervent view Alice had prospered on the strength of northern lass fake innocence and a promise that if she won she would strip off. Charlotte sympathised. And yet she took a broader view of why Alice had got so far. Beguiling boys – 'stupid boys' as Lindy put it – was part of it for sure, but Charlotte thought women bought the Alice package too. Not all women, of course: not clever, feisty young women like her who could see through the fantasy. More the sorts of women who bought glossy magazines with dozy headlines on the front.

MAKE YOUR HORMONES HORNY!

GET THIS SPRAY AND GET THE GUY!

WIN A TINY WAIST AND GREAT BIG BOOBS!

Anyway, that was the boring world of Alice: all blokes and beauty tips. Charlotte cared little for *Big Brother* but, even so, was interested to see if Alice's lead would slip as the final evening progressed leaving transvestite biker Osama – or 'Susan' as he called himself on Fridays – to take the prize. What might the outcome reveal about popular attitudes and tastes? Alice was obviously a contemporary and yet essentially conservative construction of female availability. What, though, of Osama? Did his survival to this stage signify growing acceptance of gender elasticity, a fascination with freaks, or some complex and encoded combination of the two?

Charlotte pondered these conundrums pleasurably. The gender studies option she'd taken in her first year had opened her mind to whole new ways of theorising human attraction. This had not endeared her to the more doctrinaire academics teaching her main courses but it did make biology and psychology more fun. Entertaining quarrels could be had in seminars. Essays could become sort of a game, like the one she'd been set in November.

*Elucidate the insights into human mating strategies gained from the application of evolutionary science.*

Charlotte's response had started: *The premise of this question is fundamentally flawed in that it implicitly fails to recognise how powerfully attraction is mediated by cultural expectations and social norms . . .*

Professor Lumb had only given her a C. Charlotte had told him quietly but crisply to his face that he'd done it out of intellectual fear. The incident had been a milestone on her continuing journey out of the mainstream of her discipline and into dissident waters that excited her far more. Charlotte had grasped early in her undergraduate career that most of her fellow students were orthodox and dull. She began to see herself as an independent scholar, a quester after higher forms of truth. It dawned on her that she'd been like that all her life. Throughout her childhood she'd been seen by others – particularly female peers – as an uncool good girl introvert, albeit prickly with wit if approached in the wrong way. Bullies had never bothered her. For similar reasons, though, she hadn't had a lot of friends. Too clever, that Charlotte Hawker. Too intense.

There was a light knock at the door.

'Come in.'

It was Lindy. 'You all right, Lotte?' she said.

'Yes. Just thinking about lemmings.'

'Oh yeah?' Lindy did her loopy laugh and sniffed. She always sniffed.

'Not really,' Charlotte said. 'But, speaking of blind conformity, how's your friend Alice getting on?'

'Too well,' Lindy groaned. 'They've given them this pair of giant rabbit's ears and the winner is supposed to put them on. As you can imagine . . .'

'Alice is milking it . . .'

'Too right.'

They scoffed in solidarity. Lindy, though, did not advance into the room. She knew better than to do that when Charlotte was in one of her thinking moods. Instead, she said, 'Come down and join us later, maybe? You know how we enjoy your cutting wordplay.'

'I might. Or I might go to bed.'

'Relaxing weekend, then?'

'Not relaxing, maddening – as always with my dad.'

'Oh, really? And I thought he was so *sweet*.'

'Sweet? That's a laugh.'

Lindy grinned and sniffed deeply. 'OK, I'm off! Gotta keep bashing that phone!'

She went downstairs. Charlotte didn't follow but she didn't go to bed either. There was too much to chew over – too many events with hidden meanings to unpack and too many people to analyse. She'd had a good weekend in Brayston – surprisingly. The party had been a laugh: she'd loved Nessie and Norton who had reminded her of the two sides of herself when she'd been little – the imaginative and the intense. She'd enjoyed seeing Granny and Grandad too, all the more so for inviting them herself. And then there was Boudica, Sam's fourth cousin twice removed or whatever: an extraordinary creature who'd seemed to be a big dingbat at first but had turned out to be really quite endearing. Even Moz admitted she meant well.

And Charlotte thought Moz was wonderful. It had been a bit weird when she'd appeared on the doorstep looking so – well, sexy was the word – at two o'clock on a Saturday afternoon and asked if her dad was in. But it wasn't because she was sleeping with him. Foxy Thomasina and touchy old Derek? Charlotte didn't think so! What was more, Moz had saved her from Galina. Charlotte sniggered at the memory: one minute she'd been sitting alone in the house thinking what a grouchy old wreck her father was, the next this mad woman she'd never met before was telling her he was the Lone Ranger! It had taken Charlotte twenty minutes to work out that Galina was one of the new people in the house across the close. It was Moz who had calmed her down. Putting on QVC was her idea – and opening the bottle of wine. Then Moz had started moaning amusingly about Sam and how he'd told this loopy Boudica girl, who'd appeared from nowhere at lunchtime, that she could stay with them whenever she wanted to! What was it Moz had said? It was like being trapped in a L'Oreal commercial or invaded by the dippy one from *Totally Spies*, which was Nessie's favourite TV show.

Then Charlotte had twigged that Boudica was the girl she'd met on the village green earlier that day. She smiled as she remembered telling Moz the story and the two of them going 'Bou!' 'Eeek!' 'Bou!' 'Eeek!' at each other for a while, and Galina looking confused. But then Galina had got interested in the . . . oh yeah, the sweetheart neck tunic tops, that was it. And then Derek had walked in. Charlotte sniggered. Her dad was *so* easy to read. That's *my* sparkling wine they're drinking! Those are *my* retro cocktail glasses! Those are *my* drinks coasters they're not using! And then Galina had virtually jumped on him! *So* embarrassing – for him . . . !

Charlotte straightened her back and shoulders so they pressed against the embossed swirls of the old wallpaper that lined her room. She liked doing that; liked feeling all the bones. Then she undid the top button of her trousers and spread her hands out on her belly – a mini-foetus in there, weird – and reran the sequence where she'd told Derek her big news.

*'I'm pregnant, Dad.'*

It seemed fair to say she hadn't made his day – again. It was interesting, wasn't it, that she'd dumped him in the tapas bar and yet allowed him – *wanted* him, actually – to see and smell her grubby room, encounter her grubby housemates and maybe suffer a little at Mum's hands by watching a video diary that Mum hadn't made for him? Laurent had thought it was interesting. He'd asked Charlotte about it that evening, although she hadn't said too much. Going on about your parents was such a first-year-at-uni thing, she thought – such a cliché. And everyone only said clichéd things, especially about the idea of your parents having sex. It was always 'disgusting' or 'gross'. But Charlotte – being Charlotte – had stopped doing that when she was still at school. Why should the thought of your parents having sex be so repulsive? That was how they'd made you, wasn't it?

She missed Laurent, actually – not terribly, but a bit. At the same time she was glad he wasn't there. His feelings about the bud, seed or alien invader would only get in the way.

It was after ten o'clock. Charlotte got up carefully – it was strange the way she'd started to do that – and wove through the clutter on her floor to reach her desk. Waking up her laptop she read Matthew's latest e-mail again.

Dear Sis,

As you know I am concerned that Dad is suffering from stress. I spoke to him yesterday evening your time while you were partying with Granny and Grandad next door and he was not his usual vivid, robust self . . .

**I wonder why, Charlotte thought. Now let me see . . .**

Of course at this distance it is hard to be precise. However, there are certain fairly clear indicators and I'd be interested if you noticed these. They include
  a) emotional outbursts
  b) high level of self-criticism
  c) feeling under-appreciated
  d) eating and drinking too much
  e) becoming obsessed with detail

**Sound familiar, Charlotte thought.**

The above are consistent with ENTJ personality types of which I'm convinced Dad is an example. However, I have detected in Dad an increasing tendency to intro-version: he may be shifting from being an E – meaning an Extraverted style of communication – towards being an I – an Introverted type. Stress indicators in INTJs are much like those of ENTJs, but watch out also for the following.
  a) Dad becoming careless and slovenly and, para-doxically,
  b) spending too much time tidying and cleaning

**That last one rang a bell. He'd spent a lot of time alone with that Dyson . . .**

On the strength of my suspicions I could set out for Dad

a programme of remedial strategies. For example, getting more in touch with his tender side and improving his listening skills. However, as an inveterate ESTJ I am aware that making such firm judgements may irritate an INTP – that's what I believe you to be – by seeming too controlling. So I won't.

Yours affectionately, Matthew

She wrote back saying simply, You're such a sweet Jung thing. More soon.

Matthew made her smile, which she thought was odd because she often perceived him as really just a nerd version of Dad. Still, she had to admit she was a bit like Dad in some ways too. For instance, she understood why he wouldn't answer Matthew's psychometric question-naire. She didn't want her psyche read either, thank you. On the other hand she was curious so she'd called up the Myers-Briggs Type Indicator website. There she'd dis-covered that I stood for Introversion as opposed to E for Extraversion and meant she drew her energy from the internal world of thoughts.

True, very true.

N stood for iNtuition as opposed to S for Sensing which was Matthew. N people preferred to think what things might be like rather than settle for the concrete here-and-now. They liked the big picture, they saw possibilities.

True again.

T was for Thinking rather than F for Feeling, which

meant she sought truth and fairness more than she sought harmony. Hmmm. Well, Dad would probably agree. And Mum would say he wasn't one to talk.

And, finally, Matthew reckoned she was a P which stood for Perceiving instead of a J for Judging and meant she'd rather live in a spontaneous and flexible way whereas Js wanted everything well ordered and planned.

Dad would probably agree with that too. And, actually, so would she. Charlotte made up a little song:

> *INTP*
> *Do these letters describe me?*

It was quite clever, really – the Myers-Briggs stuff, not her song. Or maybe it was just a Cosmo quiz with airs. Or too like the tick box so-called research behind evolutionary psychology. And that reminded her: wasn't she supposed to be hungry to have a baby, to obey her fundamental inner urge? She called up another website, one she'd recently logged under 'favourites' – the Brook Advisory. She scrolled through the vital passages again.

Note that the stage of pregnancy is calculated from the first day of the woman's last period.

Five or six weeks already – it was amazing, really. She'd mentioned this to Derek in the car on the way down; not to scare him, exactly, although that was some of it, but to break the silence he'd slumped into.

> To get an abortion on the NHS, you will need to be
> referred by a doctor to your local hospital or clinic. Your
> own GP, or a doctor at a local family planning clinic, or
> at Brook (if you are under 25) can do this. It is important
> to go along as soon as possible.

She hadn't actually been to a doctor yet, just the chemist
for testing kits. Perhaps she'd better find one.

> The abortion pill is a form of abortion available to
> women who are under 9 weeks pregnant. The woman
> will be given a pill to swallow and 36 to 48 hours later
> a tablet will be placed in her vagina. These two drugs
> will end most early pregnancies within the following
> four hours. A minimum of 2 visits to a hospital or clinic
> are involved.

This sounded better, Charlotte thought, than having
something sharp stuck up you. Yuk. However . . .

> This method is not always available on the NHS so you
> will need to check with the referring doctor. It is available
> privately.

Wasn't she in BUPA or something, through Dad's company policy? She couldn't remember and that meant she
would have to ask him and that would be like asking for
more money. He was already paying her tuition fees, her
accommodation fees and her living costs. That was quite

enough dependency. Anyway, there was still time left to think.

From downstairs came a huge chorus of jeering. Charlotte got up and switched on her TV. Alice was getting naked even as Osama left the house. In less than a minute she had the bunny ears on and everything else off. But Charlotte soon lost interest. She much preferred matters of life and death.

part two: summer

# chapter 10

'Hi Jade!' trilled Nessie into her Barbiemobile. 'It's me, Amber . . . oh, I'm fine. Listen, you won't *believe* what's happened? It's, like, *amazing*?'

Nessie had discovered many amazing things lately. For example, upspeak? And that the good thing about chickenpox was you could have it without feeling ill; well, you did feel ill at first but you didn't know it was chickenpox *egg-zackly* until you got the spots. And by the time you got the spots you didn't feel ill any more, just itchy, and then the spots got scabs on and you shouldn't ever scratch them because, Sam said, if you scratched one and it fell off you got a scar.

That's why she was still off school – in case a scab got knocked off by mistake. Sam said one more day off school was OK because it was the last week before the summer holidays and they wouldn't be learning much anyway. And he said Norton could stay home too because *he* might have chickenpox as well, though not the spots yet, and it wouldn't be nice to give chickenpox to other children who might be going to the seaside or Florida or France with their families next week. Sam said it was quite nice having her and Norton at home now and again though they mustn't interrupt him when he was on the phone helping people work out how to have more fun at work. But they'd got noisy and bored. So they'd visited Charlotte who lived next door – sort of, some of the time – and she'd told them she'd had chickenpox when she was seven too. And now they were in her bedroom, and Norton was doing some maths at Charlotte's desk, but Nessie was being Amber, which beat maths any day.

'So everything is, like, really cool?' Amber explained to Jade. 'I'm not at school because I'm sick even though I'm not, like, sick? I just look, like, *rully gross*? And if my teacher tells me off I'll just say "*what-everrr*".' Nessie broke off from being Amber for a moment and practised her 'what-everrr' hand gesture, a kind of throwaway flip of a wrist. Then she went back to being Amber and spoke again to Jade. 'Can you, like, hold on a moment, sweetie?' She put the Barbiemobile down and readjusted Mr Heath. She'd placed him lovingly beside her, propped against Charlotte's pillow, but he had suddenly keeled over, perhaps because he hadn't been secure there in the first place, perhaps because he'd become overwhelmed by nausea.

Checking that Norton was still absorbed under his hat, she tiptoed on to the landing. Yes, Charlotte was still there, half wrapped around the banister trying to make out what was being said downstairs. Nessie really liked it that Charlotte was doing this because she sometimes did the same thing at her own house. She listened in on Sam and Moz when she was meant to be asleep and they were downstairs doing snogging on the tiger rug – yes, she knew *all* about *that*, baby! – or, as had happened a few times lately, when they were in the kitchen 'having words' about Bou. Nessie would have liked to sit with Charlotte – they could be Girls Sharing A Secret – but in the end she thought she'd better not. Charlotte was wearing her Do Not Disturb frown which was a bit like Norton's. The voices from downstairs were deep and stern. So Nessie went back to Charlotte's bed and picked up the Barbiemobile again.

'Hi Jade! Sorr-ee! Just feeding Bouncer . . . Yeah, he's my puppy. He's so *cute*? Anyway, as I was saying. Charlotte, she's, like, my *pretend* big sister? She looks after animals that have had accidents and things? But now I have a real big sister too. Can you believe that? She just, like, *appeared* one day? Her name's Boudica who was a queen of England in the Olden Days and she had, like, really red hair. And she did fighting, though it was, you know, good fighting 'cos she had to do it, it wasn't 'cos she *wanted* to do fighting, like, for fun.

'Anyway. Boudica – that's *my* Boudica, not the Olden Days one, hee hee! – *she* has red hair too and *her* daddy is *my* daddy but my *mummy*, she *isn't* Boudica's mummy! Boudica has a different mummy who lives in America. And my daddy used to know Boudica's mummy . . . well he must have mustn't he? 'Cos, you know . . .'

Amber put Jade on hold while Nessie thought about this Bou business again. It was hard to imagine Sam had had another girlfriend long, long ago before he even knew Moz and that they had made a baby girl. Sam had explained it all to her. He'd told her that he and the other girlfriend broke up before he knew the baby had been made and that he didn't hear about the girlfriend having a baby at all until years and years later. He'd wondered if it was possible that this baby was his but he hadn't *egg-zackly* wondered about it very much. Then he'd married Moz and never told her: after all, he'd hadn't really known if there was anything to tell.

But then she, Nessie, had been born. And Sam told her he'd loved her so, so, so, so much – as much as an elephant eats, or even two elephants – that he'd begun wondering about the other baby and if he was its daddy and whether it was wondering where its daddy was. And *then* Norton was born and Sam had wondered some more. But he still hadn't said anything to Moz. Anyway . . . *then* he'd had this letter from a girl called Boudica saying I am in England where I am learning to do hair and I think you are my daddy and can I come and see you please? And *then* she'd rung him up and said she really had to see him or go mad. And *that's* when he'd told Moz. And Moz had been cross – not because he'd had a baby with another girlfriend – not *egg-zackly* – but because he'd been a wimp and never told her anything and he'd invited her – Bou, that is – over on Easter Sunday without asking Moz first.

Nessie remembered Easter Sunday because of the party and those two old people who she'd liked. Nessie thought about Bou, who was a bit like the girls in *Totally Spies*, which was cool, but not as adventurous, and she thought about Charlotte who wasn't like the girls in *Totally Spies* at all. She was more like, well, a grown-up. She had this Animal Hospital and it was brilliant. She saved mice and birds and even *snakes*. And even *insects*! That made her a bit more like a proper big sister, even though she couldn't be one really. It was all a bit confusing. So Nessie picked up the Barbiemobile again and became Amber and said to Jade, 'And what's *rully*, *rully*, like, *amazing* is that Charlotte, my pretend big sister, is going to have a baby! *Egg-zackly!* In time for Christmas!'

Amber put Jade on hold again and Nessie scratched her head. When her pretend big sister Charlotte had the baby, could she be the baby's pretend auntie? Would Norton want to be its pretend uncle? He was a bit young for it, maybe. And a bit grumpy. Hmm. Families were difficult things.

Charlotte decided to wait until the detectives had left before taking Nessie and Norton home. Going downstairs with them before that would risk exposing the children to their suspicious manner, something she could feel even from a distance in their voices, which were hard beneath a deferential veil.

'Mr Hawker? Sorry to trouble you, sir. We're police officers. You're probably aware that some of our colleagues conducted a raid on the house across the way earlier this morning – the house of Mr Lorcan O'Neill . . .'

There'd been a tricky moment earlier when one of the pair, a blunt, bearded man wearing a collar and tie under a short leather coat, had come up the stairs to find her. Charlotte had guessed that Derek had been asked who else was in the house and that the officer was checking what he'd said. Hearing his heavy footfall on the stairs she'd come out of her bedroom and intercepted him on the landing.

'Hello. You're a policeman.'

'Hello. Yes, I am.'

She'd watched his eyes assess her body, head-to-toe in a flash. In her mother's old dressing gown she'd felt nervous and exposed, even though underneath it she was wearing her new sensible knickers. Charlotte, though, did not do girlishness. When the detective grinned at her, her manner became severe.

'I expect you're seeing who else is in the house.'

'I expect I am.'

'Well, I'm Mr Hawker's daughter and in my bedroom is Natalie, the little girl who lives next door, and her brother Norton. Natalie isn't very well, which is why she's round here.'

The detective had frowned at this. 'You mean, you're looking after them?'

'That's right – to give their father a break.'

'Their father?'

'He works from home.'

'I see . . .' Charlotte had not elaborated. Let the big lump work it out all by himself. 'OK, thank you, ah . . .'

'Charlotte. But perhaps you knew that already.'

'Charlotte Hawker, isn't it?'

'That's correct'

'OK, Miss Hawker . . .'

Charlotte had scowled at the detective's back as he'd returned downstairs. She'd sensed a loaded use of the word 'Miss'. Could he see she was pregnant? Had Dad told him? Had he just guessed?

Her eavesdropping now confirmed that he was the junior partner. The one who hadn't come upstairs was doing most of the talking. She could pick out his Scottish accent but couldn't make out very much of what was being said. She knew, though, that her father was coming under pressure from his tone: a bit over-assertive, getting snippy on points of detail. At one point his voice was raised enough to carry up to her: 'Look, I don't know if I can help you unless you stop beating round the bush. Can't you be more specific? As I've already said, he once mentioned an Aunt Mary but all I know about her is that she's dead.' Then came the muffled registers of the detectives, deliberate, insistent, cold.

Derek showed them out ten minutes later. No niceties were exchanged. Charlotte returned to her bedroom.

'Time to go, Miss Nessie,' she said, rooting round for clothes.

'I'm Amber, remember?' Nessie said.

'Oh yes, sorry Amber.'

Nessie giggled. She watched as her pretend big sister tugged on a T-shirt and jeans. Nessie saw that her breasts were bigger than her mummy's, but not as big as Bou's. How interesting, she thought – no two pairs were quite the same. Was it like that with willies too? She'd have to ask Sam.

'So Amber, how was Jade?' Charlotte asked, twisting a band into her hair.

'Oh, she's, like, crazy as usual?' chirped Nessie in her Amber voice.

'Good,' Charlotte said then added, casually, 'The policemen have gone now, by the way.'

'What did they want?'

'Oh, I don't know. Nothing probably.'

'How can they want nothing?'

'I mean, they probably just wanted to tell my daddy not to worry – because they've taken Lorcan and Galina away. Would you like a last look at my tummy?'

'Yes please!'

Charlotte exposed her belly. It was definitely rounder and a straight, dark line, faint but distinct, ran down it like a seam. Nessie traced it with a finger. 'What's it called again?'

'The *linea nigra*. It means your womb is spreading outwards 'cos your baby's getting bigger.'

'How big is it now?'

'Oh, about this big.' Charlotte held up facing palms five or six inches apart. 'That's from the top of its head to its bottom. Its legs are all tucked up. I've seen them on a special photo called a scan.'

'Cute!' Nessie exclaimed. 'And when will it start kicking?'

'Quite soon, I expect. I'll let you know. Now please get your things together and help Norton get ready too. I'll be back up in a minute.'

Charlotte went down to the lounge. Derek was standing beside the television with a blue feather duster in his hand. He paused when his daughter walked into the room, but failed to make eye contact or speak. Instead he kept on flicking at the empty screen. Charlotte attempted to lighten the mood.

'Searching for hidden clues, then, Dad?'

Derek carried on flicking. Charlotte tried again.

'Many body parts stuffed in the fridge?'

'Ha bloody ha.'

Derek still didn't look her way and Charlotte dropped carefully on to the sofa, letting the silence grow. Her father opened the sliding window and shook out the feather duster with wary thoroughness. The spectacle of male domestic neurosis enthralled the smartass in Charlotte, but the demeanour of her father as he re-entered the house made the smartass feel slightly ashamed. Derek didn't look happy at all.

'So what *was* that about?'

Derek sat down heavily at the opposite end of the sofa. He was sharing the seat with her but only in the sense that sparring boxers share a ring.

'You know they've charged Lorcan with licensing offences . . .'

'Yes.'

'And that I was there with him on the night in question.'

'Being his guardian angel, according to his wife.'

'Yes, yes, Charlotte.' Derek let his eyes roll up so they focused on a more elevated point in the middle distance. 'Well, they took my details at the time and they came over today because they wanted to get a few things straight.'

'About his Aunt Mary?'

Derek looked at her sharply. 'I thought you were upstairs.'

'Sound rises, Dad. It's a scientific fact.'

Derek now spoke with extra care: 'Yes, well, they seem to think he may have been up to something else, possibly more serious. But they couldn't – or wouldn't – say exactly what. They just wanted to know what I might know about him and a certain relative but I'm glad to say I don't know very much.'

Charlotte wondered how straightforward Derek was being. She'd been awake since six-thirty feeling bright and summery and glad her morning sickness had now gone. She'd heard the police arrive outside the O'Neills' house: three carloads. A couple of hours later a string of bagged and labelled items had been carted out and placed in one of the cars. Looked like sheaves of documents, a briefcase, a computer hard disk . . . it wasn't a social call.

'So do you think he's dodgy, Dad? You must have a theory.'

'Must I?'

'Why don't you ask Galina? She adores you, doesn't she?'

'Please?'

'Sorry, Dad. I'd better get back to those kids.'

Derek remained on the sofa, wondering if he'd been snappy with her. Maybe he had. But then, Charlotte ought to know that her sense of the absurd didn't often work for him. He'd made that very clear when she'd rung him that day back in May.

'Hello, Dad. It's me.'

'Where the hell have you been hiding? I've been leaving messages for days.'

'And I've replied to them!'

'No you have *not* replied to them, Charlotte. You've taken the mickey.'

(She'd sent him a text: Don't worry, I'm not dead! Otherwise, silence.)

'Well, I've been very busy.'

'Doing what?'

'Thinking about things.'

'Thinking about what?'

'Babies . . .'

He'd guessed the rest. 'Who's going to look after it, Charlotte?'

'I will, obviously.'

'What, you're giving up university?'

'Of course not!'

'So when you're sitting in lectures or telling eminent professors they don't know the Boomtown Rats from their behinds, where will it be? Sitting in its pram taking notes?'

'In a buggy, Dad, not a pram. And what are the Boomtown Rats?'

'Answer my question, will you?'

'Oh, we'll work something out.'

'Who will?'

'The other girls and me . . .'

Derek, naturally, hadn't just left the matter there. There had been more bickering by mobile and eventually a meeting at the tapas bar in Brixton that neither of them liked. Derek had stayed sober this time and Charlotte had not invited him to drop round to her house. She'd talked about it, though, in an offhand way.

'Babies don't take up lots of room. I'll get a cot and everything. In fact, I'll probably have it in bed with me like Kalahari nomad women do.'

'Charlotte. The place you live in is a sodding zoo.'

'Just "zoo" if you don't mind. Anyway, the animals aren't dangerous. They're ill.'

But Derek hadn't meant the recovering wildlife; he'd meant Lindy and company. At this point, though, he'd given in. He'd asked all his awkward questions and got no answers he'd liked – although, in truth, no such answers were possible.

'OK, OK, you've got everything sorted. And Laurent is due back when?'

'July. After term ends.'

'So you're going to tell him then?'

'By then I think it might be difficult not to.'

'That's true,' Derek had said, but he was bluffing. Would the future new arrival be obvious by July? He couldn't remember how many months Denise had been with Charlotte and Matthew when people had begun insisting she sit down. The important thing, though, was that Laurent at least would be in the know. This would be only right and proper – if seriously overdue – and the prospect gave Derek a crumb of consolation. He had felt very alone being unable to share the unreal information that his daughter had become part of the data on teenage pregnancy. He felt no desire to beat Laurent to a pulp or force him to the altar holding a sawn-off shotgun to his head – he couldn't know who was to blame for the 'mistake' – and he hoped he and Laurent could discuss the situation man to man. At the same time he doubted that his daughter's hapless impregnator would be an ideal partner in male solidarity. That trench coat, that camera bag, that disconnected air . . .

All these considerations had been churning in Derek even as he'd risen to drive home. Then Charlotte had said, 'Dad, you haven't even asked me when it's due.'

Unusually, she'd looked a little hurt. 'OK. Oversight. Sorry. So when . . .'

'December the fifth.'

'About the time Mum comes back.'

'Yes.'

'You will have told her by then, won't you, Charlotte?'

'I can't believe you asked me that question . . .'

And that had been that for a few more weeks: no further meetings, no tetchy mobile conversations, no visits, just the odd e-mail exchange.

Derek: Everything OK?

Charlotte: Everything fine, except it's twins.

Derek: Don't, please.

Charlotte: Just my little joke.

Derek had felt helpless. Yet Charlotte's distance – emotional as well as physical – had helped him put her plight out of his mind some of the time. He couldn't let this catastrophe prevent him getting on with his new life. He developed his Vision Thing file. He worked on his report for Libby. After he'd finished it he'd visited her at home again. He'd felt a bit ashamed this time: a one-off was forgivable but twice looked like the beginning of a dependency. Yet when he'd left her he'd once again felt restored and looked ahead with confidence once more.

For a while his short-term problems fell into per-spective. The embarrassment with Lorcan had been unfortunate, true, but he'd heard nothing about it since that crazy conversation in Sam and Moz's seduction salon and Lorcan had been making himself scarce. Derek had hardly seen Galina either except once or twice when she had taken the dogs out, or as a busy silhouette in one or other of the O'Neill house's front rooms. Maybe this portended the whole thing's going away. Meanwhile, his personal life setbacks were arguably less severe than Sam's. When Sam had eventually paid his promised visit it had not been, after all, to pick Derek's brains so he could charge two hundred quid an hour for helping someone conclude they'd have a better time at work if they used biros with black ink instead of blue – or whatever it was life coaches did. Instead he'd spilled the Big News about Bou.

'Derek, there's something I want to tell you.'

'OK, Sam. I'm all ears.'

'It's a personal thing . . . don't look so worried, you haven't got BO.'

'No. I didn't think so.'

'Do you remember those adverts? Lifebuoy soap?'

'No,' Derek lied. In fact, he'd washed with nothing else.

'It's a bit shocking actually, my news . . . well, especially for me. But rather wonderful too . . .'

'So . . .?' Derek never took long to get impatient. He hated people beating about the bush. He didn't like them gushing either. Sam was one of the worst.

'I couldn't believe it when she wrote – she'd tracked me down through the telephone directory, simple as that – but I suddenly realised that for all these years I'd been wondering about her subconsciously; she'd been there in my mind and so I just *had* to contact her back, and when we finally met I just *knew* she was my child. And the amazing thing is, Derek, she felt *exactly* the same way. She just *knew* I was her dad . . .'

Sam had ploughed this squeamish ground a little longer: he'd been pondering the father–daughter bond; he'd been reading books about it; what did Derek think?

What Derek had thought was that he didn't want to discuss it – especially given the fix Charlotte was in. And anyway he'd been busy: hoovering to do; eyebrows to trim. He'd got more interested, though, when Sam had told him about Bou's mother – 'Her name's Kathy, she's a beautician. It was before I met Moz, when I worked in the City, a lifetime ago . . .' Poor old Moz, thought Derek meanly. One day, life was a bowl of cherries: nice house, two kids, husband prepared to pleasure her for entire afternoons. Then it turns out that in a former life that very same husband sired a cross between Judy Garland and Britney Spears. Was the perfect bum still securely mounted in his neighbours' hall?

All this had been deeply diverting. But as late spring had turned to summer Derek had known that reality would come crashing back in. And as he sat on his sofa that late July morning he reviewed the damage it had done. His daughter was still pregnant. The state of his marriage was still unresolved. His passing link with Lorcan had brought new worries to his door. And now Charlotte was home again with a slightly fuller figure and more colour in her cheeks and, judging by their exchanges when she'd arrived last night, becoming more maddening all the time.

'Are you staying for a while, then, Charlotte?'

'I don't know, Dad. Maybe for a few days.'

'How many is "a few"?'

'I'm being deliberately vague just to annoy you.'

'Great. Thank you. And you still haven't told your mother?'

'No. Not yet.'

'Not *anything*?'

'Nothing at all.'

'Laurent will be back soon, though?'

'Well, he's been asked to go on to Kenya, actually.'

'So when *will* you see him, then?'

'Some time. I'm not sure. Don't hassle me! I'm pregnant! Didn't you know?'

And Charlotte? As her father fretted she sent Nessie and Norton home then headed to her room. She knew Nessie was bursting to tell Sam she was pregnant, but that didn't bother her. He'd find out sooner or later. Everybody would. Nearly five months gone. No turning back now. Oh, legally she still could but she had flown past that option by a mile. All her initial shock, her continuing foreboding, her common sense telling her she was far too young for this – for becoming a mother, for God's sake – had been overtaken by feelings she could not really explain: fascination; exhilaration; the tug of transgression and mystery. The abortion clinic leaflets with their promises of consolation and pledges of support simply could not compete with the literature of gestation and its tales of the adventure unfolding at her core: her body slowly changing; the poetry of it; the quickening she would be feeling soon.

# chapter 11

'Fore!'

Derek panicked. He dropped his driver and ran forward from the tee. He yelled again, more loudly.

'*Fore!* FOOORE!'

'Easy, mate,' said Geoff. 'It's nowhere near them.'

'Jesus Christ,' said Derek. 'Jesus Christ.'

He held his head and hoped. His ball was flying straight towards two tartan-skirted, grey-haired women measuring putts on the seventh green. It wouldn't have been so bad if he hadn't been aiming down the tenth.

'Boomerang!' said Geoff brightly. 'Stay here and it'll come back in a bit.'

In fact it fell well short of the two women. Derek went weak with relief. Even as its vicious curve was taking shape he'd imagined the awful crack of Titleist on temple, seen the county-set knees buckle, felt the shame at not wanting to give a pensioner the kiss of life.

'You all right, mate?' Geoff asked.

'Yeah. Yeah. Funny, I was sure it was going to hit her. Must be the heat.'

'I say never mind. I say you'll probably get her next time.'

'Very amusing, Geoff.'

'Oh look, she's found it for you – it's buried in that bush. She's waving! Hey, you might get a snog out of this!'

But Derek had stopped listening. His game was going from dire to even worse. Geoff was already six holes up – six up after nine and cruising. Derek's mind was everywhere except the plane of Zen. In the car park he'd sat back in the Lexus and compiled a worry list.

+ *Worry One: I'm going to be a grandad and I'm only fifty-one.*

+ *Worry Two: Charlotte still hasn't told anyone she's going to have a baby – at least, no one who ought to know. Of course, she's told the bloody neighbours, starting with their bloody kids, but she still won't tell Denise. Or Laurent. Her brilliant idea is to tell Laurent first but not until he's back from Africa and now she says that might not happen for weeks. Yes, she could send him a message but she'd much rather do it face to face – presumably so she can watch him faint.*

+ *Worry Three: I am still pretending to the neighbours and to my family that I haven't left my job at QF – the one with the impressive salary.*

+ *Worry Four: My new business isn't profitable yet. In fact, there is no business – unless you count my arrangement with*

*Libby on whom I am depending to satisfy other needs. I may have to go liquid with some shares.*

*+ Worry Five: The police seem to suspect I've been into some sort of scam involving Lorcan. Well, it's possible, I suppose – on past form with Lorcan he'd make sure I was the last to know.*

*+ Worry Six: I want Charlotte to leave. I feel bad about this, but I can't help it. I don't know how to help her, she doesn't seem to want me to and I feel lousy as a result. Also, as long as she's around I can't use my new office because she still thinks it's Matthew's bedroom and will give me a hard time if she finds out. 'It's like erasing him from history,' she'll say. 'Maybe you'd like to erase me too.'*

*+ Worry Seven: I don't want Charlotte to leave. I want her to stay in Brayston so I can help her, even though I don't know how to and even though she doesn't seem to want me to. Therefore, I want her to leave and I don't want her to leave at the same time. That means I'm vacillating.*

*+ Worry Eight: I don't do vacillation.*

*+ Worry Nine: I'm not myself these days.*

Derek conceded the tenth hole then lost the eleventh after striking his ball into a nearby garden centre where it splashed down in an ornamental pond. That put Geoff eight up with only seven left to play. Game over.

'You look like death, mate,' said Geoff. 'I say forget it. I say let's finish the round for fun.'

'Sorry, Geoff, I think I should pack it in.'

'You won't be sleeping with me, then?'

'No, I have a headache. Oh, and I'm short of cash.'

'Don't worry about it, mate. I'll wait until you've made that first million.'

'Yeah, right. It's nearly in the post.'

Derek drove back to Brayston.

Haircut 100 did not sing 'Favourite Shirts'.

He wasn't in a hurry to get home. He and Charlotte had been invited to Sam and Moz's that evening and he wasn't in the mood for it at all. Nessie and Norton made him nervous and the promised presence of Bou would make for dicey chemistry. Also, it would be his first public appearance as an outed grandad-to-be – outed by the shameless Charlotte, naturally. His impatience with his daughter was such that he didn't trust himself not to have a row with her the second he walked in so he hoped he'd get back late enough for her to have already gone next door – that way her effect on him would be diluted by the surrounding company.

With that unhappy wish in mind he paused in the kitchen on his return to listen. Then, satisfied he was alone, he went up to his bedroom and selected from his wardrobe a Boden Interesting Polo in a blue coral print and a pair of mid-length khaki shorts. From his pants drawer he picked briefs, which were the wisest choice with shorts because trunks were too hot for this weather while boxers could leave you badly exposed if anyone saw up your leg, and what if Moz should make a sly remark? Perhaps long summer trousers would be better. But no: Sam would certainly be in shorts and Derek didn't want to seem uptight and a square.

He pulled on his ensemble, slipped into his sandals and went next door. Nessie showed him through to the patio where the barbecue was smoking. At the garden table Moz stirred a cocktail – some kind of Stinger, Derek assumed. Charlotte sat beside her. Bou stood behind Charlotte, doing something with her hair.

'Hi, Dad,' said Charlotte. 'Nice legs.'

'Thanks. That's really put me at my ease.'

'I spy an Interesting Polo,' Moz remarked.

'You're right. And yes, I'd love a beer before you ask.'

'I'll get it,' said Bou before anyone else could move. Leaving Charlotte she hurried away.

'Relax, Dad,' Charlotte said. 'You're among friends. So how was golf?'

'Terrible,' Derek replied. 'And yes, I know it's a stupid game.'

'Oh, I don't think it's stupid,' Charlotte said. 'Moz plays it, don't you, Moz?'

Moz sipped her drink and said, 'Yes, I've been known to swing a club occasionally.'

She and Charlotte chuckled, privately. Derek looked round for Sam. Bou came back holding a can of lager and a glass. 'Shall I pour this for you, Derek?' she asked anxiously. 'I might not be so good at it.' She wore a green bikini top and candy-striped cotton flares that barely hung on to her hips. Her hair was a Titian cascade.

'Thank you, Boudica,' said Derek a trifle formally. He took the can and the glass. 'You're very kind.'

'She *is* kind, isn't she?' said Charlotte. 'And sweet, *and* polite.'

'Maybe you and Sam should do a daughter swap,' said Moz. 'It could be on Channel 4.'

'What do you think, Dad?' Charlotte enthused. 'We could make it permanent if it worked out. Imagine having a daughter with such gorgeous golden tresses.' She reached into the pocket of her tatty cardigan and produced for his inspection a lock of Boudica's hair. 'I'm going to keep this for inspiration; it's a wonder of evolution. Beautiful, isn't it?'

'Like a princess's hair,' said Nessie.

'It's remarkable,' said Derek, carefully. He moved the conversation on. 'Where are Norton and Sam?'

'They're in the games room,' said Moz. 'I think Norton has something to show you. Why don't you go through?'

The games room was opposite the sex room, as Derek had labelled it in his subconscious (a dark part of his subconscious; he'd been in there with Lorcan, after all). He walked in expecting to find a pool or snooker table, maybe table tennis or darts, but the nearest thing to these was table football. Otherwise, the games were all specifically for children: a canvas playhouse; a Twister mat; a dance mat connected to a TV; a mini-trampoline. Norton and Sam were absorbed in something spread out on a wooden folding table.

Sam said, 'Hi, Derek! Come in!'

Norton looked up from underneath his maths hat. His silence was appraising, his features heavy with intent.

Brando as the Godfather came into Derek's mind. On the table top a series of drawings were arranged in a rough rectangle. Each was precise and extremely detailed – clearly Norton's work. Derek fetched up some bonhomie and said, 'Well, what do we have here?'

'Aha,' said Sam proudly, 'you may well ask.'

'As indeed I have.'

'Well, this is Norton's latest project. His greatest *grand projet*. And believe it or not, Derek, it is inspired by you!'

'Really?' Derek's surprise was genuine. So was his fear.

'A while ago Norton asked me what you did for a job. I told him you invented shopping centres – that's roughly right, isn't it? – and that your most famous invention was Harboreta. Well, Norton loves Harboreta. He draws maps of it sometimes.'

'Oh, really?' said Derek. 'That's nice.'

'And this,' Sam continued, indicating Norton's drawings with a sweep of his hand, 'is Norton's blueprint for his very own shopping centre, his own super mall. He'd like to ask you some questions about it.'

Sam's face glowed with pleasure. Derek knew he was trapped. He said, 'OK, Norton, shoot.'

Norton said nothing at first. Instead, he took a suck on the *Finding Nemo* drinking straw protruding from a glass of milk at his elbow. Then he pointed to one of the spread pages. Sternly, he enquired, 'Do you know what this is?'

The page contained a picture of a building. It had a

large window at the front with a strip along the top on which was crayoned the word 'SHOP'.

'Is it a shop?' asked Derek.

'Correct,' Norton said. 'What sort of shop?'

Derek hesitated, caught slightly off guard. He'd been expecting a different sort of question. A typical five-year-old would have been seeking pearls of wisdom. This, though, was becoming an interrogation. Derek looked more closely at the shop. In the window Norton had etched some long orange shapes. Some letters appeared beside them: K, A, R, I, T, S.

'I don't know,' admitted Derek. 'I don't know what sort of shop.'

'Carrots,' Norton said. 'It is a carrot shop.'

'Oh. Where you buy carrots.'

'*Of course*, where you buy carrots,' Norton said. His face went Godfather again. He frowned so hard the maths hat dipped.

'Sorry,' Derek said.

'And what is this shop?' Norton tapped a different drawing. Again it said 'SHOP' along the top and this time the window space was graced by a number of grey aquatic shapes.

'A fishmonger?' guessed Derek.

'Not correct,' Norton said.

'OK, then, what is it?'

'A shark shop,' Norton said.

'A shark shop?'

'Where you buy sharks.'

Derek's eyes narrowed. The maths hat didn't flinch.

'And this one?' continued Norton. The third picture featured a group of grinning blob people sitting in a circle. They had plates in front of them and held pencil-drawn approximations of knives and forks. Norton waited.

'It's a restaurant,' said Derek, a little sulkily.

'Correct. And what are the people eating?'

Derek pondered some reddish felt pen swirls. 'I don't know, Norton,' he said. 'I can't tell.'

'They're worms.'

'Worms?'

'Yes. Worms to eat.'

'Oh,' said Derek, dully.

Norton kept his counsel for a second. Then he said, '*Ach-ully*, I'm joking. *Ach-ully* it's spaghetti.'

'Ho, ho,' Derek said.

Sam laughed too, and slapped Derek on the shoulder. 'Well, Derek,' he said, 'he's taken quite a shine to you.'

'Has he?'

Derek scanned Norton for signs of fond appreciation but noticed none. Indeed, the child seemed to have lost all interest in him. The tip of his tongue was at the corner of his mouth and he was jotting in a notepad – a souvenir of the Science Museum.

'So, Derek,' said Sam. 'It's all go in Willow Close!'

'Certainly is,' said Derek, wondering precisely what Sam meant.

'That police raid the other morning! Incredible!'

'Yes.'

'They dropped in on you too, I hear?'

'Yes. For a few minutes.'

'Asking about Lorcan's Aunt Mary, Charlotte says.'

'Does she? Well, not exactly . . .' Derek kept smiling. He could rage at Charlotte later. 'I told them that Lorcan had once mentioned his Aunt Mary to me – his late Aunt Mary, I think – but they were asking me about some other elderly woman.'

'Oh? Who?'

'Rejoices in the name Eugenie Flange-Boggin.' Derek shrugged. 'I'd never heard of her.'

'So who is she?' Sam pressed.

'No idea,' said Derek and he meant it. The two detectives had been blindingly opaque, especially the Scottish one. What was he called again? McBride. Detective Superintendent McBride.

'I suppose they came to you because of your connection with the Doonican's business.'

'That's right,' said Derek. He didn't know if it was true but it would do. When would Sam get off this?

'They thought you might . . . know something. Anything. Little things . . .'

'Yes. But I didn't.'

'No. No. He's an enigma, Lorcan, isn't he?'

'If "enigma" is another word for "prick".'

This seemed to warn Sam off. He shifted subject suddenly. 'And, um, it's marvellous about Charlotte. You're sure it's all OK with you?'

'What, that she's pregnant? Can't say I'm overjoyed.'

'Oh, that wasn't what I meant. I meant the child-minding arrangement.'

'What childminding arrangement?'

Puzzlement briefly clouded the usual confidence of Sam's fine features. 'Sorry, I thought this was all old news.'

'Thought what was all old news?'

'Charlotte's going to look after N and N for me for a couple of weeks. Just during my usual working hours. We generally muddle through the summer with playgroups and visits to friends and Moz and I taking a few days off. But Charlotte being here is ideal. She is *so* gifted with children. Brilliant with my two – my two little ones, that is.' He laughed at his need for this caveat. 'And Bou will be around now and then, too. We'll be paying Charlotte, naturally.'

'Aren't you going on holiday?' Derek was panicking, clutching at the nearest straw. Already, he felt invaded by Charlotte's interest in his neighbours. Was he going to be overrun by it too?

'Difficult this year,' said Sam delicately. 'I may have to fly to Texas – to visit Bou's mum. And her new husband, in case you were wondering. He's a musician.' He went on, confidingly. 'You can understand, I'm sure. These things have to be done. I want to care for Bou, of course, help her any way I can, but, well . . . it's better to discuss it with Kathy.'

'And what about Moz?' asked Derek innocently. 'Doesn't she want a holiday?'

Sam cleared his throat. 'She might take off with some girlfriends for a week. Go snorkelling or something. As you can imagine things have been a little tense . . .'

'Bou takes after her mother, does she?' Derek asked.

'In appearance, you mean?' Sam swallowed hard. 'Well, yes . . .'

'I think I get the picture,' Derek said.

Sam grinned ruefully and, for the first time, Derek looked at him with sympathy. Through no real fault of his own he'd ended up in a big mess and, against the odds, was trying to resolve it nobly. Derek couldn't relate to Sam, but he could relate to that.

Derek didn't stay long next door. He was tired after golf and it was hard to fight with Charlotte when you had no privacy. She always had a fast reply for any barb you fired her way, and she had so much energy: haring after Nessie and Norton, playing badminton with Bou. 'I'll have it out with her tomorrow,' he was mumbling, trudging home, when, suddenly, through the twilight, he heard a call.

'Oh, Derek!'

She was next to the wishing well waving to him with her gardening trowel. Thinking fast, he left the pavement and headed across the road to her before she could begin heading across to him. From previous experience Derek was keen to keep Galina as far as possible from his front door. Soon he was slaloming through the gnome army on her front lawn.

'Hello, Galina. How can I help?'

'Is Lorcan. He wants to see you.'

The feeling wasn't mutual. Yet something about Galina caused Derek to resist pointing this out.

'Where is he? In the house?'

'No, no! Is in hospital!'

'Hospital? Why?'

'For stress. Let me show.'

It was Derek's first contact with either of the O'Neills since the raid. They had returned home together by taxi late that evening and left again early the next day. Derek had seen Galina coax Grace and Favour into the back of Lorcan's second car, a red Land Rover. This had reappeared on their forecourt later. However, it seemed that Lorcan had no longer been in it.

Galina bent to place her trowel in a wooden carrying box. Derek noticed that her shoulders had been burnished by the sun. Her face, though, looked sad and drawn. She stood straight and tugged off her gardening gloves. These she let fall next to the trowel and Derek, stirred to gallantry, offered to carry the box for her.

'Thank you, Derek,' she said. 'Please come inside.'

Warily, he followed her into the house. It was the first time he'd been back since the night of the Doonican's debacle and that wasn't his only distressing memory of the place. A full-on Grace and Favour might easily deflower a man in shorts. Holding the box protectively in front of his groin Derek followed Galina through to the kitchen. The extractor fan was humming and something succulent was bubbling on the stove.

'So . . . what happened?' Derek asked. He was referring to the raid but, untypically for him, didn't go directly to the point. Galina seemed too fragile for that. He hoped her grasp of English social manners was good enough to spot the hint.

'He needs *complete* rest,' said Galina. '*Complete* rest. No Doonican's. No phone call. Nothing.'

She handed Derek a shiny A5 brochure with a picture of a large old country house on the front. Above it were the words 'The Escape' and below in smaller letters, 'Sanctuary. Renewal. Rest.' Derek flicked through the pages. There were lavish photographs of elegant bedrooms, luxurious bathrooms and foaming Jacuzzis full of good-looking people whose smiles and swimwear signified that whatever wretched state they'd been in on arrival they no longer had a care in the world.

'So,' Derek said, 'Lorcan is staying in this place and wants me to pay him a visit.'

'Yes. He says just you.'

'Not you too?'

'Just you. Is to do with court case, I believe.' Galina managed a rueful smile. 'He needs your help, Derek. I am sorry for you.'

Derek's spirits headed for his feet. He said, 'This is the Doonican's thing, right? I thought I'd heard the last of that.'

Galina flustered and slipped her hands into a pair of oven mitts. 'Pah! Nonsense! They say Lorcan is the criminal! He was the one attacked!' Roughly, she seized the handles of the saucepan on the stove and carried it to the table where she stood it on a Book of Kells place mat. It steamed invitingly.

'Yes,' Derek said. 'But I was wondering, actually, about that business the other day. The, ah, visit you had from the police.' He decided not to mention that two detectives had visited him too; best to hear what Galina knew or didn't know first.

'Ach!' Galina almost spat. 'That is Hooper making trouble.' She opened a cupboard with unnecessary force and brought out a smaller saucepan and a pair of heavy earthenware bowls. She also produced a plate, which she put in front of Derek. 'Hooper will say anything to get Lorcan in trouble, and the police, they want him in trouble too.' Galina removed the lid from the large saucepan, plunged a ladle into it and filled the plate in front of Derek with rich, aromatic stew. He wasn't really hungry, but sensed that Galina was surviving on instinct and that to refuse her food might trigger a breakdown of some kind.

'Is Aunt Mary's recipe,' she said distractedly and handed Derek a knife and fork.

'The late Aunt Mary's?'

'Yes.'

He took a mouthful of the stew. Galina transferred more of it into the smaller pan.

'I take this in for him this evening. Food there is good but not like home.'

'I'll bet,' Derek said, his mouth half full. His appetite

was bigger than he'd thought. Galina stretched cling film across the smaller pan and began filling the two bowls. Absorbed now in his meal Derek didn't pay much heed. He didn't register Galina's opening the kitchen door and allowing the fragrance of the garden to flow in. Only when she put the bowls on the floor and Derek heard the approach of eight thundering paws did he realise how much peril he was in.

Grace burst into the kitchen first with Favour bounding gamely to her rear. Both plunged their rumpled features with such force into the stew that the earthenware bowls, substantial though they were, slid noisily and chaotically over the stone tiles. The faster the bowls slid, the harder the shar-pei shoved them and the higher the frantic Derek lifted his feet. He looked to Galina for help but she was rooting in the fridge, deeply preoccupied, and, for all his mounting terror, Derek was too proud to call for help.

They came for him in tandem, ears and everything else pricked. The remains of his dinner crashed to the floor, forming a splatter-gun pattern of gravy and china shards. He crashed to the floor too and was soon flailing to escape the mind-scarring sensation of drooling canine muzzle snuffling at human private parts.

'Get OUT! Get OUT! Get OUT!'

At last Galina flew to his aid. The two dogs backed reluctantly away. A short, effusive scuffle followed before Galina slammed shut the kitchen door leaving Grace and Favour whining pitifully outside, denied the conquest they had thought was theirs.

'Oh, Derek, I am so sorry!'

Galina's hands were at her mouth. Derek clambered slowly to his feet. He checked his vital areas. He had been violated but not penetrated and should be grateful for small mercies, he supposed. The floor was in a worse mess. Yet Galina's next words showed that her first priority lay elsewhere.

'Oh, Derek! Oh no!'

She was pointing at his thigh. Derek looked down and saw a long splash of stain across the right leg of his shorts, a sorely misplaced sample of Aunt Mary's recipe. As Derek considered the damage Galina rushed straight to the sink, and although Derek hastened to make light of it she was soon kneeling before him insisting he stay on the chair and dabbing at the spots with a damp cloth. Stillness fell upon the scene, and Derek welcomed the contrast with the bedlam of a few minutes before. Galina seemed absorbed and as she tugged his shorts leg taut Derek was relieved that he had changed into the briefs. Yes, he could feel stirrings. It was fitting, though, that they were well constrained by the cotton-lycra mix, for his most powerful urge as Galina bent over him was not to couple with her but to protect her from more harm. Although the thought made his heart heavy, he resolved to visit Lorcan the next day.

# chapter 12

The Escape was only half an hour's drive away but the route was convoluted and Derek lost his way twice before stumbling across the entrance by mistake. Matching stone lions sat on guard beside a pair of mildewed pillars beyond which a gravel drive unrolled. Fine old trees, evenly spaced, threw parts of this into shade and at its far end a wing of the old building jutted into view. Derek eased forward in low gear. His heart was beating quickly and he tried to draw confidence from the many stays he'd had in elegant places like this during his QF years: conferences, away days, team-building weekends. Already, all that seemed a world away.

The drive curved left at its end and widened into a car park surrounded by sturdy shrubs and fine flower beds. Derek dithered for a moment wondering which space to take and checking out the other vehicles: a BMW, a Merc, even a red Ferrari at the end. Yes, there was serious money being squandered here.

A face appeared at his lowered window. It belonged to

a young man in a grey uniform, wearing a peaked cap. 'Visitor, sir?' he said.

'Yep.'

'May I ask who you've come to see?'

'Mr Lorcan O'Neill and his solicitor.' Derek tried to say it nicely.

'Oh, yes. You're Mr Hawker.'

'Yep.'

'Over there, by the Bentley, sir, if that's OK. Then just come round to reception. Someone else will take care of you there.'

'Good.'

Perhaps he should have been friendlier, but to Derek gruff monosyllables seemed fitting for the hard-faced business he had to do. He parked and strode round to the front of the building, inwardly intoning, 'Take no crap.' It was another fine day and the heavy wooden door stood partly open. Derek pushed through it and walked into an imposing entrance hall. Burgundy carpet criss-crossed a milky marble floor. To his left, high-backed leather chairs semi-circled an elaborate fireplace. To his right, a sharp-faced woman in her thirties sat at a long table marking off a stack of documents. Derek walked over to her. A sign on the wall above her head said *Quiet please*. He nodded at it and whispered, 'How quiet would you like me to be?'

She looked up. 'You're Mr Hawker?'

'Last time I asked, yes.'

'They're expecting you. Room seven, on the first floor.'

She smiled without showing any teeth. Geoff would have said she needed a good spank.

The lift was at the far end of the hall. It was wide enough to take a fleet of wheelchairs or three full-grown male neurotics laid end to end. As he rode up Derek checked his nose for nasties and his shoulders for dandruff. He wore a black turtleneck sweater under his plain dark Paul Smith suit. With the Omega Constellation on one wrist and a silver ID bracelet on the other he felt sure he looked the part for a showdown meeting with an iffy operator of the ludicrous kind and the poor unfortunate paid to defend him.

Derek turned left out of the lift and, following a hand-painted sign, walked along a broad landing lined with fine dark wood panelling and a carpet so rich and thick you could have lost your way in it. Derek admired quality but this was the type that put him in mind of the idle rich, and that went against the grain. He was Derek Hawker, creative force of Harboreta, who'd worked his way up – quite literally – from the shop floor.

He rapped firmly on the door of Room 7. As he waited for a reply, he detected hurried activity behind it and a sound that might have been made by someone on the plump side getting quickly into a bed. Finally, the door opened. The man who faced Derek was grey-haired, of average height and aged around sixty. He wore an open-necked shirt and a cravat. His face was pouchy and ruddy, like one of those tomatoes you no longer see except on organic farms. The throwback impression was decisively confirmed the moment the man spoke.

'Aubrey Crisp. Come in.'

Crisp turned on his heel, leaving the door for Derek to close. Demonstrating the truculence he intended to maintain Derek did so using his foot. Crisp looked round in surprise at the loud slam.

'Hello, Lorcan,' Derek said.

Lorcan was propped at a slight incline on a hillock of white pillows in a high double bed. His mouth hung slightly open and his head was tilted back. He didn't speak.

Crisp said, 'Please take a seat.' Derek sat down in an easy chair and assessed the plaster mouldings. 'Now, Mr Hawker,' continued Crisp, 'the purpose of this meeting is for me to brief you on what we expect of you when Mr O'Neill's case is heard in a few weeks.'

'Assuming I'm prepared to do it,' Derek said. 'You'll have to ask me nicely.'

Crisp's next sentence seemed to get wedged in his neck and Derek saw his eyes flick quickly towards his client. 'Well, I'm given to understand that you will stand witness in Mr O'Neill's defence; otherwise we wouldn't have asked you here.'

'You make it sound,' said Derek, 'as if you're doing me a favour rather than the other way round.'

Crisp's facial pouches seemed to deepen. He gave Derek a long-suffering stare. Derek stared straight back. He might have stared at Lorcan too, but would have probably thrown up. Crisp cleared his throat. 'Very well, Mr Hawker . . .'

'Oh, call me Derek, please.'

'Very well, ah, Derek. I understand what you are saying. However, as I imagine you are probably aware, giving a little of your time to assist my client may well be of benefit to you too.'

'You mean if I don't do it he'll tell my daughter and my wife that I went to his little strip show.'

Crisp rolled with this interruption, then went on.

'It wasn't *his*, ahem, strip show, ah, Derek, as you know. Two things on the exotic dancers. One is that my client, I assure you, wanted no part in the affair, or the provision of alcoholic beverages after hours. He was forced to allow the criminals to use Doonican's as a venue because they threatened to do violence to him and to the premises if he did not. He was intimidated, terrified.'

'He didn't seem terrified when he was introducing them,' Derek said and fired a glance at Lorcan. He said to Crisp, 'Is by any chance your client dead?'

'No. But he is sedated. He's been under a lot of stress.'

'So has his wife,' Derek said. 'You might mention that to him when he wakes up.'

Crisp ignored this and continued. 'Our argument rests on the fact that the after-hours activities were forced upon my client against his will – as, in a sense, they were forced upon you too. The reason you hadn't left Doonican's earlier was that Mr O'Neill insisted you stay for reasons that, we say, are straightforward – he wanted a dependable friend to be with him for comfort and to act as a witness if, as he feared, he found himself in danger. And, of course, his fears were justified. What we're saying, Derek, is that when the police, ah, revealed themselves as it were, and Vincent Hooper, the criminal ringleader, realised an undercover operation had been taking place, he went to attack Lorcan because he thought he'd, ah, grassed him up. Do you follow?'

'Yes, I follow,' said Derek testily.

'Not that he *had* grassed him up,' Crisp went on. 'He would have been far too frightened to do that.'

'Oh yes,' said Derek. 'To be sure.'

'The point is Mr O'Neill was scared of him . . . and you, Derek, can vouch for the fact that he had good reason to be scared, precisely because you witnessed the attack. Indeed, you bravely put yourself between Hooper and my client, didn't you?'

Derek recalled his surprise when Hooper had loomed up and swung at him. He said to Crisp, 'That's one way of putting it, I suppose.'

'That's how we'll be putting it, Derek,' Crisp replied. 'And your help in doing so would be invaluable. You are a man of substance and integrity. A respectable man . . .'

'So what was I doing at a grubby do like that?' Derek asked. 'Might be pushing your luck a bit, don't you think?'

'We will, of course, be stressing that you had no idea such an event was being planned . . .'

'Well, that would be the truth at least.'

Crisp looked slightly pained. 'Mr Hawker,' he implored, 'I understand that you may feel my client, shall we say, led you astray in that regard. Took advantage, perhaps, of your good nature . . .'

'You mean he tricked me,' Derek said.

'Tricked you, if you insist. The key point here is that his reasons for doing so were understandable. And forgivable. We hope the magistrate will think the same.'

Derek looked unimpressed. 'And what was the second thing?'

'The second thing?' said Crisp. 'Oh yes. I should emphasise to you that the, ah, nature of the, ah, entertainment on the stage that evening is not of itself subject to legal proceedings, only the fact that it took place after the time specified by the licence in force. And, of course, the same applies to the selling of alcohol.'

'So?' Derek said.

'So for your sake we hope it will not feature prominently at the hearing, which may be covered by the local media. However, Mr Hawker, the prospects for the, shall we say, more colourful aspects of that evening's events and, lest we forget, your attendance at them remaining undisclosed to the public are greatly increased if Mr O'Neill is acquitted. Innocent men are, to use the vernacular, less "sexy" than the guilty in the view of the popular press.'

'You're sure about that, are you?' Derek asked.

'I have long experience in these matters, Mr Hawker.'

'I'm sure you have,' Derek snapped. 'And I've had more than enough experience of your client.'

Derek enjoyed hurling this spear but knew it would draw no response from Lorcan, just as he knew he'd have to do what Crisp had asked. His motives, though, were more complex than his fear that Charlotte – and others – would find out how he had spent Good Friday night. Yes, that pressure was unwelcome and undoubtedly real, but Derek had other reasons for agreeing to be a witness in Lorcan's defence.

'Of course, Mr Hawker, we could subpoena you,' Crisp remarked unpleasantly, as if as an afterthought, 'though that wouldn't be ideal for any of us, would it now?'

'Now you listen,' Derek said sharply. He looked across at Lorcan. 'Listen both of you. All right, I'll go to court. I'll say everything I saw and all I know. That's not a big problem for me. This whole thing may be bullshit but I don't think I need to lie. I've thought it through and the truth is I don't know much at all. I don't know whether Hooper was threatening Lorcan. I don't know what the score was with those two. I do know one thing, though . . .'

Derek got to his feet and for the first time he thought he saw Lorcan move – a slight defensive flinch. Crisp looked up uncomfortably. Derek went on.

'. . . I know that if I need to save my family's feelings from a pair of rats like you, then I'll do what I have to do. And then there's Galina to consider . . .'

Was there another flinch from Lorcan? Derek thought so.

'Galina, of course, knows nothing about all this, only the fairy story Lorcan's told her.' He began speaking to

Lorcan directly. 'All Galina knows is that her job is to clean and cook and wash your King of Ceilidh socks and help your stupid dogs to have it off . . . and be grateful – *grateful!* – to be married to a clown like you. And let me tell you, Lorcan, she ought to know the truth and if it was my place I might even tell it to her and never mind the grief it might cause me. But I'm not sure she could take it. I'm not sure she's strong enough to hear. So there's another reason I'll bullshit for you, Lorcan. To give *you* the chance to treat her honestly.'

He headed for the door but didn't hurry. He wasn't running scared. As a parting shot he said, 'And by the way, Lorcan. Who is Eugenie Flange-Boggin?' Lorcan didn't speak and nor did Crisp. Derek left none the wiser but at least he'd had the last word.

'Let's make a potion, Nessie,' called Charlotte from the bath. 'We could pretend we're witches!'

'Yes!' Nessie enthused. 'I could be Sabrina!' She was in front of Charlotte's mirror, trying dolls' clothes on Mr Heath. Norton was at Charlotte's desk writing a menu for the Worm Café.

> *Karits and Worms, 3 pence*
> *Shark and Worms, 5 pence*
> *Spaghetti and Worms, 2 pence . . .*

In the bath Charlotte noticed her ankles had started to swell. She was swelling everywhere. Maybe Dad was right and she ought to send a message to Laurent. It was difficult, though: *Dear, sweet boyfriend who I'm not missing all that much. I am going to have your child. Please don't bother coming home* . . . In a boo-hoo voice she howled to Nessie, 'Oh, I want to be Sabrina! I'm the teenager, you know!'

'Not for much longer,' Nessie replied. 'I've already got your present, by the way.'

'Oooh! I love presents! What is it?'

'That would be telling.'

'Not fair!'

'But if I tell you, it won't be a surprise.'

'Ach-ully it's earrings,' Norton said.

'You pig, Norton!' shouted Nessie. 'You've spoiled it.'

Under the maths hat Norton looked confused. Had he made a mistake? Did people *like* surprises? Why? 'I only said what the surprise was,' he said unhappily.

'Egg-zackly!'

'Don't worry,' called Charlotte. 'I didn't hear. I had my head under the water.'

'Are you sure?'

'Honestly!' Charlotte wondered what the earrings would be like.

Gripping the sides of the bath firmly, she levered herself out and threw on her mother's dressing gown. This was her most relaxed day yet since she'd become summer nanny to Nessie and Norton. And why? Because Dad had gone out, of course – somewhere. She re-joined the children and surveyed the bedlam of her bedroom for clean clothes. Socks? Not needed really. Just as well. Big bra, T-shirt, those knickers would still do, and . . . where were they? Over there, under the chair, her new roomy joggers with the drawstring. Maternity wear: what a bore. She'd scanned a few net pages: Earth Mother dresses; smock tops with little flowers. No thank you.

'I wonder how my daddy is,' said Nessie.

'Oh,' said Charlotte, 'Is he ill?'

'He's got a cold.'

'Poor Sam.'

'He says it's stress-related.'

'Oh?'

'With all the excitement about Bou.'

'I see . . .' Charlotte laced her joggers thoughtfully. 'It's nearly lunchtime, Nessie. Perhaps we could go to your house and make your daddy some medicine. We could pretend to be doctors.'

'Yeah, brilliant,' Nessie said.

The three of them trooped round to see Sam. He was in the kitchen, sneezing. He'd already set plates for Nessie and Norton and offered Charlotte a sandwich too. Charlotte had decided she liked Sam, even though Moz was fed up with him. They were a fascinating family. The children were archetypes, a serious, technical boy, a chatty, touchy-feely girl. IQ and EQ. And yet in many ways their parents were the opposite way round, their mother steely and determined, their father mellow and nurturing, each turning conventional wisdoms upside down. They'd make great case study material for her future Ph.D. and maybe she could bring in the whole Bou business too. Better tread carefully there, though.

'Have you been working today, Sam?' she asked.

'Struggling on,' Sam answered thickly. 'When I haven't been blowing my nose.'

Nessie and Norton took their places and Sam began to serve them the nearest thing to salad they would eat: chopped apple and raisins, cucumber, crisps and cheese.

'Nessie,' said Charlotte shortly, 'is that toy cash register still up in your room?'

'Yes.'

'Shall I run up and get it? We'll be needing it this afternoon.'

'I'll come with you,' Nessie said.

'No you won't,' said Sam sternly. 'You have to eat your lunch. Charlotte's a big girl now. She can fetch it on her own.'

With that, Charlotte was gone. But when she got upstairs she didn't go directly to the children's room. Instead, she padded softly to another further down the landing whose door she was pleased to see stood open. She peered round it nervously, ears pricked for any sound suggesting she might, after all, find herself with infant company. There was a box of mansize tissues on Sam's desk. His waste-paper basket stood underneath. Charlotte couldn't help but speed-scan his bookcase. Such intriguing titles! *The Life Coaching Handbook*. *52 Ways To Handle It: A Life Coaching Year*. *Be Your Own Life Coach: How To Take Control Of Your Life And Achieve Your Wildest*

*Dreams* – and what was this? Michael Kimmel: *Manhood In America* and, hey! Lynne Segal: *Why Feminism?* Wow! Charlotte had read that one – radical stuff!

For once, though, Charlotte did not divert down a sidetrack from her main task. She went over to the basket and saw immediately that crumpled tissues filled it to the brim. Stooping silently, she picked out the soggiest she could see. Revolting but effective – she was pleased.

With the tissue in her pocket she hurried to fetch the cash register and found it reasonably quickly in Norton and Nessie's crowded bedroom. Moz had explained to her that the children, if they wanted, could have bedrooms of their own but were happier to share. 'For chalk and cheese they're very close,' she'd said. Charlotte smiled at the clutter around her: books, dolls, puzzles, make-up, microscopes. If they'd been mixed up more together she might almost have been in her own bedroom during her primary school years.

She went to head downstairs. But then she froze. One hand held the cash register, the other went to her tummy, slightly to the left side. It was a curious sensation, a butterfly tremor on the inside. It startled her, for all that she'd keenly expected it. The first kicks. Charlotte caught her breath and wiped a lone tear from one eye.

Derek didn't go straight home after leaving the Escape. Instead he drove towards Hertford and located on its outskirts a new housing development called Park Lanes. An all-weather signboard mounted on a wooden post said, 'Show homes open! This way!' but Derek's mood did not match the punctuation. He'd been full of fire with Lorcan and Crisp but in the aftermath he was subdued. It had only been bravado and even that felt flat in the absence of someone to talk to. At QF he'd have related such a showdown as a hilarious war story, one everyone around him would have been eager to hear. He might even have told it to Denise. In his changed circumstances, though, he didn't have an audience. Instead of launching a brave new life he was increasingly alone in a shrinking private world, and had better get used to the idea.

The show homes weren't too bad. Avoiding the selling agents – whose patter he would once have quarrelled with yet loved – Derek imagined the existence he might lead in a three-bedroom semi. One bedroom for sleeping in, another for work – assuming he had any work – another for visitors, assuming he had any of those. Would Charlotte come to see him with the child? But he was rushing too far ahead, an old failing. There would be details to deal with, big difficult details, like borrowing money against Hawker House or agreeing with Denise that they should sell it. Could he and Denise agree on anything again? Where would Charlotte and the baby end up living? Should he look for a new job? How saleable in the modern age was any ex-executive, aged fifty-one?

Solving complex problems used to be Derek's forte: he'd weigh all the options, cut to the chase and plot a forward path with brio. Now he saw only gloom in every permutation as he guided the Lexus back to Brayston through the Friday afternoon commuter rush. For once he hoped to find Charlotte in the house. Maybe now was the time for him to be honest with her about his lack of job, about everything, even what had gone wrong between him and Denise. She was a grown-up now. She deserved to know these things. Instead of Charlotte, though, he found a note.

Gone back to uni for weekend. C.
PS Does Matthew know what you've done to his room?

# chapter 13

Charlotte returned on the Sunday evening, arriving from the station by taxi. Derek was waiting for her in the porch – she'd phoned ahead to ask him to be ready with the fare.

'Sorry about that, Dad,' she chimed from the back seat as Derek paid the driver.

'I could have fetched you in the car, you know,' he said.

'I know.'

'I'd have fetched you from Brixton if you'd asked.'

'I know that too. Don't worry. I'll pay you back out of my wages.'

'I wasn't thinking of the money,' Derek said. But Charlotte wasn't listening. She was tugging at something down beside her feet – a shabby rectangular basket with a lid. She handed it to Derek. From inside it came a mew.

'Don't worry, Dad,' said Charlotte, seeing her father's face. 'He's had his bits removed. That's why he's so subdued.'

Derek sympathised. But if surgery was meant to render

a budding tomcat passive it did not seem to have worked in this case. Sensing freedom the cat had begun clawing at its wicker cage. With each scratch Derek felt future torment for the lounge upholstery.

'He's called Scrag,' Charlotte explained. 'He's only a kitten. I found him cowering at the end of our road. He was the runt of the litter, I suppose.' From the boot she was heaving a see-through plastic suitcase full of books and a bulging laundry bag. Derek rushed to help her. She resisted at first – 'I'm not an invalid, you know' – then thought again. 'OK, if you take these I'll bring the rest.'

'The rest' turned out to be two mice that Scrag had traumatised and were now recovering in a glass tank and three goldfish Charlotte had liberated from a funfair in Brockwell Park. 'I thought the children would enjoy them,' she explained, inspecting the fish for travel stress inside their mobile home of a thick polythene bag.

'Why have you brought a cat?' growled Derek.

'The others are all away. I can't leave him on his own.'

'What if I don't want it in the house?'

'There's not much "what if" about it, by the sound of it. But try not to worry, Dad. He'll stay outside all day and in my room with a litter tray at night. I mean, it is still *my* room, isn't it?'

Derek sighed and wandered off. Charlotte was back and blooming.

The new pattern of life at Hawker House formed rapidly. Charlotte gave the mice to Nessie and Norton – they would make up for their hamster, which had expired in January. The goldfish moved into the glass tank vacated by the mice. The puny eunuch Scrag mostly slept next to Mr Heath on Charlotte's bed, rising occasionally to nibble from foil trays of expensive kitten food and/or to deposit excreta in or sometimes fairly near the proper place. This too gave enormous pleasure to the next-door children whom Charlotte brought on to the premises for at least part of each day. And Derek? He mostly hid.

His hiding places varied. Sometimes he hid in his bedroom, sometimes in his office – in which he had an extension for the cordless phone installed – and sometimes in the car, which he may or may not have driven somewhere first. He and his daughter's lives were suddenly at once adjacent and yet so separate that they touched only now and then. Both made an effort to do things together and rub along more cosily. Both found the going hard.

In the supermarket Derek bought ready meals and booze where Charlotte bought organic fruit and veg. They queued at different checkouts. They ate in staggered shifts. In the evenings Derek watched sport on the big lounge television while Charlotte visited Moz or went to her room to write and read. The only TV she watched was the Open University. Peace of a sort prevailed but was threatened constantly by mutual incomprehension. One evening it was disturbed by appalling high-pitched squeals from the garden. Scrag had caught a frog.

Charlotte, knowing the sound, rushed outside to save it and, to aid its recovery, allowed it to squat in the kitchen sink. Derek was horrified.

'You can't leave it in there! It's not hygienic!'

'It's an amphibian, Dad, not a disease.'

'I don't want an amphibian in my sink!'

'Since when was it *your* sink, anyway?'

It was years since they'd been so intimate and the intimacy was fraught. Derek was annoyed by Charlotte's habit of letting her wet washing lie for hours in the machine but he didn't want to move it – he was too embarrassed to handle his daughter's underwear. He didn't like Charlotte's being too long out of his sight and yet felt uncomfortable around her. He expended lots of energy tracking her, second-guessing her, listening to her movements through a closed door. Was she in her bedroom? If he stepped out on to the landing did he risk bumping into her? Was she going out soon? Was she out already and, if so, when would she be home? The turbulence caused Derek to observe his comfort rituals more strictly: to fold his pants with still greater precision, to commune with the Dyson daily, to slip out to stroke the Lexus frequently.

Nessie and Norton perturbed him too. He had to be fair to Charlotte: most of the time she entertained them in their own garden or took them for walks to the village pond (the probable source of the Scrag-molested frog, to which it was ceremonially returned). Yet their presence in the house, even when they were physically absent, quickly grew. First came the fridge magnets. *NeSsie is A NOOdle. chaRlotTe is a gOat. AMBer is A Pop sTar. NORton is 3 + 2 oR 1 + 4 or 5 + 0.*

Then, one sunny morning, the two of them and Charlotte encamped on the Hawker patio to 'do art'. Derek cowered in his office pretending to 'do work'; then, after they'd gone off for a picnic, sneaked down to see what the damage was. He found the kitchen table groaning with painted cardboard boxes and wiggly lengths of rolled out plasticine. He glared at them in confusion until their significance hit him: Norton's elaborate mall blueprint had only been the first stage of a much larger enterprise; building work was now getting under way. He tackled Charlotte about it later.

'Can you put those children's magnificent creations somewhere else?'

'Don't worry, Dad, I'm going to move them now.'

'Going to move them where?'

'Upstairs.'

'Where upstairs?'

'Into your old office. You don't use it now, do you?'

'No, but . . .'

It was her most direct reference to Derek's annexing Matthew's bedroom. Now he was discovering how she would make him suffer for his sin. It gave her moral leverage: he'd destroyed her brother's birthright and all she wanted, by contrast, was to borrow some of the space he had so readily vacated. And it got worse.

'Anyway, Dad, it's only a few boxes.'

'But why can't they make it in their house, for God's sake?'

'Because it's Derek World.'

'What?'

'That's what Norton wants to call it and Nessie agrees. They know you are a mall – sorry, leisure destination – expert and they've named it in your honour. That's why they want it to be here; and so they can call on your specialist knowledge if they need to.'

'Is that a threat or a promise?'

'A threat, obviously.'

It was all a new experience for Derek. For the first time in his life when faced by novel challenges he wanted to retreat. The fact of Charlotte's pregnancy was one thing; her refusal to put other family members in the picture – especially Denise – heightened his feeling of impotence. And on the few occasions when she asked him for his help he didn't quite know where to put himself. OK, he knew it was a wind-up when she asked him if he'd join her in some antenatal exercise routines – 'Dad, it will do wonders for your pelvic floor muscles.' But when he drove her – as he insisted – to her hospital appointments he was genuinely torn. Should he wait in the car park or go with her? When he did the former, he felt mean. When he did the latter, he worried that people were thinking he was the father-to-be. Or else that he was simply a Bad Parent – what other sort raised daughters who fell pregnant out of wedlock at nineteen?

Increasingly, he slipped into a limbo. August was racing by and both the baby and Denise were scheduled to arrive in December. Something had to give – but what or who or how he couldn't see. When he wasn't repositioning bath towels on his heated rail or picking through his CDs for mournful pop blasts from his past – the Beatles singing 'Yesterday', the antiseptic aah-baahs of 'I'm Not In Love' by 10cc – he drifted into hazy speculation. Once or twice late at night he pondered what it might be like to caress Galina's milky Belarusan breasts and rotate their nipples into rigid raspberries with his thumbs. His heart wasn't in it, though. He went to sleep instead. More often, he thought about Denise. Was she playing away on the banks of the Yangtze River? Was she rolling in the Nan Shan Mountains' lovely flowers with some sexpot called Sun or Li?

Their few e-mail exchanges were exercises in evasion.

Denise: What is Charlotte up to?

Derek: What do you mean?

Denise: I mean is she all right?

Derek: I think so . . . but what do I know?

Denise: Nothing probably.

Did Denise know anything, something or nothing? He couldn't know without asking yet to ask would have aroused her suspicions.

Denise: How is Charlotte?

Derek: Fine, I think. Why?

Denise: Have you seen Laurent lately?

Derek: He's still in Africa – isn't he?

In all this uncertainty Derek's only consolation was Libby. He relished their meetings. He knew it was madness to keep on seeing her but he couldn't help himself. First the intimate business upstairs then the talk over coffee – it was all part of the service.

'I'm going to be a grandfather,' said Derek, who still had trouble believing it.

'You should be a fortune-teller,' Libby replied.

'Very funny.'

Libby blew a smoke ring and made a small moue of a smile. 'Oh well, I like to keep my clients entertained.'

Derek went on. 'Just the idea of it is frightening. The reality . . .' He shrugged.

'Denise still doesn't know?' Libby asked.

'Correct, apparently.'

'And the father doesn't either? Young Laurent, is it?'

'No.'

'And her brother?'

'No again.'

'When *is* she going to tell them?'

'I don't know. And I don't think she does either.'

'Who *does* know?'

'The neighbours, basically, and her revolting student friends. Still, it isn't something you can keep secret now she's beginning to . . .'

'She's getting a bump, is she?'

'A bump . . .' Denise had always talked about having a bump. Derek finished his coffee. 'I should be getting back. That first million won't make itself.'

'True,' said Libby sagely. 'But your life will be full of riches anyway.'

'I hope so,' Derek said.

'I *know* so.' Libby laughed.

It wasn't love or anything. But he needed her, badly.

Charlotte, by contrast, needed no one; to be exact she needed no one else to make her feel complete. She only needed company for mental stimulation: Moz, for example, whose views she sought often, usually during the evening over the low part of the garden fence.

'Moz?'

'Yes?'

'I've got a big question for you.'

Moz was flat on her back on the grass, lifting weights. She said, 'Do you ever have the other sort?'

'No. How important are fathers, do you think?'

'That's pretty big. It all depends. Sam is very important to Nessie and Norton.'

'That's true.' Charlotte was getting to like Sam.

'And it would appear,' continued Moz, 'that he is important to Boudica too.'

'Yes,' Charlotte agreed. 'You see, what *I* think is that fathers are important mostly as an *idea*. Do you see what I mean?'

'No.'

'OK. A lot of children never know their fathers and yet they grow up happy and well balanced, as long as they're not mistreated or poor.'

Moz lowered her weights. She arched an eyebrow at Charlotte in that way of hers – a mannerism Charlotte admired – and said, 'So?'

'So they didn't really need a father, did they?'

'But,' said Moz, 'like Bou, a lot of children who've never known their fathers track them down. It seems to be a powerful natural urge.'

'But is it?' Charlotte demanded happily. 'You see, that is my point. If Bou's mother . . .'

'The lovely Kathy,' Moz put in, wrinkling her nose. Sam would be flying off to see her in the next couple of days.

'What if the lovely Kathy had told Bou a lie? Say she'd told Bou that she'd become pregnant with her because of a one-night stand with some man she didn't know and never saw again; or from an anonymous sperm donor. Or what if she'd told her Sam was dead? What would Bou have done then? Would she have been devastated because she'd never know her father? Or would her life have gone on much the same?'

'I don't know,' said Moz. 'But I've a feeling you think you do.'

'I think her life would have gone on much the same. But once she knew about Sam, and once she was old enough to go and find him, the *idea* of having a father took hold of her imagination. When I asked her about it she almost put it that way herself. She talked about this need to find out where she came from and so on. But where did that need come from? Did it come from some inborn genetic drive that every human has or was Bou really inspired by society's *believing* it is natural to want to know your dad?'

'What do you think?' asked Moz, becoming interested.

'What *I* think is that these things aren't clear,' Charlotte said. 'Some children who track down fathers they've never known – or mothers they've never known too if they've been adopted – are very disappointed when they find them. They realise they have nothing in common *except* a biological link. Others are thrilled to meet each other and become very close. At the same time . . .' Charlotte's momentum was unstoppable. She was waving her arms about. 'At the *same time*, children can go through their entire lives thinking their mum's husband or partner is their father and being perfectly happy with him when, in fact, if DNA tests were done they'd find out he isn't their father at all – genetically speaking, that is.'

'I see,' said Moz. 'And what is your conclusion, professor?'

'It all invites the question what *is* a father, in fact? If by a father we mean a male adult carer who is devoted to the upbringing of a child, does that man need to have provided the sperm that helped create the child in order to do the job? Answer? Of *course* not!'

'You're the expert,' Moz said.

'Look at gay men who bring up children. They're very good at it. Yet only one of them, if that, will have a genetic link with each child. And, of course, we all know that loads of biological fathers are crap at being parents

and their children would be better off without them.'
Charlotte clapped her hands and looked triumphant.
'QED,' she said.

'Is that what you do in biology and psychology?' asked
Moz. 'I thought it was all mazes and rats.'

'Some of it is and some of it's about people,' Charlotte
said. 'That's where I get into arguments.' She giggled.

'What about?' asked Moz.

'Oh, the teachers think the secrets of the human family
are all in the genes,' explained Charlotte airily. 'But *I*
think it's *much* more interesting than that.'

'"Interesting",' said Moz. 'That's a good word for it.'
She got up carefully and shook out her arms and legs.
'So, Charlotte, does this theory of yours have something
to do with what you're thinking about Laurent?'

'Hmph!' Charlotte frowned playfully. 'I knew you were
going to say that.'

And Charlotte *was* pondering the problem of Laurent.
She was doing it every day. On the one hand, she was
quite sure her baby wasn't going to need him – or anyone
but her and a few mates. On the other, she didn't want to
be mean to her boyfriend – her *sort of* boyfriend as she
had begun to think of him. It was a complicated problem
and, therefore, fascinating – as was the whole business of
Bou. All things considered Willow Close was turning out
to be a good place to be pregnant for the summer. Even
being with Dad wasn't so bad, although he certainly was
weird: always lurking in his new office (the one he'd
stolen from Matthew, the beast); always fussing round

the washing machine (if he wanted to use it why didn't he just take her stuff out?); always tidying things.

Some days, Charlotte was tempted to share these observations with her mother, but didn't want to risk revealing that she was spending all her time at Hawker House – it might make Denise jealous and, worse, might prompt her to ask Derek about it, and Derek might weaken and give her big secret away. So when Denise asked about Derek as, in her e-mails, she occasionally did, Charlotte kept it brief.

Denise: Have you seen your father lately?

Charlotte: Often enough.

Denise: How is he?

Charlotte: Hoovering, usually.

Denise: That's nice for him.

Charlotte: I know – that's what's so worrying.

Denise: Any more big news to tell me?

Charlotte: No, just busy being brilliant as usual.

It hurt Charlotte to be opaque in this way. In her head she remained convinced that it was best for everyone if she kept Denise in ignorance for as long as possible but, despite the impression she often gave, she didn't have a heart of stone. As she grew through the stages of her second trimester each antenatal examination, conversation with a midwife or ultrasonic scan made her think more about her mother and how different these experiences might have been if Denise, rather than Derek, had been around. Where Derek was diffident, Denise would have been hands-on, full of memories and questions.

Where Derek was awkward, Denise would have been in her element, looking on the bright side, making herself essential, filling in all the gaps left by . . . well, in some ways by Laurent. Hand-holding – that sort of thing, Charlotte supposed. Stuff Derek was no use for at all.

She stayed in good spirits, though. She had many projects on the go. Thanks to her careful nurturing Scrag put on weight and took up daytime residence in the conservatory where he could laze uninterrupted. She had her studies, of course. And Nessie and Norton were a delight. Their work on Derek World continued and soon the bedrock elements of Norton's master plan were all in place. On the floor of Derek's old office, the cardboard box emporia – Karit Shop, Shark Shop, Worm Café and, of course, Maths Hats R Us, to name but four – were arranged in a triangle serviced by a Scalextric highway. At its centre stood a silver foil ice rink upon which pirouetted three My Scene girls with their pet dogs, a detachment of pirates from the Early Learning Centre, two sheep and a goat. Development work continued round the perimeter where Bob the Builder and two clones put the finishing touches to a swimming pool in which a plastic Tigger cavorted with a troop of chimpanzees. A large cardboard clock was propped against Derek's old desk. At last came the day of the Grand Opening at which Derek was the reluctant honoured guest.

'What do you think, Dad?' Charlotte asked. She stood with an arm round each of the children. Nessie was beaming in a floaty summer frock – Amber had been on the phone all day to Jade discussing what outfit to wear. Norton, beneath the maths hat, looked fiercely proud. Derek tried to get into the spirit. 'Well, it's certainly ambitious,' he said.

'Ambitious – what does that mean?' Charlotte asked.

'It means,' said Derek hurriedly, 'that I really like it. You've all worked very hard.'

'Is it as good as Harboreta?' Charlotte pressed.

'Well, yes,' said Derek. 'Except . . .'

'Except what?'

'Except you don't have clocks in malls.'

'Why not?'

'Because you don't want people to know the time.'

'Why not?'

'Because if they don't know the time they might stay longer.'

'That's so *evil*,' Charlotte said.

Nessie thanked Derek for coming and handed him a pink plastic champagne glass. Norton removed the clock. Charlotte hustled Derek out on to the landing. 'You're so thoughtless!' she hissed. 'You could have really upset them.'

'I was only giving them the benefit of my specialist knowledge,' Derek protested.

'They're *children*, you idiot!' Charlotte snapped.

Later that night she lay in bed, contemplating her belly. The kicking was frequent now, her weight starting to slow her down. She was still annoyed with Derek. Fathers, who needs them, she thought. Her laptop rested open at her side. She thought she'd check her e-mails before she went to sleep. A new one had arrived. It was from Laurent. Its subject was 'coming home'.

Allo Charlotte. It is fixed I will be in Paris at the end of August. Do you want to see me there? Or will I come to see you?

Charlotte spent a long time composing her reply. She spent even longer agonising over whether to send it.

Allo Laurent. I feel bad about this. But I'm going to Australia with my dad for a few weeks. My nerdy brother lives there, remember? I won't be able to see you until October, probably. Maybe you ought to find another girlfriend (that's a joke, probably).

'God help me,' she murmured, then clicked on the 'send now' icon and it was gone.

Down the landing Derek was suffering too. As he put his Remington PG200 Rechargeable Grooming Kit to work, Charlotte's angry words kept coming back to him – '*They're children, you idiot!*' – and he was haunted by the sort of thing Matthew would say – '*You sound more tense than usual lately – lacking your usual wit and energy . . .*' Most of all, he was thinking about tomorrow – the day he was due to give evidence for Lorcan in court. 'Be brave,

Derek Hawker,' he said to himself as he went back into the bedroom and lay on his marital bed, no longer the sole occupant of the house yet somehow feeling even more alone.

# chapter 14

Dennis Boam JP looked at his watch, checked with his fellow magistrates and his clerk, and nodded to the usher to call the first witness. It was 10.47 so not too much time had been lost while the wheelchair was stowed away and the defendant helped on to the chair in the dock. None the less, Boam remained perturbed. Earlier he'd called Crisp over for a private word.

'Forgive me, but are you sure your client is fit for this? Mentally, that is?'

'Yes, your worship, although he won't be giving evidence. And I shall be presenting expert evidence that he's been under heavy stress.'

'I see. And the, um, ecclesiastical clothing?'

'Mr O'Neill's attire is simply an expression of his cultural inheritance and deep religious faith.'

'Surely he doesn't always dress like that. He runs a pub, doesn't he?'

'You surmise rightly, sir. He reserves his spiritual garb for more formal occasions.'

'And the, ah, mitre? Is that the right word for it?'

'He will, of course, remove it before proceedings start.'

Now Boam shook his head and took stock of everyone else in court: Alex Welch the purposeful young prosecutor and his assistants; Crisp's haughty young secretary in that appalling orange twin set he'd seen her in before; the smart young man on the public benches who was obviously a policeman with some interest in the case. No one in the press seats. But then, Boam supposed, on the lists this one had looked pretty dull. He wondered if it would turn out that way.

The first witness walked in. It was the gaunt police officer who'd led the Doonican's raid and spoken to Derek in the aftermath. As he took the stand his demeanour signalled he thought nonsense was afoot and that he didn't plan on putting up with it. He took his oath. Then Welch got to his feet and asked him to identify himself.

'Inspector Colin Spackman, Hertfordshire Police.'

Welch asked Spackman questions about the background to the bust. The answers were commanding and concise. There had been rumours about 'lock-ins' – customers being invited to stay on after hours. Two weeks prior to Good Friday he'd sent three plain-clothed constables to investigate. The rumours proved correct: behind shuttered windows and bolted doors alcohol was served until the small hours and there had been an entertainer too – in this case a blue comedian. The constables had learned that a further lock-in was planned for a fortnight's time. And so the Good Friday operation had been planned. 'They were taking liberties,' said Spackman. 'It had all got out of hand.'

He continued by describing how he and his team had infiltrated the sports bar then been ushered through to the music lounge after the regular punters had gone home. He recounted the introduction of the strippers and his successful purchase of an alcoholic drink – 'At that point I called time.' Welch asked him more about the drink and an exhibit was produced: a half-empty bottle bearing the label Kilkenny Kicker.

'And this was the illicit liquor Mr O'Neill made available to his after-hours customers?'

'That's correct.'

'Along with the usual beverages – beer, spirits and so on?'

'Yes.'

'Who was serving the drinks?'

'Mr O'Neill, some of the time. And another man – one of the heavies he'd hired.'

'And who introduced the strippers?'

'Mr O'Neill.'

'So he took the lead in all the evening's nefarious action?'

'He was in the thick of it, yes.'

Welch resumed his seat, looking pleased. Crisp rose to cross-examine. He put it to Spackman that he had omitted one significant detail from his account.

'After you revealed that you were a policeman there was a fight, Inspector Spackman, wasn't there?'

'There was a scuffle, yes. I'd hardly call it a fight.'

'A scuffle, a fight, call it what you like. The point is there was an attempt to attack Mr O'Neill.'

'I didn't see the incident kick off. I know one of the heavies struck another man – one of the punters.'

'Yes, Inspector Spackman. The "heavy" as you call him did indeed strike another man. The man he struck is a friend of Mr O'Neill who nobly and bravely protected him against an extremely violent thug whose name is Vincent Hooper. We shall be hearing evidence from that blameless friend – Mr Hawker – a little later. But first, Inspector Spackman, can you confirm that Vincent Hooper was, in fact, arrested in connection with this . . . scuffle, as you call it?'

'I can.'

'Can you confirm that he was, none the less, never charged?'

'Yes.'

'Why wasn't he charged?'

Spackman looked uncomfortable. He blustered. 'As I said, I didn't see much of the incident. It looked like a case of handbags. And the other man didn't want to make anything of it. I spoke to him myself.'

'I see,' said Crisp. He rustled a few papers. Then he said, 'And you and or other officers questioned Hooper and his associates – the other "heavies" – about their part in the after-hours activities, didn't you?'

'Correct, yes.'

'But you didn't arrest them in that connection, did you?'

'No.'

'And in the end only my client, Mr O'Neill, faces charges. That's rather strange, isn't it?'

Spackman shrugged. His earlier vigour was subsiding. 'Mr O'Neill is the proprietor . . .'

Crisp affected disappointment. 'Dear, dear, Inspector, that really won't do, will it? Tell me – can you tell me where Vincent Hooper and his associates are at present?'

Spackman summoned a disbelieving laugh. 'No, I can't.'

'No, you cannot, can you, Inspector? And I put it to you that the reason for that is simple – they've gone to ground, haven't they?'

'I wouldn't know, Mr Crisp.'

'They went to ground very quickly – and for one simple reason. They know the truth about what was *really* going on that night in Doonican's, don't they?'

'Do they?' Spackman made a stab at weary impatience.

'Yes, they do, Inspector – as would you had you bothered to investigate the matter properly. It never crossed your mind, did it, that the reason Vincent Hooper tried to attack Mr O'Neill is because he believed – quite falsely, as I'm sure you can confirm – that the raid was the result of Mr O'Neill's informing the police that he was being forced, against his will, to let Hooper and his chums use his premises as an illegal entertainment venue?'

'No. It didn't cross my mind.'

'Of course, Mr O'Neill had not informed on Hooper –

much as he would have liked to – for a very simple reason. He was terrified – terrified of the terrible vengeance Hooper would take if his racket were exposed. Indeed, he attempted to tell you that on the actual night, didn't he?'

'Well . . .' Spackman blew out his cheeks. 'It's hard to say. He wasn't very coherent. He kept calling for the Virgin Mary. And Dr Ian Paisley, as I recall.'

Crisp's cross-examination continued in this vein, painting a picture of incompetent policemen failing to comprehend that his client, 'a peaceful, sensitive man of profoundly ecumenical religious beliefs', was the helpless victim of Hooper and his gang. Lorcan, suitably, sat in suffering silence throughout and maintained it impressively even during the evidence of the next witness, the youthful plain-clothed officer Constable Glenn Branch, who blushingly described the descent of his chinos.

Crisp, though, did not dwell on this. It would have been a diversion from his central strategy: 'Like Hooper and the others who profited from the cruel misuse of Mr O'Neill, the strippers have disappeared into thin air – haven't they, Constable?'

'I hope so,' Glenn replied, looking round nervously.

While all this went on, Derek sat fidgeting in the lobby. He had arrived at nine as Crisp had asked him to and been through one more rehearsal. 'Remember,' Crisp had stressed, 'to secure my client's innocence we need to portray him as *an* innocent – an innocent at large – who has been ruthlessly misused by evil men.'

'Yes, Aubrey. And may all your bacon sandwiches have wings.'

Derek felt enriched by this display of insolence. The lawyer's casual condescension lit a fire in him, brought out a chippy streak. It was invigorating. In fact, he'd been feeling robust since waking. It had been a relief to be finally doing something after the anxiety of the night before. He'd made his pants decision with uncomplicated relish – if ever there was a boxer shorts day this had to be it – and rolled on freshly laundered socks. His suit choice was conservative – single-breasted, slate grey check – while his shirt and tie selection radiated class. Every thread said 'man of substance'. Even Charlotte had seemed impressed.

'When is the Queen expecting you?'

'Just after she's chopped off your head.'

'No, seriously – you look very posh.'

David Bowie circa 2002 was how Derek would have put it, but 'posh' was the nearest to a compliment he was likely to get. He'd pulled *Station to Station* from his CD collection and let the Lexus cruise to the finger-snap groove of 'Golden Years'. But though his cool customer mood had helped him deep-freeze Crisp it didn't last. These days, his good vibes never did. The lobby seemed to teem with lads in rough trade casuals and he started to feel conspicuous and prim. Rutted copies of the *Sun* began mounting on the tables.

Styrofoam beakers accumulated on the arms of the bolted down chairs. Derek's head began to pound with the desire to tidy up and fetch the pack of Flash anti-bacterial wet wipes from the car. Then his thoughts switched back to home.

*What if the house is burning down?*

*What if I didn't close the freezer door?*

Derek began fidgeting. He got up and paced. Finally, he caved in. Use of mobile phones was not permitted in the lobby, but was OK in the canteen. He walked out to it in a fluster, fumbling for his phone, and found a corner next to a vending machine. He called home, heard the connection and waited for the ring. Then an intercom announced his name.

'Mr Derek Hawker?'

Sod's Law timing! Shit! The phone was ringing now. Come on, Charlotte, answer it!

'Mr Derek Hawker please?'

*What if the house is burning down? What if . . .*

'MR DEREK HAWKER?'

He switched the mobile off and rushed to the court-room.

Charlotte picked the phone up at the second it stopped ringing. 'How *annoying*!' she exclaimed and dialled 1471. The robot voice disgorged the caller's number. She recognised it as her father's mobile. What was he playing at? Was he checking up on her? Was he spying? She punched 3 to call him back but got only a recorded message. *It has not been possible to connect your call. Please try again later.*

Charlotte returned the handset to its plinth and took a vexed look round. She was in Matthew's bedroom – as she still thought of it – which was the best room from which to spot anyone entering the close; in this case, the postman on his second delivery. He usually came at twelve o'clock. Was it nearly that yet? Charlotte never wore a watch and there was no clock in the room; except there'd be one on the laptop, wouldn't there?

Emboldened by irritation she went to Derek's iBook, prised it open and switched it on. As it went through its start-up motions she peeped down the landing to check on Nessie and Norton. They were still wonderfully absorbed, as they had been all morning. An integrated public transport system was falling into place, enabling sundry rubber monsters and pouting Li'l Bratz to be conveyed to Derek World by Brio wooden railtrack.

Charlotte turned to the iBook. The clock said 11.53. Again she looked out of the window towards the entrance to the close but saw no one. Then . . . why not? He'd never know. If he could nose round in her business she could nose round in his. Charlotte moved the cursor to the mail icon and double-clicked. Her father's inbox appeared. It made revealing reading. I Luv Lexus Club – quality cruisin'. Dyson Unofficial – Kissed Your Clear Bin™ lately? Jockey Talk – real pants are back! And then: Elizabeth Ford – my pleasure.

What was *that* about? Spam probably. Mucky stuff. Why hadn't he deleted it? She opened it.

Dear Derek,

It would be my pleasure to keep you as my client after our present agreement has expired. I am delighted you enjoy my services. I'm sure we can discuss it at our next date.

In confidence, Libby

Charlotte read the message. She read it again. 'In confidence'? There was an address at the bottom – 7 Kidley Road, Welwyn Garden City. Then the doorbell rang. Charlotte jumped like a discovered thief. She cried, 'I'll get it, children!' and bolted downstairs at much greater speed than pregnant women should. The postman held out a parcel that was too big for the letter box – 'something for your dad, I think' – and a letter, bearing her college's crest – 'something for you, too'.

She accepted the items with a flat 'thank you' to conceal the excitement she felt. She closed the door and let the parcel thud to the ground – some mail order catalogue by the looks of it – and opened the letter greedily. It took only a few seconds to find the key sentences.

'I *knew* it. I just *knew* it!' she exclaimed.

'What did you know, Charlotte?' Nessie asked.

Charlotte looked up sharply. She didn't realise she'd been followed. 'Oh, nothing. Nothing important. How are things in Derek World?'

In the witness box Derek took the proffered Bible and read from the accompanying card – 'I solemnly swear that the evidence I shall give shall be the truth, the whole truth and nothing but the truth . . .' He meant what he was saying – he'd just about convinced himself of that – but had a harder time believing the amazing state of Lorcan whom he was seeing for the first time that day. Bishop O'Neill of Brayston? Could this be real?

'Very well, Mr Crisp,' said Boam.

Crisp rose and cleared his throat. 'Please give your full name.'

'Derek Lester Hawker.'

'And let it be clear for the record that you are a near neighbour of the defendant, Mr O'Neill – indeed you live directly opposite him, don't you? In the village of Brayston?'

'Yes, I do.'

'And you were with Mr O'Neill at Doonican's Irish pub on Good Friday night when the alleged offences took place?'

'That's correct.'

'Thank you. Now, if I might . . .'

'I'm sorry,' Derek said. 'Could I have a glass of water?'

Crisp looked a bit put out – he was just getting into his stride. 'Well, yes, of course.'

Derek was playing for time. If Lorcan's rig-out hadn't been unsettling enough he'd now spotted the man on the public bench. It had to be him – McBride, the Scottish detective who'd called on him the day the O'Neills' house was raided.

'When you're ready, Mr Hawker . . .' drawled Crisp.

There was no turning back. Derek stuck his chin out bravely. 'Yes, I'm ready now,' he said.

Crisp's questions were carefully framed. They drew from Derek an account of the fateful evening that was much the same in substance as Spackman's but different in emphasis. Where Spackman had depicted Lorcan as the sole architect and beneficiary of the lock-in, Derek's evidence laid stress on the prominence of Hooper and his mates. He described seeing Lorcan speak to them in the sports bar and how struck he'd been by Hooper's lack of friendliness. He recalled Hooper's 'menacing manner' while the strippers did their stuff and his 'business-like detachment' from it.

'And how would you describe Mr O'Neill's demeanour?' asked Crisp.

'Agitated,' said Derek.

'Intimidated?'

'It seems very possible, yes. He certainly looked scared.'

'I see. And you waited for Mr O'Neill, didn't you, so that after the police had finished speaking to him he wouldn't have to travel home alone?'

'Yes.'

'How was he during that journey?'

'Hysterical,' Derek said. 'He prayed a lot and asked for his mother.'

'And when he got home?'

'His wife was there to meet him. I helped her to calm him down.'

'And tell me, Mr Hawker, does Mrs O'Neill know

all the facts about what went on that evening?'

'No, she does not.'

'And why is that?'

Derek picked his words deftly: 'Because Mr O'Neill didn't want to worry her. She is under the impression that this trial is about a few yobs misbehaving at Doonican's and one of them – this Mr Hooper – assaulting me. I've gone along with this white lie to spare Mrs O'Neill's feelings.'

'And do you believe, Mr Hawker, that that is indeed what this trial ought to be about?'

'Well, Mr Hooper did try to attack Mr O'Neill and ended up hitting me. He is certainly a very violent man.'

'Finally, Mr Hawker, given your knowledge of Mr O'Neill, do you find it credible that this gentle and fragile character, this God-fearing individual, could have been responsible for the provision of such coarse entertainment?'

'The more I think of it,' said Derek, 'the less likely it seems that Mr O'Neill is capable of being in any way responsible.'

'Thank you, Mr Hawker. That will be all.'

Sam fetched Nessie and Norton just after half past three. He'd been back from Houston for two days. Moz had taken off on her golfing holiday the morning after his return. Charlotte studied his face for signs of emotional trauma. She noticed none.

'How have they been, Charlotte?' he asked. 'It's the first time they've spent a whole day round here, isn't it?'

'Oh, they've been very good. Derek World is still expanding and some penguins have moved on to the ice rink.'

Sam did his concerned face. 'Derek himself – he won't think they're taking over, will he? I mean, there's not a lot of mess or anything?'

'Oh no,' said Charlotte vaguely.

'Any news from court?'

'No, nothing.'

'He'll be back soon, I expect. Court proceedings usually finish around four. Did he say?'

'Um . . .' Charlotte signalled 'search me' with her hands. 'Something like that . . . How's Bou?'

Sam smiled. 'She'll be here on Friday.'

'Oh, she can come to my birthday tea, then. Nessie's making a cake.'

'Bad luck – about the cake, I mean. Boudica will love the party. You know . . .' Sam became earnest. 'It's been really great for her, having your company, Charlotte. You've been like a sister to her.'

'Oh, I find her interesting,' said Charlotte. 'It was a big thing for her to do, coming to look for you. Risky.'

'Risky?'

'What if you hadn't liked each other? What if you'd discovered that, you know, you weren't really her father after all?'

'Fair point,' said Sam, who was getting used to Charlotte's spiky candour. He laughed. 'Don't worry, Kathy's quite certain who was responsible. It was quite nice to see her, actually. She's changed a lot: much calmer, rather like me. Now where are those two pests?' He called to Nessie and Norton, who were avoiding him upstairs. 'Hurry up now, kids. We mustn't keep Charlotte from her intellectual struggles.'

No, Charlotte thought; or from her moral ones, either.

Derek's Omega Constellation said it was 3.46 p.m. The clock on the courtroom wall said 3.48 but he didn't let it worry him. All of his attention was fixed on Dennis Boam.

'Well, here we are at last,' Boam said. His tone was that of a wizened traveller on completing a long, strange and surprisingly enlightening journey. He continued, 'It has been a rather extraordinary case with some contentious and extremely, ah, colourful evidence. And reaching a verdict has taken a little time . . .'

Derek gnawed a knuckle. He noticed that Lorcan was staring at the ceiling, possibly to summon a celestial stairway down which would amble a job lot of apostles led, of course, by God.

Boam and his colleagues exchanged knowing looks. 'However,' Boam went on, 'after long consideration we have reached a decision. Guilt, of course, must be established beyond reasonable doubt and on that basis we find the defendant . . .' he allowed himself a moment of dramatic hesitation, 'not guilty of all charges.'

Boam thanked his clerk for his assistance. Welch and Crisp shook hands. Lorcan's trance state remained undisturbed as the usher wrestled with his wheelchair. Derek got up to leave and, as he did so, made accidental eye contact with McBride, who gave him a quick nod that just might have been friendly. But Derek didn't wait to find out. Before anyone could waylay him he pushed through the swing doors into the corridor and followed the 'exit' signs with rapid strides. The Lexus was in a car park a ten-minute walk from the court. Derek did it in five. Only when enwombed by leather upholstery did he permit himself a deep sigh of relief; and even that was strongly qualified.

Yes, he had helped Lorcan get off which meant Galina would be spared from knowing what had really happened at Doonican's. Yes, if Crisp was right, he'd got himself out of jail too, for there'd been no one in the press seats all day. Yet there remained so much that wasn't right. He'd managed to give his evidence without telling any lies but he still had to fib to Charlotte. He'd have to keep alive the falsehood that the trial had been about assault, that he had been the victim and the defendant had been the elusive Hooper – and he'd have to hope that Lorcan would stick to the same story. As if he wasn't keeping enough secrets: from Charlotte, his relationship with Libby; from Denise to name but one the fact of Charlotte's pregnancy; from everyone his resignation from his job. And what about the freezer? Had he left its door open or not?

# chapter 15

'Charlotte?'

'Yes Norton?'

'Would you play chest with me?'

'Why don't you set out the pieces first?'

'*Ach-ully*, I have to set out the pieces first,' Norton said, 'otherwise we wouldn't be able to play chest, would we?'

'Actually, Norton, no.'

'Norton,' put in Moz from across the Hawkers' dining-room table. 'Don't be grumpy with Charlotte, please.'

'It's not nice on her birthday, is it?' added Sam.

'*Egg-zackly*,' Nessie confirmed.

Norton said nothing and kept his head down. It was good to keep your head down when you were being told off because the front of your maths hat went more over your eyes so you couldn't see who was telling you off and that meant you could pretend they weren't telling you off really. And Norton wanted Charlotte to play chest with him so it wasn't sensible to be told off again. He wanted

Charlotte to play chest because she knew how to play it properly. Some people didn't know how to play chest properly. Some people thought the littlest pieces, the ones that can only take other pieces diagonally, are called prawns. But they aren't called prawns, they're called pawns. And if you don't know they're called pawns you don't know much about chest.

'Norton,' said Boudica. 'Shall I play chest with you?'

Norton said nothing again, although this time the nothing wasn't only a nothing because he did a little growl too quietly for anyone to hear. Boudica didn't know how to play chest. She wasn't an intellectual. Maybe Derek would play with him later. Norton liked Derek. He knew about shops and was a bit grumpy, like him.

'Cheer up, Norton,' said Charlotte. 'If you like you can help me cut the cake up into eighths.'

'The cake made by me, Natalie Blake,' put in Nessie, 'just in case anyone forgets.'

'There's no danger of that,' said Moz. 'Sam and I are still clearing up the mess.'

'Oh, I'm so sorry,' said Boudica, who'd helped with the icing.

'Don't worry, darling,' said Sam a bit defensively. 'Moz is only joking.'

'Oh yes,' said Moz, 'it was only a joke.'

There was a mildly awkward lull before Norton announced, 'Cutting the cake into eighths would be a joke.'

Charlotte, who was removing the twenty candles and

sundry party popper streamers from the magnificent pink confection, asked him why.

'Because there aren't eight people,' Norton said. 'There are seven: you, me, Nessie, Sam, Moz, Boudica and Derek when he comes back.'

'So,' said Charlotte. 'There will be one piece left over. Does it matter?'

'Yes,' said Norton. 'It does matter.'

'Why does it matter, Nor?' asked Moz.

'Because there will be one piece left over.'

'I know. But *why* does it matter?'

'Because it *does*,' said Norton. His maths hat was very low now, but it couldn't hide his unhappy face. 'Because it *does*!'

'All right, all right, all right,' said Sam soothingly, putting an arm round his troubled little boy. 'How about if we give the piece left over to someone else?'

'But there *isn't* anyone else!'

'We could give it to Scrag,' offered Charlotte.

'Or Jade?' said Nessie in her Amber voice.

'No, no, NO!' shouted Norton. 'They aren't people! They aren't real!'

'I have an idea,' said Moz. 'We could share the eighth piece between us.' She smiled at Norton, coaxingly. 'Then we'd all have one big piece and one little piece.'

'No,' said Norton flatly. 'The little piece would be too silly.'

'OK, OK, Norton,' said Sam. 'What do *you* think we should do?'

'It has to be in sevenths.'

'Sevenths?' said Sam. 'Oh, *Norton* . . .'

'Sevenths it is, then,' said Charlotte, smothering a smile with her hand. 'So who's got a protractor?'

Luckily, she did. And Norton, of course, had his calculator on him. Soon a cake-sized circle was being cut from a piece of paper and its circumference marked at intervals of 51.428571 degrees to serve as a template for the slicing. The others chatted among themselves.

'How's the baby?' Boudica asked Charlotte.

'Very well,' said Charlotte. 'I'm having a scan tomorrow. You can come with me if you want.'

'Wow, that would be cool,' Bou enthused.

'Can I come too?' asked Nessie.

'Of course you can. There's plenty of room in Dad's car.'

'Maybe I'd better take you this time,' said Sam, 'if you're planning on bringing all these guests.'

'Will the scan tell you its sex?' asked Boudica.

'It might.'

'Will you want to know?'

'Oh, yes.'

'Have you chosen the baby's name yet?' Nessie asked.

'No. I'm still thinking.'

'But what if it was born this minute?' asked Nessie. 'You wouldn't know what to call it!'

'If it was born this minute we'd all get a big shock,' said Charlotte. 'And we don't want that to happen. If it was born this early it might not live.'

'That would be *terrible*,' said Nessie, clutching theatrically at Charlotte's arm.

'It would,' Charlotte agreed. 'Now, are those sevenths ready? I'm *dying* to try Nessie's cake.'

But before the knife could be wielded the phone rang. It rang twice then went silent again. 'Dad's picked it up, upstairs,' said Charlotte. 'I wonder what he's been doing up there.' She could already hear him on his way.

'It's Mum,' he said as he came into the dining room and held out the cordless from his office, keeping his thumb over the mouthpiece.

Charlotte rose amid a sudden quiet. Despite the physical distance – or in a way because of it – Denise loomed large in the lives of every adult in the room. She was the Mum Who Doesn't Know, especially in the mind of Moz who often struggled with feelings of helpless disloyalty. Charlotte eased herself out from the table and took the phone. 'I'll talk to her upstairs,' she said and left the room.

Charlotte waited until she was up on the landing before speaking.

'Hello, Mum.'

Down a wind tunnel of a line Denise burst into song.

> *'Happy birthday to you!*
> *Happy birthday to you!*
> *Happy birthday dear Charlotte . . .'*

'Thanks, Mum, that'll do.'

'Don't you like my singing then?'

'Yes, yes, of course I do.'

God, Mum was so insecure.

'What's it like not being a teenager?'

'About the same as being one day short of not being a teenager.'

'Oh, Charlotte, you're so *serious* . . .'

'That's true.'

She'd made it to her room and was trying to get comfortable sitting on her bed. Mr Heath was flopped beside her, and Charlotte noticed that the stitches in his back were coming loose – maybe his stuffing concealed precious jewels. Scrag's litter tray needed changing. She touched her belly, gently. Oh, Mother, she thought, if you could see me now . . .

'Did my card arrive?' Denise asked.

'Yes, yesterday. It's beautiful.'

'Did Dad get you a cake?'

'I've had a cake, yes.' Charlotte hedged. She'd known the call was coming but was only now realising how unprepared she was to receive it. She didn't want to say Nessie had made the cake because Denise would be curious about how she'd become so friendly with the neighbours. Charlotte could imagine the questions that would follow. *Are you seeing them a lot, then? How come? Are you spending a lot of time at home?*

Denise spoke again. 'Any nice presents?'

'A few.'

Charlotte thought desperately. There were the earrings and the book on baby animals from Nessie and Norton, the book on baby humans from Sam and Moz . . .

'What were they?' asked Denise.

'Dad's given me some money,' she said. 'To buy whatever I want.'

'Nothing lovely to unwrap, then?'

'No, Mum. Nothing lovely to unwrap.'

'That's a shame.'

Charlotte knew what Denise was thinking: if *I'd* been there you'd have had lots of lovely presents to unwrap . . .

'Well, I don't mind really,' Charlotte said, making an effort to sound less stroppy.

'Anyway, darling,' said Denise. 'How is Laurent?'

Charlotte faltered. She couldn't think what would be the best thing to say.

'Darling, are you still there?'

'Yes, Mum, sorry. Well, Laurent . . .'

She winced recalling the e-mail exchange she'd had with her sort of boyfriend earlier in the day.

Laurent: Allo Charlotte, cherie. Happy birthday! Are you enjoying Sydney?

Charlotte: Allo Laurent. Sydney is great. I will be on the beach later.

Laurent: What, in the winter?

Charlotte: Not sunbathing! Walking!

Phew, she'd thought, that was a close thing.

Laurent: I hope you were joking about finding a new girlfriend.

**Charlotte:** I don't have an old girlfriend, actually (that's definitely a joke, by the way. I'm saving lesbianism for when I retire.).

**Laurent:** I am missing you, Charlotte.

**Charlotte:** Good.

Denise was sounding worried. 'Charlotte? Where have you gone?'

'Mum, I'm not going to see Laurent for a while.'

'Oh, why's that?'

'Well, he's still in Africa.'

'He's coming back, isn't he?'

'Yes, he's coming back but not for a while and, well, he's very sweet and everything but he's been gone for ages and, you know. It wasn't very serious.'

'You make it sound as if it's over. You never told me things weren't going well.'

'There wasn't much to tell.'

'Even so. Are you coping?'

'Oh, Mum. I'm a grown-up. I don't need rescuing.'

'Oh well, pardon me for sticking my nose in.'

'I didn't mean that, Mum. It's sort of like . . . a trial separation.'

'Oh well. Like mother like daughter, I suppose.'

'Anyway, Mum, how are things with you? Are the pandas more fun than Dad?'

From here the conversation went more smoothly. Denise relayed a string of anecdotes about the children she was teaching, the food she was eating, the sanitation she was enduring and the embarrassment of accidentally saying surreal things in Mandarin. Charlotte punctuated these with the occasional 'Really?' and 'How amazing!' Her responses were banal not because she didn't care what her mother was saying nor because, in other circumstances, she wouldn't have found her stories diverting. It was simply because Denise sounded so very far away and was so very evidently in the dark. Dad was keeping his word, then. Even so, it felt strange. Charlotte mentioned that Derek had started ironing his socks, which wasn't true but made her mother laugh. She signed off cheerily.

'Oh, well, darling, I'd better be going now. See you in December! By-eee!'

If not before, thought Charlotte.

Switching off the handset she reflected for a minute, feeling rather bad about herself. What was she thinking, being so icy with her mother? Why was she so irritated by her dad? Was it logical to feel so very crowded by the people whose support she was going to need most?

And that wasn't the end of Charlotte's problems. For the first time in her life she understood why people said that there were some things it was better not to know. Kneeling carefully by the bed so as not to pull any muscles, she reached under her mattress and retrieved the envelope she'd received from her college the other day. It was from Howard Milling, her favourite biology professor. She was his star student which was why he didn't mind doing her a favour – a big one. She opened the envelope and read the letter through again.

*Dear Charlotte,*

 *I enclose the results of the DNA tests you asked me to do. As you'll see the samples you provided did not produce a match, suggesting there is no biological link between the two people concerned. Of course, as you know, the results of such tests are far less reliable when the samples used have not been collected in the preferred way – buccal cell collection by mouth swab, as you know – so I don't think firm conclusions should be drawn. Anyway, Charlotte, I only did this for you because I respect your ethics and admire you as a student. I trust you will use this informa-tion cautiously if at all.*

 *Yours faithfully, Howard*
*PS The red hair was very beautiful. I can't say quite the same thing for the snot!*

Charlotte put the letter back in its hiding place and went down to her birthday guests. She passed Derek coming up the other way.

He gripped the edges of the en suite bathroom sink, looked into the mirror and saw his eyeballs staring back. Derek knew better than most – *much* better than most – that there are ways of being fifty-odd these days – the Tony Blair way, the David Bowie, the Richard Branson – without appearing to be knocking on. Yet the time was sure to come when the glaze of enduring youthfulness would crack to reveal a man hiding from truths he had to face: that early-maturing private pension plan; aggressive younger motorists calling him 'grandad'; the ever-grimmer recognition that time was counting down to the grave. It might count for fifty years. It might count for five days. At his age, you couldn't know.

'Will they *ever* go home?' he asked. He'd had enough of Charlotte's birthday party. He'd had enough of everything. For ten years he'd scorned the notion of the midlife crisis, buoyed by the glory of Harboreta and by the belief that his move to Willow Close was not only a monument to his past success but the platform from which he could enjoy more. And suddenly his appetite had left him. Leaving QF, he now saw, had been a sort of self-delusion: not a radical refreshment but a futile flight from disillusion. He hadn't got his solo act sorted at all. He hadn't posted his website, he'd never chased up contacts and even the sporadic oddball responses to his Chambers of Commerce listing had dried up: Libby's had been the only sane one he'd received.

The world of products and shopping just didn't thrill him any more. As an early-thirties young buck roaming retail's Brave New World the slap of his first morocco leather Filofax on his first boss-class desk propelled him to those realms of deep sensation others entered by snorting cocaine. There had been many highs of this kind: getting acquainted with the steel-and-rubber-dotted body of the Braun Micron Universal electric shaver; his initial sighting of the cover of the Human League album *Dare*; his first visit to the Neasden IKEA. Now everything felt old and tired, and he did too.

'Derek? Are you up here?'

It was Sam on the landing. Derek jumped in surprise and then felt guilty for sneaking away. Charlotte showing the old home videos had been the last straw . . . 'Look, there's me with my fishing net collecting crabs!' 'Look, there's Dad hiding in the beach hut worrying about his hair!' . . . but he knew he was failing in his duty. That duty was to be fun-loving and easy-going and joining in the general joshing about his long-lost younger self on this, his clever daughter's twentieth birthday. He couldn't cut it, though. He'd had to take refuge in gloom. Now Happy Sam was dragging him back into the light.

'Coming, Sam,' he called.

He made his way past the bed and Denise's dressing table and then out through the door. Sam stood there smiling. Norton was waiting with him, holding his hand.

'Sorry about this,' Sam said. 'Norton wants me to look at the model mall and I didn't like to just barge around . . . knowing you were up here somewhere . . .'

'Oh, that's all right.' Derek felt Sam's eyes peering into his. Did he look as dreadful as he felt?

'Norton says it's down here.' Sam pointed to the old office door.

'Yeah, yeah, that's right,' Derek said. From somewhere he rustled up some social graces. 'Let me show you.'

They walked together into Derek World, careful to avoid crushing viaducts, destroying block-built houses or trampling window-shopping members of Sylvanian Families.

'Wow, it's grown even bigger,' Sam enthused. 'But, Derek, this looks like your study. Don't you mind?'

'Oh, it's fine. I'm using another room for work.' He tried to change the subject. 'I see they've built a church,' he said with false enthusiasm. 'Dedicated to St Lego.'

'It's for weddings,' Norton said.

'Weddings in a shopping mall,' said Sam. 'I suppose it could catch on.'

'It was Nessie's idea,' said Norton.

'Girls, eh?' said Derek. 'Who needs them?'

'Derek?'

'Yes, Norton?'

'One day will you play chest with me?'

'Pardon?'

'And Derek?'

'Yes?'

'How many seconds is it till I'm six?'

'You've got me there, I'm afraid.' He chuckled in a mannered fashion, hoping for sympathy from Sam.

'Eight million, eight hundred and twelve thousand, eight hundred and ninety-two,' said Norton.

'Approximately,' said Sam. 'We worked it out downstairs.'

'And Sam?' said Norton.

'Yes?'

'I need a poo.'

He trotted directly from the room with one hand clutching his bottom, just in case. Sam and Derek looked at one another. They hadn't been in such close proximity since the evening Sam had visited to tell all about Bou. Derek froze a little.

Sam broke the ice. 'The time,' he said, 'is seven-fifteen.'

Derek checked. 'Seven-eighteen, as it happens.'

'Close enough. Norton is very regular, you see.'

Derek didn't know what to say: defecation cycles weren't his thing. He was glad, then, that Sam moved the subject on. 'He's also very clever, isn't he?' It wasn't said boastfully. More regretfully, if anything.

'He is clever, yes,' Derek agreed. 'In fact, it's frightening.'

'But you see, Derek,' said Sam, 'there are some things he can't do.'

Derek felt strangely cornered. It seemed Sam was feeding him lines and he couldn't help but say them. 'What things can't he do?'

'He can't relax. And he can't swim. It's a nervous thing. So's the hat.'

Again, Derek felt tugged along. 'I haven't noticed him being nervous. He seems full of confidence to me.'

'Oh, he does get nervous,' said Sam, in a tone of quiet yet absolute certainty. 'I think he gets it from me.'

'I hadn't noticed you . . .'

'People don't,' said Sam. 'But it is there, lurking.'

'Oh,' said Derek. 'Really?' He recognised his own nervousness now. It was the same type that had assailed him on the day he resigned, sitting with Amelia Hardwick in her new soft corner: the closeness of another person's attention to him, its inhibiting effect.

'I made my money in the City in the Eighties,' Sam said. 'Quite a lot of it. Enough to fly off to New York and have flings with beauty queens.'

Now Derek was floundering. Where was Sam leading him now? He latched on to a stray detail. 'I thought Kathy was a beautician?'

'She is. She was a beauty queen before.' Sam was very earnest. 'I haven't mentioned that to Moz. She's suffered enough, don't you think? Anyway, I burned out in the City. I made a mountain of money, then I got scared. I panicked all the time. It was terrifying.'

Again Sam left a space. Again Derek filled it. 'What did you do?' he said.

'I lived on tranquillisers for two years. Then I took up yoga. It was at Moz's health club. I met her and she saved me, basically.'

This seemed to be the end of the story. Derek was just wondering what would happen next when Norton called.

'Sam. I'm lonely.'

Sam led the way to the bathroom. Derek followed him – somehow this seemed understood. Norton was sitting on the toilet, frowning ruminatively. Derek leaned against the doorframe. Sam perched on the edge of the bath and said, 'I'd started to notice people were dying – people I thought of as contemporaries or as part of my youth. It's a regular thing now. Pop stars from your teenage or who you loved when you were twenty or thirty: George Harrison; Ian Dury; Joe Strummer. You start reading the obituaries page in newspapers and there are more and

more people in them you've heard of. Anyway, anyway
. . . Norton, have you finished yet?'

'No.'

'OK, but don't be long please. So, anyway, Derek, I'll
be fifty next year.'

'Fifty?' Derek was almost appalled. He'd always had
Sam down as much nearer forty, like Moz.

'Yes, fifty. It will be ten years since I finally, at long last,
sat down and thought clearly. I asked myself, what are the
simple things that would make my life better? Well, I'd
found Moz by then which gave me a new perspective. I
decided, one, that I had to have a job I found fulfilling –
hence the line of business I'm in now; two, that when we
had children I would be in a position to watch them
growing up; three, that I was going to lead a calmer,
gentler life . . .'

'I've finished, Sam,' said Norton.

'OK,' said Sam, 'let's do your bum.' He tore off some
toilet paper. Norton leaned forward helpfully. Normally,
Derek would have made an excuse and left but he hung
bravely on.

'So what are you going to do, Derek?' asked Sam as he
went about his task. 'At this moment in your life, what do
you most want?'

'I want to do the right thing,' Derek said.

'And what is the right thing?'

'I've got to get Charlotte to tell Denise about the baby.
Or let me tell her. She has to know.'

'OK. Anything else?'

'I've got to get her to tell Laurent.'

'OK. When are you going to do that?'

'In the next few days. Is that a good idea?'

'My opinion doesn't count. Only yours.'

'I know I have to do it.'

'Fine then,' said Sam.

Norton climbed down from the toilet and pulled up his shorts. Sam flushed and went to the basin to wash his hands. That task complete he turned again to Norton. 'Well, I suppose we'd better be going home. Say thanks for having us, Norton.'

'Thanks for having us, Derek,' Norton said.

'And by the way, Derek,' said Sam. 'You've just been life coached.'

# chapter 16

'Now Sam, try this.'

Lorcan reached for one of the two tumblers. Galina held the tray. Sam followed his host's example in knocking back his inch of muddy liquor in one go. Derek observed this from a distance some way beyond surprise.

'Phwah!' gasped Sam. 'That's lethal. What is it?'

'Kilkenny Kicker. From the county of my birth.'

Derek mouthed this line as Lorcan spoke it. Galina accepted the two men's empty glasses with a solicitous dip. Derek wanted to spit. He stood alone at the corner of the O'Neills' patio. The sun blazed down. It was the last Sunday in August, and a long, tormenting summer would soon be coming to a close. Pity the months to follow would be worse. Derek was now resolute about his course of action. He would level with Charlotte and then do the deed. But although he was convinced it was the right thing he still dreaded making that phone call to Denise.

He looked uninterestedly around the O'Neills' garden

where little groups of guests balanced petits fours on plates and sipped what might have been Doonican's house Lambrusco. Estate agents, were they? Vets? The Sodomy sub-section of the Mid-Herts Wife-swapping Society? Derek didn't know and didn't care. He was present out of duty and to escape from Charlotte for a while. She'd threatened to come over and embarrass him, of course – 'Think of the headlines, Dad: Father Faints In Flower Bed At Daughter's Pregnant Shame!' – but he didn't think she would. He'd left her buried in books about inherited connections between temperament and genes, no doubt to help her write an essay about why the books were rubbish and their authors complete fools.

'Would you care for a drink, sir?'

A waitress from the caterers presented a tray of sparkling glasses.

'Is it legal?' Derek asked, taking two.

The waitress giggled and left. It was the best conversation Derek had had so far. He was usually adept at social gatherings, cracking jokes and telling tales with verve and confidence. Perhaps he could amuse himself by bumping into Crisp who stood twenty yards away wearing a yachting cap and pushing cocktail sausages into his face. Derek thought he might sidle over Sam's way if only Lorcan would go and foist his funny hooch on someone else. Or perhaps he'd chat to Galina, despite the danger of her insisting on knitting him a sweater or massaging his feet.

But hello, who was this? A new guest caught Derek's

interest – and would, as it turned out, return the compliment before the day was through. He'd arrived quietly and had moved quickly to join the group standing furthest from the house. He was young and tall and casually smart – Derek recognised the Hackett threads enhancing the straight-backed good looks – and would have cut a striking figure in any company, let alone the assembled spivs and oddities from the local squirearchy. It was obvious he had become the main attraction for those near him. Crisp's secretary was among them and looked up at him through lowered lashes before braying her approval at something he said. An elderly man with a handlebar moustache threw back his head and guffawed. Yet Derek sensed that the newcomer's immediate audience was not the sole focus of his attention. Although the young man was apparently at ease, he seemed alert for action should the need arise.

And then calamity! From a copse of apple trees at the far end of the garden came Grace and Favour at high speed. Long leather leads whipped the ground behind them and trailed loose twigs and leaves. Plainly, they had been tethered to ensure visitors' safety. Plainly, they had broken free. They charged towards the group in which the young man stood. One of them – it turned out to be Grace – powered directly into the rear end of the man with the handlebar moustache, her muzzle boring for his anus with heat-seeking accuracy. This, though, was as nothing compared with the peril now threatening Crisp's secretary. Derek thanked the heavens he was wearing long trousers as Favour leaped at her and Derek glimpsed the blade of livid pink. Crisp's secretary shrieked. Her vol-au-vents were scattered, her skirt flew up, she fell forward on her knees and . . . and . . .

At that second the young man intervened. Initially his conduct seemed bizarre. Throwing back his head he let out a series of what could only be called howls: plaintive sounds, yet urgent and strangely cautionary. At the same time he bent his body into a curious pose and held it rigidly. It was similar to the type struck by martial arts experts except for the hands with which he described mystic patterns, the fingers rippling like the tentacles of sea anemones. Grace was the first of the two dogs to desist. Then Favour dismounted, meekly. Both sat neatly on the grass until, with every head now turned his way, the young man drew himself up to his full, impressive height and composed his entire frame into a vast balletic shape, one arm outstretched towards the copse from which the two shamed shar-pei had emerged. Together, they trotted calmly back into it and out of sight.

There was a great round of applause. The young man could have taken a bow but instead gave a helping hand to Crisp's secretary as she and the man with the handlebar moustache scraped up the fragments of their shattered dignity. Galina rushed over fretfully, gushing apologies. Others gathered round, trilling and tittering about the spectacle they'd seen. Only one person seemed unenthused. It was Lorcan. He simply stared. Derek called over to him. 'You should have that fellow living here,

Lorcan. He'd save everyone a lot of grief. Who is he, anyway?' Lorcan, though, didn't speak. He turned towards the kitchen, went inside and disappeared.

What was up with him? Derek made his way over to the young man. Once close to him he faltered, because others were crowding round their hero and Derek had no appetite for small talk. In the event, though, he had no need, for the young man seemed to spot him, excused himself and walked straight over to Derek, offering his right hand.

'Grainger. William Grainger. You're Mr Hawker, I believe.'

'Yes, I am. How did . . .'

'The driving force behind the famous Harboreta.'

'That's right. Have we . . .'

'No, we've never met. But I have my spies, Mr Hawker. They're everywhere.'

William released Derek's hand and laughed. Derek laughed too. It wasn't heartfelt, though, and Derek sensed that William's had been a little hollow too. Something about this towering specimen was too intense for humour. What was more, that remark about the spies seemed oddly likely to be true.

'And what's your connection with Lorcan then, William?' Derek asked.

William laughed uncommittedly again. 'Oh, that's a very long story, Mr Hawker. It would take a whole lifetime to tell. Let me ask you something if I may.'

'Go ahead,' Derek said. He was intrigued.

'What was your motivation?'

'For Harboreta? Well . . .'

'No, no, no.' William smiled, a little sharkishly. 'For getting Lorcan . . .' He said the name deliberately, perhaps with irony. 'For getting Lorcan off the hook?'

A tiny chill went through Derek, in spite of the heat. He played for time. 'What do you mean?'

'Come on now, Derek. Don't tease.'

'Tease?' William's presence seemed to engulf him. Derek said, suspiciously, 'Are you with the police?'

'No. Good guess, though. But tell me this, Derek. Did he have something on you? Or did you just feel sorry for him? It can happen, you know. You wouldn't be the first.'

'What do you mean?'

'Or were you being noble? Trying to save a damsel from even worse distress?' His eyes rolled heavily in the direction of Galina. She was chatting frantically to Crisp's secretary and Sam. Before Derek could answer William went on, 'I think maybe that's a part of it. Maybe a little of the other stuff too, but I suspect you're a pretty solid fellow. And not someone who takes kindly to being pushed around. My spies think so too.'

'I don't . . .'

'He spotted me, didn't he?' said William.

'Spotted you?'

'Lorcan. He picked me out during the business with the dogs. That's why he's run away. What do you reckon, Derek? Has he vamoosed in that nice Audi or is he somewhere in the house?'

Derek was flummoxed; mute. William slapped him on the shoulder. It was a light slap as slaps from Hercules clones go. 'Don't worry,' William said. 'You're a good man, I sense it. Maybe you and me can help each other. After all, it may suit us both to sort dear old Lorcan out.' As he completed this speech William's face turned stony. Derek saw that he was shaking slightly, struggling to marshal powerful passions. William seemed to sense that his veneer was wearing thin. 'I'd better leave now,' he said, 'before I say too much.'

Abruptly, he walked away towards the house. Derek watched him go, covering the ground in massive strides. Others watched him too. The young man – whoever he was – was a force of nature. Even a force of nature, though, must use the lavatory some time, and perhaps that was where the other guests assumed he was heading. Derek watched him disappear, wishing he hadn't had so much to drink. And when after a few minutes he too went into the house he hoped concern wasn't written all over him. He reached the bottom of the stairs just as William bounded down them and made for the front door.

'What have you done?' demanded Derek fearfully.

'Don't worry, Derek,' William said darkly. 'I haven't hurt him; just made sure he knows that he'll be seeing me again.'

With that William Grainger swashbuckled from the house and cut a swath through the gnome army without a backward glance.

\*   \*   \*

It took a while before the guests sensed anything amiss. When Lorcan's absence was first noticed Galina covered gamely, explaining that her husband had been under such pressure lately that he needed a lie down – 'It catch up with him! Phut! I put him to sleep!' But there was no point in dissembling once the ambulance arrived, taking everyone, including Galina, by surprise. As Lorcan was wheeled out on a stretcher Derek saw he'd gone into his celestial suffering trance again, although self-evidently its full disengaging effect had not kicked in until after he had made his phone call to the Escape. Within an hour all the guests except Sam and Derek had gone. The caterers cleared up and went soon after. Sam left at the same time, explaining that it was Nessie and Norton's bedtime. That left Galina and Derek alone in the front room.

'Derek, I am frightening,' she said.

'Why's that?' Derek was getting used to her distinctive use of English. He'd also worked out the way to calm her down: a jewellery demonstration proceeded silently on QVC.

'I am frightening of what he has been doing,' Galina explained.

'Doing?'

Galina put her sunburned head in her hands. 'The police, when they take me. They ask me all about these things, and this and that, and how Lorcan get his money. And all this Lady Thing-Boggin.'

'Thing-Boggin?' Derek cottoned on, but opted not to show it. 'Go on.'

'I say I don't knowing any Lady Thing-Boggin. They say Lorcan is getting money from her. I say I don't know this. All I know is Lorcan romance me in Sittingbourne and looking after his Aunt Mary. They ask me about her and I say I never meet her, then she die. Then we marry. Then we living here. Then . . .' She threw her hands up and made a parp of resignation. 'Everything go mad.'

Derek nursed a glass of Jamesons. He was still reeling from the afternoon's events. 'Who was that William chap?' he asked.

'Who is knowing? Not me.'

'He was good with the dogs.'

Galina groaned. 'These bloody animals, driving me mad! Grace back in season again soon and Lorcan want them shagging every day. Pah! Favour put it everywhere but in his wife!'

Derek flinched at the mental image. He changed the subject quickly back to crime. 'What happened to Lorcan after they took him from here? Was he charged with anything? I'm sorry, I know I shouldn't ask.'

'What happening to Lorcan? I don't know. He come, he go, he stay at the Escape . . .' Her shoulders slumped. 'Galina should be living back to Minsk, I believe.'

Derek's heart filled with pity. He hinted, 'You said before that it was all to do with Hooper.'

'Is nothing to do with Hooper.'

'Are you sure?'

'I am sure, I am not sure. I don't think I am knowing Lorcan any more.'

235

Derek ran out of questions; at least, he ran out of the strength needed to ask them. Galina's attention shifted to 'a captivating array of diamonique best sellers set in fine sterling silver or radiant yellow gold.' It was dark outside. Derek got wearily to his feet. 'Will you be all right, Galina? I'd better go and see how Charlotte is.'

At Hawker House Charlotte examined her tummy. Was that his head or his bottom she could feel? She examined her emotions too. How was she responding to the new shape she was taking? What difference was it making that her latest scan had transformed the 'it' into a 'he'?

*It's a boy!*

She tried the words out in her head.

*It's a girl!*

She tried that as well, to see if it made her sad. Then she tried: *Charlotte, the baby's dead.*

Or might it be '*Your* baby's dead'? They liked you to hold them, the ones that didn't live. She'd been reading about it. Apparently, it helped you cope. Charlotte imagined holding a dead baby: 'the' baby, *her* baby, 'him'. Funny, he was alive not long ago. Little devils, aren't they, kids?

She looked at the clock in her bedroom. It was nearly nine o'clock. Charlotte rose carefully from her book-cluttered bed and walked across the landing to the guest room. From there she spied through the blind at the O'Neills' – the tenth time she'd done so in the two hours since returning from next door. She'd been into town with Moz and the children: Nessie and Norton hadn't wanted to go to Lorcan's party for fear of those scary dogs and Moz hadn't fancied it either – that couple were too weird. For her part, Charlotte wanted to spend time with her older friend while she still could. The summer was nearly over and next week the kids would be back at school. Her final year at university would be starting soon – she was as bent on going through with it as ever – and she was at the frontier of her third trimester. December had appeared on her personal horizon. She'd begun imagining Christmas with two feuding parents and a stack of baby gifts all coloured blue. And a baby boy too.

There was no sign of life at the O'Neills' and the caterers' van had gone. Where had Dad got to? She had to have it out with him: until then she couldn't rest. Irritated now, she returned to her room and pored over the front page of the *Herts Gossiper* again. She'd picked it up secretly while out with Moz and the kids, purely for the purpose of sneering – desperate little free sheet full of tacky ads, she'd thought. Well, that much had proved right. But there'd been more.

The front door slammed. Taking the newspaper with her Charlotte hurried to the top of the stairs and looked down into the hall. Derek stood there, deep in thought.

'Hello,' she said loudly.

He looked up. 'Hello.'

'You all right?'

'Yes. And you?'

'Fine, thank you. You're late.'

'I helped with the clearing up.'

'That's nice.'

Derek felt the innuendo but ignored it. He wasn't in the mood for trading barbs. He waited for the next one as Charlotte came down the stairs. She wore a smock frock and her hair in pigtails. He thought she looked like a child again now that her waist had disappeared.

'What's the matter, Charlotte?'

'Nothing. Just that you seem to spend a lot of time round there. With her.'

'Charlotte, her husband is in some sort of very serious trouble and has just been carted off to his rest home again. She's all on her own. I feel a bit sorry for her.'

'A bit sexy for her, more like . . .'

'Don't be ridiculous.'

'. . . and why wouldn't you? She's always all over you.'

Derek looked at her squarely. 'Charlotte, you're being vile.'

'It's an ideal arrangement really: middle-aged man whose wife has run away; nice, handy doormat across the road . . .'

'Shut up, Charlotte!'

'. . . unlike Mum.'

'I said, SHUT UP!'

Charlotte did shut up but not through fear. He'd snapped and she had not which in her mind made her advantage still greater. Fuming, Derek went through to the lounge. Charlotte followed quietly. She said, 'And who is Elizabeth Ford?'

If they'd been in a movie the background music would have begun throbbing to show their hearts were beating faster.

'How do you know about her?'

'She rang while you were out.'

'She didn't.'

'Yes she did.'

'She didn't, Charlotte. She hasn't got the landline number.'

This was a lie. But Derek had asked Libby not to call him on it.

'Made sure of that, did you? Wouldn't want your daughter picking up when she called.'

This, on the other hand, was true. But Derek was making a comeback. He could see he'd called Charlotte's bluff.

'And,' he continued, 'if she'd needed me urgently, she'd have called on my mobile – which is here in my pocket.' He produced it, clinchingly. 'Have you been prying in my office, Charlotte?'

'Matthew's bedroom you mean? No.'

'You've been looking in my laptop, haven't you?'

'No.'

'OK, let's try 1471.' He started for the phone.

'It won't be on there now.'

'Oh?'

'Someone else called.'

'Who?'

'Lindy.'

'OK, I'll have a chat with her.' The phone was in his hand.

'All right, all right,' said Charlotte. She slumped on to the sofa, panting slightly. 'I peeked. Ages ago. Not much of a sneak, am I?' She laughed dizzily. All this was just too daft.

'It's a business relationship,' said Derek.

'If that's how you like to describe it.'

'She owns a shop.'

'Yeah. A knocking shop.'

'What?'

'Nice little place in Welwyn Garden City. What do the neighbours think?'

Derek paused. A few pieces of the puzzle began falling into place.

'It's a children's clothes shop, idiot. Called Kids Nite Out.' He added, rashly, 'I'll take you there if you want,' and immediately hoped she wouldn't hold him to it. At that point Charlotte hurled the rolled up free sheet. It hit Derek in the chest. 'Nice shot,' he said as it fell harmlessly to the floor. What a pathetic gesture. He'd won.

'Have a look at it,' said Charlotte.

'I don't think I could cope with the excitement,' Derek said but bent to pick it from the carpet anyway.

'Front page,' Charlotte said, eyes fixed on the wall.

Derek looked.

## STRIP–O–PLOD!

### LAP GIRL UNDRESSED COP BUT
### PUB LANDLORD GOES FREE

Derek read.

A secret raid on a local Irish pub went badly wrong when a plainclothes cop was dragged on stage during an illegal strip show. Constable Glenn Branch of Hertfordshire Police thought he was operating undercover. But he ended the night badly exposed – truncheon and all!

#### LOCK IN

The strip show took place on Good Friday after a 'lock-in' at Doonican's theme pub. Landlord Lorcan O'Neill was charged with licensing offences but acquitted after a Hertford magistrate heard he'd only allowed the lock-in because local thugs forced him to.

#### THUMPED

Inspector Colin Spackman who led the fateful raid claimed O'Neill had organised the whole event. But Doonican's punter Derek Hawker said different. He described being thumped by the thug leader as he tried to attack O'Neill because he thought he'd grassed him up.

#### POPE

O'Neill got off after a psychologist said he was a fantasist and easily taken in. His solicitor Aubrey Crisp refused to comment on why his client had taken the witness box dressed like the Pope.

As he had done in crisis situations before Derek sat down at the opposite end of the sofa from Charlotte. He looked at her and said, 'This paper will never catch on, you know. They just can't get their facts right.'

'Don't bullshit me, Dad,' Charlotte replied. A bitter tear ran down her face.

'I'm not bullshitting you, Charlotte.'

'That's all lies then, is it?'

Derek tossed the paper on the coffee table and sighed. 'It isn't all lies, no. It doesn't tell the whole story, though.' He felt ragged and furious. Who had leaked the story? Not Lorcan, surely. Maybe one of Glenn's mates? But there was something else as well: a faint trace of relief. 'Shall I tell you the whole story?'

'If you want to.'

He took her through it in detail: why he'd gone to Doonican's, how Lorcan had made him stay, the white lie he'd told Galina about what had gone on and how that lie had grown and grown. He told her, too, about Lorcan's hint at blackmail at Sam and Moz's Easter party and his encounter with Crisp at the Escape. 'I didn't want you to know what I'd got mixed up in that night. If I'd told you how it happened you'd have laughed in my face.'

'Probably,' Charlotte said.

'And I did feel for Galina. She still knows nothing about all this so far as I can tell.'

'Won't she see the paper?'

'She hasn't seen it yet and nor had anyone else who was over the road; or if they had they never said. Maybe she'll never see it. She might never find out. It's possible, you know. She is completely isolated over there. She just does what Lorcan asks her to and believes what Lorcan tells her. Although I think that raid on their house the other week has got her thinking.'

Charlotte asked, 'But was he really innocent, Dad?'

'The truth is, Charlotte, I don't know. I just told the court what I'd seen and what I thought. It is just possible. When you look closely at the evidence against him it didn't really amount to solid proof. That's what the magistrate thought too.'

'And what about this horrible story in the paper?' Charlotte asked. 'What will everybody think? What about people at work? What about your boss?'

'I haven't got a job, Charlotte.'

'What do you mean?'

'I resigned just before Easter. It was that day I came to Brixton to see you. Do you remember? Laurent was there and you gave me your keys so I could go round to your house.'

Charlotte looked puzzled. 'Oh. Why didn't you say?'

'I was going to. But you were so bloody unfriendly!'

'Was I?'

Derek could only raise his eyebrows. Did Grace and Favour bark? Did Scrag miaow? He asked her, 'Did you know then? About the baby?'

'Yes, I suppose I did.'

'How do you mean, "suppose"?'

'My period was late. I'd used a home testing kit. But I

hadn't seen a doctor to confirm it. And I couldn't believe it. Or didn't want to.'

'And Laurent?'

'He flew off the next day.'

'You know we have to tell him, Charlotte.'

'Yes, I know.'

'You know we have to tell Mum too.'

She pursed her lips and nodded. For the first time in many weeks, Derek did what he used to be so good at: he considered several options and reached a clear decision quickly.

'I'll start with my mum and dad,' he said. 'We'll take it together from there.'

# chapter 17

Derek set off for Folkestone early, leaving with the first light of dawn. Soon he was cruising through the eastern fringes of east London passing landmarks that delighted his father, whatever insults others hurled their way: Canary Wharf to the right; the Millennium Dome. Once through the Blackwall Tunnel familiar road signs showed ahead: Channel Tunnel; Dover. 'You idiot,' Derek said, and shook his head. The cause was a flashback to his first visit to the O'Neills' house and Lorcan's account of the wooing of Galina – 'Then I showed her the seaside: Dover.' She'd been outside with the shar-pei when he'd said it. Only now did Derek remember Dover doesn't have a beach.

He motored swiftly through sparse traffic and reached the elder community village before eight – much earlier than he'd predicted when he'd phoned the previous evening. He knew his parents would be up, though, Phyllis in the kitchen trying out some new concept in potato peelers, Les down the back garden polishing his mountain bike and releasing morning wind. Derek showed his visitor pass at the security gate. The guard was a regular and Derek rustled up the usual quips. Inside, though, he was pensive. Before creeping out to the Lexus he'd looked in on the sleeping Charlotte, curled up with her arms round Mr Heath. He didn't like leaving her. He was anxious, too, about how his mum and dad would respond to what he'd come to tell them. They were, of course, upbeat and broad-minded. But Charlotte meant the world to them and, for all their impressive vigour, fragility shadowed them more closely every day.

Observing the speed limit of 10 miles per hour Derek drove on until he reached his parents' bungalow. It stood well back off the road and was fronted by a neat lawn and weed-free flower beds which local gardeners were employed to help maintain. Derek parked in the drive, got out and saw Phyllis waving from the living-room window. A sticker on it read 'I Love The Chunnel'. Les appeared at the front door wearing a grey silk dressing gown. 'We were just starting our breakfast,' he said, and performed a rapid knees-bend exercise. '*Aimes tu croissants? Aimes tu pain au chocolat?*'

With a saddening soul, Derek walked in. From the hallway wall Matthew and Charlotte as children smiled at him from photographs. He and Denise hung there too, done up for their wedding day like some Power Pop band's video, then beaming, Next-attired, with one small infant and then with two. The weight of tarnished hopes and under-fulfilled promise began to press on Derek as he heard Phyllis plumping cushions and Lester made him listen to 'Don't Worry, Be Happy' as performed by Big Mouth Billy Bass.

He sniffed the air discreetly. There was still no lurking trace of that stagnant old-age smell. Entering the living room, though, confirmed his impression, growing for some while, that Lester and Phyllis no longer had quite their former will or perhaps the inclination to throw things out as they used to do. Although they were still thrilled by novelty their past, at last, was settling immovably on them. The TV was huge and wide screen but an old Sanyo music centre was now a fixture in the corner – unlike the Triumph Spitfire it wasn't a preserved treasure but a relic they hadn't got round to replacing. A few vinyl records were stacked beneath it. Derek couldn't see which they were but childhood memories stirred in him anyway: 'Downtown' with Petula Clark; the soundtrack from the hit musical *Hair!*; budget-priced non-stop bossa nova party albums with covers showing girls in hot pants chasing balloons.

'Hello, Derek,' said Phyllis. 'Let's sit down.'

Derek kissed his mother and sat in his usual place on the low-level leather sofa. Dressed in stretch leggings and a sweatshirt, she handed him a plate of pastries and a mug of tea then sat down in the armchair opposite. Les settled next to Derek. They knew something was coming. Just as he was subconsciously preparing for their deaths, they had been preparing for bad news.

'Mum and Dad, I've something to tell you. It's about Charlotte.'

'Charlotte?' Les was alarmed.

'Is she all right?' Phyllis asked.

'Yes, yes, she's fine.' Derek's hand shot to his father's arm. 'Except she's going to have a baby.'

He sketched the basics quickly: it was an accident, she's kept it secret from everyone, even the father, even Denise, and yes-I-know-it's-mad-but-you-know-Charlotte. They were shocked, obviously – so shocked at first that Phyllis's hand shook and Derek was concerned – yet they rationalised quickly. Many worse things happen – much worse. Yes, it was unfortunate but Charlotte had made her decision and all that mattered now was that she and her baby should be OK. Their main worries were for the future. Could Charlotte look after a baby and continue with her studies? Would she live in Brixton or Brayston or look for somewhere else? What about the father? What about Denise?

'I don't know what's going to happen with the father,' Derek said.

'He's French, isn't he?' said Lester, looking on the bright side.

'Half-French. He's not a bad chap, really, but he's only a kid – and a bit of a dopey one at that. I don't know how he's going to cope when he finds out. I can't see them making a go of it as a couple. The way Charlotte's been behaving I'd be surprised if she even wanted him around.' Derek shrugged. 'It's hard to know what's going to happen. It's even harder to know what's best. Still, I'm going to break the news to Denise later today. Maybe she'll have some brilliant idea.'

As soon as he'd finished the sentence Derek knew the

time for evasion was over. There could be no more white lies, no more presenting unpalatable truths in a favourable light. As when he'd been caught out in some deception as a child he sensed his mother looking at him, indulgent but insistent, waiting for him to own up. 'You've probably guessed, both of you, that Denise and I haven't been getting on so well lately . . .'

They had guessed, of course: her flying off like that, him left all alone, it hadn't sounded right. Derek asked for their forgiveness for not telling them previously. They gave it, readily. 'What will happen?' Phyllis asked softly.

'God knows, Mum,' said Derek. 'All I can say is it doesn't look too brilliant just now.'

It was after two o'clock when Derek kissed his parents goodbye and held them extra close – every time he had to part from them these days he knew it might be the last time he ever saw one of them, or maybe both. It couldn't go on for ever: the job lots of Viagra ordered from the net, the cruising with the roller-blading pack. 'You don't think badly of Charlotte, do you?' he asked as he got into the Lexus.

'Of *course* not,' replied Phyllis.

'Not for one minute,' echoed Les.

'And anyway,' said Phyllis, 'it means we'll be great-grandparents . . .'

'By Christmas!' finished Lester.

At first, his parents' optimism, so dauntless and touching, only deepened Derek's melancholy. Yet by the time he'd filtered back on to the M20 relief had done its work and his spirits were perking up. Dealing with Denise and Laurent would be more difficult, of course. But now he had momentum. Soon the job would be done.

He was past the Ashford exit when he thought to check his BlackBerry. He pulled over to consult it. Old age, he thought; makes you more scared of taking risks. To his shock there was a message from Sam Blake. It was tagged 're Charlotte' and it said: Charlotte gone to hospital – ring Moz now!

Her number followed. Derek called it with a pounding heart.

'Hello.'

'Moz? It's Derek.'

She was outdoors – he could tell that from the background noise. Her tone was urgent. 'Where are you, Derek?'

'Kent. Has something happened?'

'It certainly has . . .'

She gave him the vital details. He calculated he could make it in two hours.

'Moz,' he said.

'Yes?'

'Please take care of them for me.'

# part three: dragonfly

# chapter 18

'Take off my dress,' she said.

'Yes, mistress,' came the reply.

'Take off my bra.'

'Yes, mistress.'

'Take off my knickers.'

'Yes, mistress.'

'And don't let me catch you wearing them again.'

The two women laughed loudly. A waiter glanced over and several fellow diners looked up from their meals.

'That must be the silliest joke ever,' said Angela, the younger of the pair.

'I was told it by a boy called Kevin,' said Denise. 'I was only eight. We were alone in the PE cupboard, me in just my navy blues and vest. It was my first erotic experience. Those were the days.'

She sighed and looked out at the Tokyo traffic. Eight months into her adventure she'd become accustomed to a fairly frugal existence but it was nice to taste a bit of First World luxury for a weekend. And it was wonderful to see her old friend Angela again, especially looking so happy and so well. She was as warm and sane as ever and her children were so beautiful: little Estelle perched in the baby seat chatting to a felt rabbit called Ron; baby Lois snoozing milkily in the cotton sling lashed across her mother's chest.

'So what's the famous Joseph Stone doing at this moment?' Denise asked.

Angela laughed. 'I don't know about famous. He is making a bit more money these days, though. He's with this dealer who's sold a lot of his sports portraits and reckons he can sell more. Joe's hoping he'll be interested in his more serious stuff as well – you know, those intimate domestic scenes he loves to do – but he's not holding his breath.'

'Quite a catch, wasn't he?' Denise said.

'You didn't think so when I first told you about him: three kids, barely solvent, no proper job . . .'

'A cook in the kitchen, a nurse in the nursery and a whore in the bedroom, you said.'

'Did *I* say that?'

'Don't play the innocent with me, Angela Slade. It was on the evening after you first, ahem, made his acquaintance. You went into the experience in quite a lot of detail, I recall.'

'You'll make me blush.'

'I shouldn't think so. It's never happened before.'

Denise smiled at her unlikely friend. Motherhood and marriage obviously suited her. This had seemed

improbable ten years or so ago. They'd met at a con-
ference on homelessness and children in Camden. On
the face of it they had little in common yet, thrown
together in a workshop, they'd really hit it off. Denise
had been charmed by Angela, attractively androgynous
and very self-possessed for a young woman in her early
twenties who had come down from Derbyshire only a
year or so before. She was living on her own in a flat in
Croydon and – as Denise, being Denise, had quickly
learned – had already had a succession of interesting
boyfriends, all of them nice, none of them quite right.
But that was before Joseph.

Denise, by contrast, had been faithfully married for so
long that her two children were already half grown. By
then she and Derek had moved from Edmonton to a
desirable Victorian terrace in Barnet with lots of original
features but fashionably furnished, all mod cons. She was
still teaching back then: three days a week, which gave
her her own money and left time for motherhood and a
few good works. Her husband was gregarious and go-
ahead and although they often quarrelled the heart of
their marriage seemed sound. Oh, he could be deaf to
those around him, impatient and driven. But they loved
each other, Denise had been quite sure.

It was only recently that she'd been besieged by painful
questions. Had she fooled herself into thinking she'd been
content? Had she expended so much energy keeping
those around her happy that her life – her youthful life –
had ended up too tame and compromised? There was a

balance to be struck between doing what was needed to keep everyone else cheery and putting others first to the point where you felt bitter and left out. She'd long been aware of this conflict within her, yet never found a way to resolve it. Instead she had dismissed it, put it off. But now she couldn't hide from the troubling realities that Matthew had insisted on pointing out.

'Hi, Mum! How's Chongqing?' he'd asked when she'd called him.

'Well, it's not exactly Brayston. Not exactly Willow Close. But we've got a happy team here. I'm making sure everyone rubs along.'

'That's fantastic, Mum! But make sure you look after yourself too.'

'Oh, don't worry about me.'

'But I do worry, Mum. You know, at your time of life and the Dad thing and everything . . .'

'Oh, Matthew . . .'

'The thing is, Mum, your questionnaire responses indicate a classic ESFJ. You are friendly, warm and practical, you love harmony and your instinct is to put others first . . .'

'Thank you, my darling.'

'. . . but . . .'

'But? I don't like the sound of that.'

'But that often means you put your own needs last and, well, that isn't always good for you – because you like to get your own way too.'

'Oh, really, Matthew? Thanks.'

'This isn't personal, Mum. ESFJs often take things too personally. They feel rejected and lose energy and go around insisting that the future is all gloom.'

'Well now, let me think: I'm forty-eight years old, my children have left home, my career is non-existent, my marriage is on the rocks . . .'

'This is only feedback, Mum, not an attack. I can send you a full ESFJ type analysis if you want. It contains material on how to become more effective . . .'

'Well, Matthew, you're the expert. I'm only your mother. What do I know?'

Denise felt bad about that little exchange: she shouldn't have thrown a strop. She felt bad about Charlotte too. That telephone call she made on Charlotte's birthday. The bit about Laurent kept coming back.

*'You make it sound as if it's over. You never told me things weren't going well.'*

*'There wasn't much to tell.'*

*'Even so. Are you coping?'*

*'Oh, Mum. I'm a grown-up. I don't need rescuing.'*

*'Oh well, pardon me for sticking my nose in.'*

So that was how things stood with her children: her son thought she had a victim complex and her daughter didn't want her to be concerned about her. Wonderful. Great. Fine. As for Derek, she had no clear idea how things stood with him. How odd it was, Denise thought, that Angela was suddenly so hitched and so maternal – not only to her two daughters but to Gloria her adolescent stepdaughter and her two younger stepsons

Jed and Billy – while she, Denise, was suddenly so all alone.

Estelle read a cardboard book. Lois mewled mildly in the sling. In the twenty years since Charlotte was born Denise had ached physically for a third child only now and again. She felt that ache now, though, and as she did so saw herself back home in Brayston meandering plumply through the menopause in an anorak and unfashionable jeans. She said: 'You do realise, don't you, Angela, that I'll probably never have sex again?'

'Oh, rubbish,' Angela said.

'Angela, my love, I'm forty-eight years old with a saggy bosom and fat legs.'

'Oh, Denise . . .'

'Where's Kevin from the PE cupboard when I need him?'

'Oh, Denise, Denise, Denise . . .'

Angela touched Denise's hand. Denise used her napkin to mop a seeping tear. 'I wonder what Derek's doing,' she mused darkly. 'Probably bonking his boss's silly secretary.' Her mobile lay beside her plate. Lifting it to her ear she did a cutting impersonation of Amelia's PA: 'Good morning! Quintessential Futures! Sophie speaking! Guess what colour my thong is today!'

Angela said, 'Oh, stop it, or you'll have me crying too,' and as if to underline the point Denise's mobile promptly rang. Denise didn't answer straight away but checked who the call was from. Her eyes popped wide.

'My God,' she said, 'it's him!'

'Who, Derek?'

'Yes!' The ringing stopped. Denise said, 'What does he want?' The phone began to ring again.

'Answer it,' Angela said. 'It might be important.'

Denise took the call.

'Hello, Derek . . . Yes . . . What? . . . *What?*'

Derek switched off his mobile and went back through the sliding doors. He had no headspace for Denise and no time either; he'd deal with her later. He paused to get his bearings. In the haste of his arrival he hadn't memorised the route and the queue at the reception desk was long and unmoving. Damaged human traffic traversed the circular hall propped up or wheeled by auxiliaries with tired eyes. Friends and relatives of patients sat joylessly on plastic bucket chairs waiting for . . . whatever. What floor was the neonatal unit on? When Moz had met him here twenty minutes or so ago she'd rushed him into a lift. He'd try to retrace that journey. Better to get lost looking than to wait in line and rot.

He rode up to the first floor – so far so right. Follow the signs down a corridor, left, left . . . A nurse came round a corner. 'I'm looking for Dr Coulton. Is he through there?'

His hand was on the nurse's elbow. She took a half step back.

'He might well be. You can try.'

'Thank you.'

Beside the unit door, Derek pressed the intercom,

ignoring the security guard's non-committal stare. While waiting he steeled himself. Be calm, now. No more rows. The ward manager was expecting him. She half opened the door.

'I got through,' Derek said, a little sheepishly.

'OK. You can have a word with the consultant now.'

She let him in and Derek said, 'I'm sorry about that earlier. This is all a bit dramatic, obviously.'

'Never mind. I've seen worse.'

'I made an idiot of myself.'

'You're not the first.'

She led him into a side office. Dr Coulton sat behind his desk. He looked up over his glasses. 'Come in, Mr Hawker,' he said. 'Sit down.' Derek sat. 'Oh, by the way,' said Dr Coulton, 'your heroic neighbour – she's gone to the canteen. She says to meet her there in your own time.'

'Thank you.' Derek fidgeted and cleared his throat. 'Dr Coulton, I'd like to apologise for how I acted earlier...'

'That's all right, Mr Hawker.'

'I'm sure you're not a dimwit...'

'That's all right.'

'Or a gormless bureaucrat...'

'Mr Hawker, please...'

'Or a horse's arse.'

'Mr Hawker, *please*,' said Dr Coulton loudly. 'I accept your apology. You simply have to understand that we cannot be too careful about who we let in here, especially if they are in an emotional state.'

'I understand,' said Derek. 'I've calmed down now.' In fact his head was an inferno. A tinderbox of tension had been set ablaze by Denise's closing words.

*'You never told me about this! All this time and YOU NEVER TOLD ME ABOUT IT! What if he dies, Derek? What if I never see him and he dies?'*

'Now, about your daughter and her child – your grandson.'

It was still difficult for Derek to take in the details. But the general impression – one of sustained emergency – became still more starkly clear. Some things he knew from Moz already. Charlotte had felt pains when she woke up and she'd decided she would mention them to Moz. On her advice, as a precaution, Charlotte had called the hospital midwife, who'd suggested she go in. Her waters had broken all over Moz's Previa en route.

'The local hospital called us immediately,' Dr Coulton said. 'They can't cope with very premature births there. Luckily we had a space.'

Less luckily, Charlotte and Moz had been unable to call Derek: neither knew his number and though Charlotte had it stored in her mobile she'd left that somewhere at Hawker House. She remembered Derek's e-mail address and Sam was detailed to message him, hoping he'd taken the BlackBerry with him. He had – but didn't look at it until the epidural was already taking effect. Drugs had been administered to slow the labour down, but by the time the ambulance was nosing through London it was clear they hadn't worked. The contractions were coming quickly. Then the baby's heart began decreasing.

'Prolapsed umbilical cord,' said Dr Coulton, 'Very serious. Blocks the blood and oxygen supply. An emergency caesarian is the only option then.'

Charlotte had gone into theatre at about three-thirty. The baby had been born by four o'clock – just as the general anaesthetic took effect, and about the same time as Derek had been having kittens in a traffic jam. 'She's recovering at the moment,' Dr Coulton said, 'so you can't see her for a while, I'm afraid. But you can see the little boy.'

'How is he?' Derek asked. He almost prayed.

'He's in an incubator, which is absolutely standard for babies born as prematurely as this. Your daughter's notes say she was in her twenty-sixth week, but calculating dates isn't a precise science so it's possible she was nearer twenty-five – and that can make a big difference. He's been put on a ventilator. We're watching everything else carefully.'

Watchfulness. Care. Basic parent business. It was illogical, he knew, but Derek felt responsible for Charlotte's plight – and that he'd failed her.

'Now, I should warn you, Mr Hawker, that he's very, very tiny – one pound and ten ounces. And very pre-mature babies can have a rather shocking appearance. They don't look terribly cuddly. Indeed, they can look as if they'd break if they were even touched . . .'

'I understand,' Derek said.

Dr Coulton looked carefully at him: one final check, perhaps, before allowing the lunatic who'd called him a dimwit to gaze upon a fragile being whose own mother had yet to see him, except in an instant Polaroid. 'Very well, a nurse will take you through.'

'One last thing,' Derek asked.

'Uh hmm?'

'What are his chances, doctor?'

'I hope better than fifty-fifty,' Dr Coulton replied.

# chapter 19

The clatter of wheels on track shook up a thousand memories. Her body was on a train heading away from Heathrow airport but her memory was in the kitchen – *her* kitchen – in Brayston. There were many scenes to pick from but her subconscious selected the morning Matthew received his news from Oxford telling him he'd got his first in Economics and Management. The family had celebrated over breakfast, toasting the young conqueror with orange juice and tea. Already he was weighing the provisional job offers he'd received. Laying her head against her overnight bag Denise reviewed each family member's response to his triumph: Derek putting a range of clever counter-arguments to each one Matthew advanced for accepting a position overseas – this was how he'd shown that he was pleased; Charlotte listening closely yet remaining detached; Denise herself seized by a sudden fright that almost overpowered her impulse to keep things jolly and light.

The outskirts of west London hurtled by. Denise tried

to block out the chatter of three young women across the aisle. Each had her hair done in exactly the same way – blonde highlights with deliberate stray wisps – each displayed an inch of midriff, each had made an effort to Kylie-up her lips. In other circumstances Denise would have enjoyed listening in on their conversation and perhaps found a way of joining it. On this occasion, though, she almost resented them with their mouths full of giggles and heads buzzing with banalities. Charlotte, with her shabby clothes and absence of make-up, had become the mother of a boy who didn't yet have a name and might not even last the day. Why couldn't those silly girls keep quiet?

At least the train was fast. In another ten minutes it pulled into Paddington station and Denise hit the platform running. Where was he, the moron? She hadn't wanted to be met. But there he was, craning his neck to see her. As she approached him he went to take her bag but she hung on to it. She snapped, 'Where are the taxis?' and ducked his attempt to kiss her cheek.

'Just over there,' he said and she walked on. 'Denise,' he said, 'I know all this . . .'

'I don't want to talk about it, Derek.'

'Denise, I just think . . .'

'Don't talk to me, Derek.'

'But . . .'

'Don't talk to me at all.'

When they reached the hospital Denise left Derek standing and set off to see Charlotte on her own. She'd noticed that he'd not reacted to her seething fury, but she vowed not to be fooled. He'd soon get down to insisting he'd been right. Well, she wouldn't be submitting or strategically retreating as was so often her way. First, though, she had to wear a mask of calm. She worked on it as she hurried to the neonatal unit, not caring if she looked dreadful or smelled.

Her first sight of the intensive care ward shook her. The walls were a summer yellow and there were lots of teddy bears, but the technology was ominous. Alarms buzzed everywhere. She saw the clear box of the incubator, then the face of Charlotte who looked up from her pillow glassily and smiled.

'Hello, darling.'

'Hello, Mum.'

Denise faltered. She wanted to touch Charlotte but didn't know quite how. On the long road from Tokyo she'd foreseen hugs, loving and forgiving, but Charlotte looked too beaten up. A series of clear tubes converged at a needle junction protruding from the back of her left hand. Sensing her mother's need Charlotte raised her right one. Denise clasped it. She said, 'How is he?' She didn't have the nerve to look.

'He's tiny. And hairy,' Charlotte said.

'Yes, but . . .'

'They're hopeful he'll be all right. But it's always touch and go.'

Touch and go. Denise took courage from her daughter and peered at the boy through the plastic. Tubes protruded cruelly from him too, from his throat and mouth. Wires ran to a monitor from tiny pads placed on his chest.

'I was only twenty-six weeks,' Charlotte said. 'If that.'

'I know. Poor thing, I know.'

Derek had told her that when he'd at last answered her frantic calls from Japan. She'd been halfway to the airport by then after a mad dash from her hotel. 'It's a lot better than twenty-four,' he'd said, 'and at twenty-three, most don't survive.'

'I know all that,' she'd snapped, thinking hark at the world expert, although, in truth, she'd only known it because Angela had told her as she'd bolted from the restaurant. Lois had arrived ten days early, which was nothing these days. It would have been in Denise's. And *three months* early was best not thought about back then. One pound, ten ounces; a scrap, a shrimp. Desperate.

'Have you held him yet?' whispered Denise.

'No. Touching only, through those holes in the side. And I have to use a breast pump. Stupid thing.'

This was all new to Denise. She felt out of her depth. 'What are you going call him?' she asked nervously. Amid all the uncertainty the question seemed trite.

'I still don't know.'

'He's got to have a name.'

'I can't think of one. Not for a boy.'

'We could have thought of one together, if I'd known.'

'Yes, Mum, I know.'

'Sorry. I didn't mean . . .' A wave of disappointment

broke over Denise. 'This is all so difficult to take in. If I'd been here we could have . . . I don't know, we could have talked about these things.'

'That's true.'

'I should never have gone away.'

'Mum, that's daft. You had to do it – you know you did.'

Denise blew her nose. 'Oh, now I'm being pathetic. I should be asking about you.'

'Well, I'm a bit of a mess.'

Denise wanted to say, 'This whole thing is a mess, every-thing's a mess, we've all made this bloody mess.' Instead, she said, 'That'll teach you to sleep with a Frenchman.'

'They're the worst, are they?'

'I wouldn't know,' Denise replied, truthfully. She'd slept with four men in her life, all of them English. She'd half wondered if she might meet somebody while in China but it turned out to have been wise to have wondered rather than hoped. Derek was still her most recent conquest. 'You're not a mess,' she said to Charlotte. 'You might feel like one, but you're not.'

'It's all my fault,' Charlotte said.

'It's not.'

'Whose fault is it, then?'

'It's no one's fault,' Denise said, knowing she didn't sound convincing; knowing, too, that she didn't want to.

'Where is Dad, anyway?' said Charlotte.

'Somewhere else.' Denise was pleased – message received.

'You're cross with him, aren't you?'

'I could murder him. I shouldn't say that, but I can't help it.'

'He wanted me to tell you, but I wouldn't.'

'He should have told me anyway.'

'I made him promise not to. I knew you'd come straight back. I didn't want to spoil your fun.'

'Oh, Charlotte.'

'Oh, come on, Mum. I was going to tell you soon.'

'When?'

'Probably today.' Even in her anxious, stitched and shattered state, Charlotte tittered at the irony.

'And what about Laurent?' asked Denise.

'Yes, well, that's a bit more tricky.'

'Doesn't he know anything about all this?'

'Nothing.'

'Where is he?'

'In Kenya, taking pictures.'

'Still?'

'He's enjoying himself.'

'What are you going to do?'

'Well, I told him I was going on a long holiday with Dad. Which was true, in a way.'

'Where does he think you are?'

'In Sydney, with Matthew. That's the bit that isn't true.'

'*Charlotte* . . .'

'I know, but . . . well I thought that if he thought I was in Australia he probably wouldn't suggest, you know . . . popping by when he gets home . . .'

Denise absorbed the import of this. 'But darling, you'll

have to tell him eventually,' she said. 'It isn't fair on him, and in the end he'll find out anyway. You can't hide from him for ever.'

'I know, I know. It's just that . . . I don't think I can cope with him at the moment. I don't know what to do with him. I don't know how he's going to feel or what he's going to want or whether I want him around at all. I just want to get through this; and get through it with my baby. Right now, he's all I can think about. Mum, do you understand?'

Denise nodded. 'Oh, yes. Yes, I do.'

'Are you cross with me too?'

'No.'

'Not even a bit?'

'Not even a bit.'

Charlotte said, 'Are you and Dad speaking?'

'Not really. But we'll get round to it. What's he been up to all this time?'

'Oh, this and that.'

'Such as?'

'I think he'd better tell you that himself.'

'Are you *ever* going to speak to me, Denise?'

'I shouldn't think so, no.'

Derek's question came from over his shoulder as he waited at a red light. Denise had gone for the back seat. She added sharply, 'What would you like me to say?'

'Oh, I don't know – wonderful to see you, darling, can't wait for a nice cuppa . . .'

'You're not very funny, are you, Derek?'

'Uh-oh,' Derek said as the Lexus pulled away. 'I'm not very funny. Silly me.'

Denise thumped the upholstery. Derek felt its pain. Both of them resumed their former silence – best wait to scream and yell in the privacy of home. Derek, though, mused that Denise looked rather well despite the imprints of worry and fatigue. Her face was a bit leaner and her legs, emerging from a pair of baggy orange shorts, were tanned and toned. All that hill climbing, he supposed; all that spying on pandas from the bamboo. He, on the other hand, had put on weight and was generally all over the place. Their time apart had been intended for mature reflection on what had gone wrong in the empty nest. Further giant changes had not been anticipated. Now, everything had changed.

Dusk had gathered as they entered Willow Close. Derek led the way from the garage to the house and as Denise let her bag fall to the kitchen floor she wondered for the first time which bed she would sleep in; which room. Derek began filling the kettle, which made her feel like a guest. She noticed the fridge magnets. *ChaRloTte is A geNiuS. NeSsiE Is a niT. 3(2x + 4y) = woRms, WalrUs aND ChiPs.*

'It's the neighbours' kids,' Derek explained. 'She's been looking after them.' He placed two mugs beside the teapot with enormous care as if any sound they made on contact with the work surface would shatter the veneer of civility.

'She told me,' Denise said.

'What else did she tell you?' He tried to sound casual, but the question was too direct.

'Why, have you got something to hide?'

'Well, what do you think?' The kettle noise grew louder as the water reached boiling point.

'I'm going upstairs,' Denise said.

She shouldered her bag again and left Derek to the PG Tips. Her legs ached as she reached the landing. Which way to turn next? She checked the guest room first. It was just as she'd left it. For that reason as much as any she put her things down there. For a similar one she chose the family bathroom rather than go through her bedroom – was it still hers? – to the en suite. She peeped into Charlotte's room on the way. Books, papers, goldfish, clothes and clutter everywhere – the old bedlam had resumed. And what was that in the corner? Not a tray of cat litter! She tried to imagine Charlotte waking alone amid all this, feeling the gripe of her contractions and with no one for company but Mr Heath. Thank goodness for Moz.

In the bathroom she turned the taps on and stripped off, liking the coolness of the tiles beneath her feet. Standing before the full-length mirror she lifted her chin and squared her shoulders, which made some of creases at her neck disappear. They were spreading, though, like cracks in a cartoon dam, and would one day form a torrent between her breasts. Way back, she'd liked to let her nipples graze the palms of Derek's hands. Such harlotry seemed foolish now, the idea of it absurd.

'I've got your tea here, Denise.'

He was outside the bathroom door. She reached her old dressing gown quickly from the peg. The detritus in the pockets confirmed Charlotte had been using it: tissues, hair bands, a pencil sharpener. Denise opened the door just enough to take the mug.

'Thank you.'

'That's all right.'

She closed the door again, quickly switched off the taps then went back to the door to listen. The bath was hot and full and bubbling and she was longing to get in, but felt unable to relax until he'd gone – she didn't want him knocking to ask her some question or, worse, to come in. What was he doing, anyway? She heard him plodding to his office, open and close the door. Then he was in Matthew's room – what did he want in there? Finally, she heard him go into the bedroom – his bedroom, her bedroom, their bedroom, who could tell? – before, at last, he made his way downstairs.

Denise pondered. The bath was so inviting, but she was curious too. Quickly, and on tiptoe, she hurried to Derek's old office, looked in and saw the glory that was Derek World. She skittered back along the landing and stole a glance into the bedroom. She was pleased to see her mother's dressing table. It reminded her she must visit her father – she had a lot of explaining to do. Finally, she approached the metal nameplate announcing *Matthew's Room*. She pushed open the door. She said 'Bloody hell', forgot about her bath and went back downstairs.

Derek was reclining on the lounge sofa. He seemed to be expecting her.

'What have you done to Matthew's room?' she asked quietly.

'Denise,' Derek said. 'You'd better sit down. I've got a few things to explain.'

'More than a few things, Derek. More than a few.' She wasn't talking quietly now.

'Just get off your high horse, will you?'

'I'm *not* on my high horse. I've rushed halfway across the world, I'm sick with worry, and now I find half my house has been rearranged.'

'It isn't only your house, darling. And it wasn't even your room.'

'Have I got a bloody room at all?'

The doorbell rang.

'I'll get it,' Derek said. 'It's probably Moz.'

Denise kicked the sofa. She heard Derek open the front door and say, 'What the . . .' Two more voices reached her. One of them she recognised. Tightening the dressing gown cord she dashed in delight and disbelief out to the hall. The young woman she saw there was tall and fair and swinging a huge rucksack down from her back. Derek was saying, 'Here, Hayley, let me give you a hand.'

Matthew was lugging in a suitcase when he saw her. 'Mum!' he said, astounded. 'What are you doing here?'

# chapter 20

Matthew lay in bed beset by all kinds of confusion. God knows, he'd factored Encountering Emotional Turmoil into his Surprise Visit Project but only his father's, not his mother's too – and definitely not his own. And now here he was hiding under the guest room duvet at 6.14 a.m. with no idea at all what he should do. His one consolation was diagnosing his dilemma as typically ESTJ: his impulse was to take control but his respect for seniority – that of his parents in this case – prevented him from telling them what to do. The fallout from this was typical too: acute mental anguish and a retreat into silence and despair.

'Good morning, Big Bunny,' said Hayley sleepily.

'Good morning, Bunny Love.'

Hayley felt for Matthew's penis, which was limp. 'Where's Big Bunny's carrot?' she enquired.

'Hiding in its veggie patch.'

'Would it like to hide in Bunny Love's?'

Still beneath the duvet, Matthew sighed. Normally, the

answer would have been a hearty yes but after two long, jet-lagged days, with his parents barely speaking and everyone wretched with worry about Charlotte and the baby, he was too depressed for sex. This was tough on Hayley who had worked hard to lift the gloom. The Erogenous Tableware catalogue had helped. Denise at any rate had been engaged.

'It's so ingenious, Hayley! That cruet, for example. The testicles are for ketchup, I presume?' she had exclaimed.

'Ketchup, mustard, relish, whatever. That's the beauty of having four – two with the pepper grinder, two with the salt.'

'And very artistic. Quite abstract, some of it. The avocado dishes. You don't see it at first. Then you look a little longer...'

'Forbidden fruit, eh?'

'Hmm. And those dinner plates ... well!'

'Handmade and dishwasher friendly, too.'

This houseparty mood hadn't won Derek over, though. He'd slipped away with a packet of biscuits and a beer. Matthew had tracked him to his ex-bedroom and found his father staring blankly at his Vision Thing file. They'd had a rather forced debate about pitching globally in cyber terrain then Matthew had forced the pace, as was his way.

'Dad, are you feeling unappreciated?' he'd asked.

'Matthew, I have no job and no income. I've brought my marriage to the brink of ruin. My daughter can't stand me. And I've stolen my son's bedroom. How much appreciation have I earned, do you think?'

'Being too self-critical is a strong ENTJ trait when under stress.'

'Yeah, yeah. Here, have a Hobnob. And Matthew, be a pal – fetch me another Grolsch.'

'So is too much eating and drinking. And, if you don't mind me saying, you seem prone to emotional outbursts.'

'MATTHEW, WILL YOU STOP ANALYSING ME?'

Matthew was still coming to terms with this explosion; with the entire Hawker family chemistry. Even Charlotte wasn't being her usual icy logical self though he forgave her, obviously (he'd been to see her; he'd seen the baby). Who, though, was hiding what from whom? Who was cross with whom and why? The subtleties were too complex. Hayley snuggled up against his bony flank and he was glad. 'Bunny Love,' he said. 'Remind me what I say about myself.'

'OK. You must improve your listening skills. You mustn't interrupt or . . .'

'Talk other people down. I know.'

'But you just did it!'

'You're right. Oh, no. Oh, no!'

'And Big Bunny must be more gentle and own up to his tender side.'

'Right again.'

'I know I'm being a bit fluffy.'

'Not fluffy. Just ESFP.'

Matthew held Hayley close. He listened to Denise's footsteps heading to the family bathroom. He knew they were Denise's not only by their lightness compared with

Derek's but also because she was borrowing Charlotte's bedroom and not making use of the en suite. In fact, she *could* have used the en suite because Derek had already left for London – Matthew had heard that too. But maybe she didn't want to. Maybe Mum was so fed up with Dad she couldn't even stand to wash in the same sink.

Such thoughts upset Matthew greatly – more, much more, he sensed, than either of his parents knew. Still, he had to fight off his depression for the sake of Hayley. He must look beyond the short term. He must try to relax, go more with the flow. He knew his type functioned better if they could accept that sometimes pleasant surprises came out of disorder – maybe he'd get one this afternoon. He reached his phone from the bedside table and sent Derek a text.

Hi Dad. C U @ golf @ 3. Matthew.

Derek read Matthew's message at 8.23 according to his mobile, at 8.24 according to his Omega Constellation and at 8.25 according to his BlackBerry. To avoid thinking about the message and, therefore, about Matthew, he phoned the Speaking Clock and spent several futile minutes trying to synchronise the three timepieces. He knew Matthew would say that getting too caught up in detail was a sign of an ENTJ under stress. So he stopped. But he still couldn't stop thinking about Matthew. He replied to the text.

Looking forward to it.

This was untrue, but at least it mended a fence. A four-ball was planned with Geoff and Moz – should be an experience.

Derek finished his tea. He was in a café near the hospital. Charlotte was allowed visitors from nine o'clock and he intended being there bang on time – hence his early start and time to kill. The previous day Charlotte had been told she and the baby might soon move from intensive care to the high dependency ward, which would indicate that the child had survived the most immediate dangers. Derek's fingers were crossed. Surely something had to go right soon. And that reminded him. He wanted to bring Libby up to speed. He paid his bill and went outside, preferring to speak to her from the more anonymous setting of the street. She answered straight away.

'Libby? It's Derek here. I expect you're rushing out.'

'I am, but that's all right.' It was a Thursday, one of her above board days, as she put it.

'I'm sorry to call like this. It's not about business.'

'Oh?'

'I thought you ought to know that Charlotte's baby's been born.'

'Yes. I had a feeling you were going to say that.'

'You would. It's very, very early.'

'How are they both?'

'Getting better, I hope. Anyway, I'm near the hospital and I'm about to go and see her so I'll tell you more about it when I see you next. The other thing is Denise has come home.'

'How nice. I'd love to meet her.'

'That isn't very funny.'

'She's broad-minded, isn't she?'

'Not where you're concerned she wouldn't be. She'd slaughter me.'

'Oh, that's a shame. Why don't you bring her with you next time? Make it a threesome. I do discounts for groups, you know.'

'Don't even think about it. The point is, remember not to use my landline number.'

'OK. Goodbye.'

'Goodbye.'

Derek headed for the hospital.

At Hawker House Moz joined Denise for morning coffee. She wanted to have a catch-up conversation before the afternoon of golf. It was a change to spend a day off in this way. Normally she passed them having a filthy time with Sam. But though the ice was melting, as yet there'd been no return to hours on end of pleasuring as usual. Moz had thought she had the measure of Sam's past – the excesses, the breakdown, the gradual recovery – but now felt haunted by a piece of it she'd known nothing about. Benign being though she was, Bou had come into her life like a spectre. Moz was adjusting, but remained unsure of her bearings. In this she had something in common with Denise.

They sat sipping caffè lattes in the conservatory. Scrag lay in his basket, sound asleep. Matthew and Hayley had gone out for a walk.

'I feel terrible,' Moz said.

'What about?' asked Denise.

'Knowing about Charlotte when you didn't.'

'That's not your fault, darling, is it?'

'I know, but . . . I still feel bad about it. I would have told you if I could have. But she was adamant you weren't to know. Derek isn't making that up.'

'I know he isn't.' Denise touched Moz's arm. 'But he should have told me anyway, the big sap. And then you end up having to cope with the emergency as well . . . I'll always be grateful to you for that.'

'Oh, listen. Charlotte has been a godsend this holiday – if "holiday" is the right word. Nessie and Norton love her. She'll make a fantastic mum.'

'Let's hope so,' said Denise. She did not elaborate. Charlotte was hoping to be able to hold and feed the baby today but he was still so fragile and there was too much that could go wrong: eye problems, breathing problems, cerebral palsy . . . She sipped her coffee, then said: 'So, Moz, how are you and your new addition getting along?'

'The all-conquering Boudica? My stepdaughter from nowhere?' Moz shook her head. 'What can I say? She's so sweet-natured and so . . . so *pleased* with Sam. That's the only way I can put it. All she thinks about is families. She was talking the other day about this lad she works with – Jamie, I think he's called – whose elder brother died in a motorbike accident and how difficult it is for everyone who's left. I should be grateful, I suppose. Nothing like that has happened to me yet. And Sam is a good father. He's an all-round good man. It's just that I can't help feeling . . .'

'Jealous?'

Moz nodded and looked shamefaced. 'Pitiful, isn't it? Still, I suppose we're all spooked by our partners' exes, aren't we?'

'Oh yes,' said Denise sounding more certain than she felt. Did she feel haunted by Derek's old flames? She did not. There'd only been a couple and he'd never talked about them much. 'Not serious,' he'd said, 'not like my punky little minx.' And had *he* been jealous of *her* exes? No, dammit.

Looking Moz in the eye Denise said, 'How has he been – just generally – while I've been away?'

'He's seemed OK. Of course, at first I didn't know him very well. I think he was a bit edgy round me at first – probably thought we'd been gossiping about him. We hadn't, though, had we? Not *really*. I mean, I knew you wanted a break, a change of scene. But you never mentioned things were difficult.'

'You guessed, though.'

'I had an inkling.'

'Did you have an inkling he'd left his job?'

'No!'

'Yes. He left it before Easter.'

'Hah!' Moz was wide-eyed. 'He's been telling us he's been working from home!'

'Well he has, but not for Quintessential Futures. He

says he's set himself up as a freelance consultant, though he doesn't seem to be getting much work.' Denise rolled her eyes. 'I asked him why he did it and he said he didn't know! He said he just woke up one morning and needed a new challenge! He wanted to build something with his own hands!'

'What a guy,' said Moz.

'It's a good thing we haven't got a big mortgage,' said Denise. 'You know how hard it can be financially when people divorce.'

'Divorce?'

'We've talked about it, but I'm not sure we can afford it. Neither of us has got a job. I'd have to go back to teaching. And then there's Charlotte to think of.'

'Of course, of course . . .'

'Perhaps you and he could have a chat about all that when you're at golf.'

'That *would* be relaxing.'

'And Matthew always has lots of opinions.'

'Fine, fine . . .'

'And watch out for Geoff. He thinks he's a ladies' man.'

'Thanks, Denise. I can hardly wait.'

They both uttered hollow laughs. Then, from the house, came the call of the phone. Denise jumped up. 'It might be Derek,' she explained. 'He's at the hospital.'

She walked back along the patio and into the kitchen. Each footstep increased her dread. It might be Derek. It might be Charlotte. In her head it was Charlotte every time.

*'Oh, Mum. Oh, Mum.'*

*'Oh, darling, I'm so sorry.'*

*'He was so little.'*

*'I know, I know.'*

*'I can't bear it, Mum. I want him back so much.'*

Denise lifted the receiver. 'Hello.'

It wasn't Charlotte. It wasn't Derek. It was a woman whose voice she'd never heard before. 'Is Derek there?' the woman asked.

'Not at the moment,' Denise said. 'Who's calling?'

'Oh, just a friend – a business friend. Elizabeth Ford. Perhaps I'll try his mobile.'

'You've got that number then, have you?'

'Oh *yes*,' the woman said. 'Sorry to disturb you.'

She hung up before Denise could speak again. Just a friend – a business friend . . . Denise tapped out 1471 and listened. She wrote the number on her hand.


Derek only noticed he was still wearing his slippers as he waited for a nurse to let him in. Such a sartorial blooper would have been unimaginable even a month earlier and its significance hit Derek like a wrecking ball. 'I'm in a desperate state,' he said.

'Pardon?' said the nurse. Transfixed by the slapstick condition of his feet, Derek hadn't noticed her open the door.

'It's nothing, really,' he said. 'I'm only going off my head.'

The nurse let him in, cautiously. He headed straight for Charlotte.

'Hello, Dad.'

'Hello, Charlotte.' Derek forgot about his slippers. He looked in the incubator. Something wasn't right.

'He's had a bad night,' Charlotte said.

'What's the problem?'

'He's picked up an infection.' Charlotte said it listlessly. Her face was very pale.

'What does that mean?'

'Drugs. Changing his tubes. He's been crying and hot . . . It means I still can't hold him. It means I have to stay in here with all these bloody machines.'

Derek knew she'd hoped for better after a week: a move down the scale of fear where she could at last make proper contact with her son. That, though, was on hold. The whole world seemed on hold. Derek pulled his chair closer to Charlotte. 'It's going to be all right, you know. He's already through the hardest part.'

'I just feel so useless.'

'You're not useless, Charlotte.'

'Yes I am.'

Me too, thought Derek. Me too.

Never before had Derek been so conscious of the lunacy of golf. As he and his three playing partners headed down each fairway he could almost hear Charlotte's voice on the early autumn breeze.

*'Perfectly good countryside carved up in the name of hitting a little ball into a hole.'*

At least, that was how she felt before discovering that

Moz played. The quartet were driving at the par four eighth, scene of Derek's chip-in against Geoff on that joyful day in spring, the one after his first encounter with Libby. The self-confidence, the single Pringle, the gung ho gimme on the eighteenth – where had that New Life promise gone? Derek was trying to keep the faith but Fate seemed to be against him. And Matthew was on his case again.

'All I'm saying to you, Dad, is life is precious.'

'Yes, Matthew, yes.'

'It is, isn't it, Geoff?'

'I should say so, yes. I say live it while you can.' Geoff wasn't really concentrating. He was too busy admiring Moz's behind as she bent to tee up her ball. He asked her, 'Does your husband play?'

'No. He does yoga.'

'Yoga?'

'He finds it more relaxing.'

'I say good luck to him.'

'Also it's given him exceptional suppleness and stamina.'

'He needs it, probably.'

Moz seemed not to spot the innuendo. Or, if she did, she chose to respond to it by lashing her drive far down the centre of the fairway. Her prowess once again brought murmurs of admiration from the men.

'Excellent shot,' said Matthew.

'Good hit, Moz,' said Derek.

'Not bad for a girl,' said Geoff.

It was Geoff's turn next. He swaggered to the tee, all saloon bar swank. He's put on weight, thought Derek. Like me. What had always seemed like big, bluff bonhomie suddenly looked more like plain, old-fashioned fat. The easy style was still there though: the hitch of the wrists, the waggle of the hips . . . but then came something more than the usual smooth swish. Rather, it was a full-blooded, lacerating hit and Geoff grunted at the moment of contact. He held his follow-through in that way of his as his ball hurtled into space and out-flew Moz's by some distance.

'Fine strike,' said Matthew.

'Terrific, Tiger,' said Derek.

'Mustn't be out-driven by a lady, eh?' said Moz.

'Uuuuuuh,' said Geoff. 'Uuuuuh. Ug.'

His hands still held the driver, but the remainder of him sagged. In slow motion he collapsed. Derek and Matthew ran to him, flustered and concerned. It was Moz who showed the most presence of mind. 'Ambulance, please,' she snapped into her mobile. 'I've just witnessed a heart attack, I think.'

# chapter 21

Denise's father Ronald wore a traditional striped apron, plaid carpet slippers of a type now rarely seen and a jumper he had owned for a dozen years; or, in Denise's mental calendar, since a good five years A.M. – After Mum. Even in its shapeless state this made the sweater still new in Denise's eyes, as was anything and everything Ronald had accumulated since that shocking day when the tumours finished their work and her mother passed away in the bedroom where Ronald still slept today. Denise had been thirty, her brother Richard thirty-two. Matthew and Charlotte had been too young to understand. Derek had been very good about it, she had to admit.

'What's for dinner tonight, then, Dad?'

'Lamb hotpot.'

'Do you need any help?'

'Nooo!'

He was reaching the heavy casserole dish down from a high shelf. The casserole dish was B.M. Denise even remembered being in the shop when it was bought, she sitting holding her Tressy doll – 'Her! Hair! Grows!' went the jingle on the TV ad – and Richard saying Tressy had funny eyes. The casserole came in a choice of brown or blue, which was quite daring at the time, especially for Worcester. Richard had said 'blue' and Denise had said 'brown' and Ronald had laughed and said, 'Carole, looks like we'll have to toss a coin.' Brown had won, which was good even though, secretly, Denise had preferred blue too.

'Heard from Richard lately, Dad?' He was down from the chair now. Denise breathed more easily.

'He visited the other week. Have you called him yet?'

'Yes. I told him about Charlotte. He didn't know what to say.'

Ronald set the casserole dish down on the table and scraped in chopped onions and mushrooms. Then he went to the fridge to fetch the meat. Before opening the door he said, 'You don't see each other much, do you?'

'I know, Dad, I know . . .'

Denise got on with Richard well enough, but they weren't close. He was a senior manager with an insurance company and lived with his wife and three children in a suburb of Leeds. The geographical distance had increased their lack of contact over the years, leaving little more than an annual Christmas visit. This bothered Ronald, and now and then he let his daughter know it. She caught herself hoping he let Richard know it too, then felt ashamed at being so competitive. Her mother too would have wanted her and Richard to stay in closer touch.

All this went through Denise's head as the kitchen clock chimed half past two (that was B.M. too). Tormenting herself about her late mother was only a respite, though. Soon Denise's mind was once again spinning with Charlotte and the poorly child. She'd been to see them the previous afternoon, after Derek's morning visit. Nothing had changed: baby still hot; Charlotte still blue. Denise felt better in her conscience for being with her father, yet worse for not being with Charlotte. She also felt bad not seeing Matthew and Hayley off at the airport. But Matthew was quite right. 'You can't be everywhere, Mum,' he'd said, 'and Charlotte will have the rest of us to put up with anyway.' He, Derek and Hayley were going to drop in on her en route to Heathrow. Before that they were going to drop in on Geoff. A heart attack! On the golf course! 'Collapsed like a sack of onions,' Moz had said. Death's shadow was everywhere.

'How do Phyl and Lester feel about Charlotte's situation?' Ronald asked.

'They've been very good, apparently. I haven't spoken to them yet.'

'Well, they are very good, aren't they, to be fair,' Ronald said. He found Lester and Phyllis entertaining. He was very different from them, with his retired head teacher manner and his fondness for solid objects from the past: furniture, books, pots and pans. Yet despite being so different he and Carole had always got on well with Derek's parents, each recognising and admiring the others' distinctiveness.

'And how is Derek?' Ronald asked. He was checking through the lamb pieces, which Denise was pleased to see he'd got the butcher to chop up. Ronald had the beginnings of arthritis in his fingers. Denise wondered again how many years of self-sufficiency he had left. She'd discussed it with him bluntly when making her decision about going to China. 'Better go now than later, I expect,' he'd said with enough impishness to reassure her. Even so, a new part of her future had presented itself. Decisions she made about her own life would be influenced more and more by her father's increasing dependence.

'Answer my question,' Ronald said.

'Oh, Derek's all right.'

'Hmmmph,' said Ronald, shooting her a look.

Denise did not resent this. In fact, she appreciated his waiting an hour before bringing it up. Her father was considerate, as her mother had always said. 'Oh, Dad . . . I suppose the truth is I haven't got room in my head for him as well as Charlotte.'

'Are you fed up with him?'

'Yes.' With elbows on the table, Denise let her jaw rest on the heels of her hands. 'I shouldn't be really. I know he kept me in the dark because Charlotte insisted and I believe him when he said he would have told me by now if the pregnancy had gone on normally. But I'm fed up with him anyway.'

'I see,' Ronald said.

'Sorry, Dad. I know you like him.'

'It isn't that, love.' Ronald got up from the table and

went over to the dusty corner where he kept his wine. Picking a bottle of red he pulled the cork with a low pop and brought the bottle and two glasses to the table. Denise watched in quiet rapture as the wine babbled into the glasses, a sound and sight she'd first loved as a child.

'It's so hard to know what's best,' she said.

'Are you thinking of splitting up?'

'Yes. Though nothing's decided yet.'

Ronald pushed a glass her way. 'Has he got somebody else?'

'I don't know.'

'Do you suspect him?'

'To be honest, Dad, I don't know that either.'

'What about you? Have you got someone else?'

'Don't be daft!'

Ronald looked surprised. He stopped his own glass halfway to his lips. 'What's daft about that? You're still young . . . and as lively as ever.'

Denise smiled at him. 'You're biased.'

'Going to China was pretty lively,' he said.

'That's not the same as chasing boys,' said Denise. But Ronald's mind had already moved ahead.

'Denise?'

'Yes?'

'Have you heard of empty nest syndrome?'

Oh no, thought Denise. He's been surfing the net again. 'Yes, Dad, I have. Sounds like I've had a case of it.'

'Your mother and I went through it too.'

'You never told me that.' Denise's shock was genuine.

'We didn't know that's what it was. They hadn't come up with a name for it back then!'

Denise looked at him in wonder. She felt a little foolish. Shouldn't she have noticed at the time? 'Are you saying you and Mum might have split up?'

'No. We never got to that point. It was a simple thing, really. Richard had gone, of course. Then you went off to college. Took your Buzzcocks records with you, thank God – it was the Buzzcocks, wasn't it?'

'And the Rezillos, yes.'

'Well, you left a gap. Your mother and I weren't ready for it. It was tricky for a while.'

'How did you work it out?'

'We had to find a new way of being together. New interests, new things to think about and say.' Ronald leaned forward. 'And I'm glad we did. As I found out when she died, it's difficult being alone.'

But I wouldn't be alone, thought Denise. I'd have Charlotte with me. And the baby, too. Wouldn't I? Her father spoke again. 'All I'm saying to you, love, is don't throw something good away until you're sure it can't be fixed.'

'Well, well,' said Derek. 'Everything you ever wanted to know about Geoffrey Lunt and never got a sniff of, even though you'd asked.' He was in a stunned state again, yet this time the effect on him was different: brightly enlightening; almost pleasant – in a competitive sort of way.

'So that was all news to you, Dad, was it?' Matthew asked.

'Totally,' said Derek.

'It was amazing,' enthused Hayley from the Lexus's back seat. 'I thought I was going to cry!'

They were heading away from Letchworth having been to visit Geoff who was convalescing at his parents' home. The first shock had been discovering that it was Geoff's home too. The second had been learning that this had been the case for most of the previous twenty years. It was not, however, Geoff who had revealed these details. He'd received his trio of visitors quite boisterously and with an implied insistence that he'd be hang-gliding for England any time soon. 'I say these things happen,' he'd insisted. 'I say, "Geoffrey, it's a setback, but don't let it grind you down."'

Yet after they'd left him to sleep, his mother and father had detained them and, in low, worried voices, spilled the fascinating beans about their son. It seemed the younger Geoff had been a formidable cricketer, an aggressive seam bowler and hitter of huge sixes in the Andrew Flintoff mould. 'Could have been county standard,' said Mr Lunt senior, 'if he'd taken it more seriously. But that's Geoffrey for you, I'm afraid.'

The Lunts had lived in Surrey then, and Geoff – lo and behold – had married a local girl called Tina. 'For a few years, they seemed happy enough,' said Mrs Lunt, a plain-spoken woman who gave the impression of having waited years to get this stuff off her chest. 'Then, one day, out of nowhere, Tina did a midnight flit.'

Her seducer had been a stringy wicket keeper called Pete Coombe. Together, they'd disappeared without a trace. It was months before Tina got in touch. In an emotional letter forwarded by her solicitor she'd explained to Geoff that she'd seen no future with him – no life for herself or with him as company and, worst of all, no commitment to children. Mrs Lunt related this sad tale with deep dismay. Mr Lunt shook his head. 'We'd moved up here by then. Geoff was broken-hearted. He couldn't stand to be alone, so he sold his house in Guildford and moved in with us. It was meant to be temporary, but that's the way it's carried on. He's got his flat in the Barbican where he stays some of the time but it's hardly a home, is it?'

Mrs Lunt concurred. 'He has his job, of course, but otherwise he's drifting. I knew something like this was going to happen. Geoffrey overdoes it, and he's lonely. It's time he found another girl and settled down.'

Derek turned this story over and over in his head as he continued the drive into London. One part of it in particular resonated. It seemed that after Tina disappeared some of Geoff's cricket team-mates had vowed to track Coombe down and extract retribution. This didn't surprise Derek, and nor did it surprise him that the threat was never carried out. It was not, though, the reason the story struck a chord with him. He wondered whether those would-be avenging team-mates had given a second's thought to *why* Tina would want to leave Geoff; *why* she would abandon a comfortable life as a housewife in a decrepit Vauxhall Viva with a man who didn't even own a proper set of whites. Derek, though, reckoned he understood. He felt strangely vindicated, even in the midst of his own marital crisis. By the time he'd found a parking space and he, Matthew and Hayley were making their way to the neonatal unit he felt in better spirits than he had for weeks.

'Hello, Charlotte,' he said, leading the way.

'Hello, Dad.'

'How's the little lad?'

'A bit better today.'

'I knew it,' Derek said.

'How did you know?'

'Don't ask me. I just did.'

Matthew introduced Hayley whom the ward manager had 'just this once' allowed in. She might have made the exception more readily had she known the therapeutic impact Matthew's girlfriend would make.

'Oh my, he's so *gorgeous*! He's so *adorable*! He's so *sweet*!'

The effect of Hayley's enthusiasm, so unbuttoned and genuine, was to lift the pessimism of all the Hawker family members. Soon, Matthew too was oochie-cooing like a veteran through the holes in his tiny nephew's incubator. For the first time in a week Derek saw Charlotte smile and as he took in the scene he felt refreshment reach a parched part of his heart. As Matthew and Hayley doted, he perched next to his daughter, looked at her straight and said, 'We still have to tell Laurent.'

'*We* do?'

'I do. One of us.'

Charlotte did not agree or disagree. But there was acceptance in her tone. 'I expect he's back in Paris. He was due to arrive this week. He'll be wondering where I am soon in any case. But Dad . . .'

'What?'

'I have something else to tell you.'

'Oh my God . . .'

Her voice fell to a whisper and she kept one eye on Hayley and Matthew. 'Dad. It's Boudica. She might not be Sam's daughter.'

'Charlotte. She is.'

'I did a DNA test. Well, I got one done.'

'Charlotte. Tell me I'm dreaming.'

'Dad, I used the lock of hair. Remember, the golden tresses?'

'Charlotte. You are mad.'

'And, er, a tissue full of Sam's snot.'

Derek let his head fall into his hands.

'You see, I just couldn't believe it,' Charlotte said. 'Not without scientific proof. And, well, I couldn't resist finding out. But then again . . .'

'Then again what?'

'The way they are together. So what if they aren't related by blood? They are so happy with each other. And Moz is getting used to it. And anyway, the mother is convinced and the test might not be right. The thing is, Dad, I don't know what to do.'

Derek raised his head again. 'Guess what, Charlotte?'

he said. 'I don't either. And I don't know what I'm going to do with you. But in the meantime, please, please tell me where I can find the father of your child.'

'Assuming he *is* the father.'

'Don't start!'

'I'm not starting! But you must promise to tell him face to face.'

'I promise, you monster. How do I find him?'

'I wrote down the phone number of his flat in Paris. And the address.'

'Where did you write them, Charlotte?'

'On a bit of paper.'

'And where's the bit of paper?'

'Somewhere you wouldn't have found it.'

'So where?'

Charlotte bit her lip. 'You'll think I'm silly.'

'I already think you're silly.'

'It's on a bit of paper in the back of Mr Heath.'

Derek had no need to stand listening in the kitchen. Charlotte was in hospital, Matthew and Hayley were on an Oz-bound aeroplane and Denise was staying with her father in Worcester. Once again, he had Hawker House to himself. But he listened anyway, almost out of nostalgia for the days before Charlotte's shattering appearance at the top of the stairs.

*'I'm pregnant, Dad.'*

Derek had travelled a very long way since then, and his journey was far from over. He checked his Omega Constellation – it was nearly 9.20 p.m. Too late to do much except extract Mr Heath's secret and eat something before bed. He'd start the search for Laurent the next day. 'Cannelloni, I think,' he informed the microwave and got some from the freezer.

The greeting 'Good evening, Derek' interrupted his removal of the cardboard packaging. 'Sorry to drop in on you in this unorthodox manner – force of habit, I'm afraid.'

Derek stepped back and said, '*Whaaaa-ut?*' He dropped the cannelloni on his foot.

'Don't worry,' said William coolly. 'I'm not going to hurt you. My police officer friend wouldn't allow it anyway.'

Derek spun round and was met by an outstretched hand. At the arm's opposite end was the rest of the Scottish detective: the senior partner of the pair who'd dropped in on him in July, the one who'd watched the lunacy of the Doonican's trial.

'Good to see you again, Derek,' he said.

'Is it?' Derek said. He hoped it was, he really did.

'You do remember me, don't you? Duncan McBride?' Derek was mute, terrified.

'I should say straight away,' Duncan continued, 'that this is an unofficial visit. However, William and I hope you will conclude that the ends will more than justify the means.' He bent and picked up the cannelloni. Handing it to Derek, he said, 'Shall we continue our conversation in the lounge?'

'After you've prepared your meal, obviously,' put in William soothingly. 'Shall I assist you?'

Derek offered no resistance as William took the cannelloni, tore off the plastic film and placed it in the microwave.

'Now,' he said, 'where do you keep your cutlery?'

It took the pair nearly an hour to state their business. For most of it Derek sat open-mouthed. At the end William set out his proposition.

'So, Derek,' he said. 'What do you say? Are you out or are you in?'

'I'm in,' Derek replied. 'But could you hold on for five minutes? I've got an ageing panda to unstitch.'

# chapter 22

Galina looked down from the window. Derek held the ladder tightly and mouthed a tense 'OK?' Galina gave a short nod and eased the sash window up. Derek reached for her hand. Her resolute expression made him ashamed he was so fearful to be a whole flight above the ground. It was 9.20 a.m. – a bit early to dice with death.

'Where is he?' Derek hissed.

'Is in the bath.'

'Good.'

Derek climbed two more rungs and half climbed, half tumbled over the sill. He landed in a heap on thickly carpeted floor. Hauling himself to his haunches he looked round to see a small but elegant lounge distinguished by a chaise longue and a polished walnut table of classical design. Galina peered down at him and whispered, 'I go back. You hold.' She disappeared through the room's only door. It opened on to another room, one Derek had seen before.

Still gasping from his exertions Derek returned to the

window. With cat-like confidence another, more athletic figure was on the way up. It reached Derek's side with a soundless vault and with finger pressed to lips tugged him by the arm to the crack of the slightly open door. They both listened, furtively. No noise came directly from within but from somewhere adjacent to it they made out an echoing refrain. Derek recalled the ditty from his childhood – Delaney's Donkey.

The rendition provoked a mild wince in Derek. It brought a painful grimace, though, to the other listener's face; the face of William, who softly urged Derek to 'Go!' then swung the door smartly open and advanced. Derek stole behind him, entering once again the luxurious bedroom where he'd had his first encounter with Aubrey Crisp. He was back at the Escape. This time, though, his arrival was unscheduled and his host was about to be caught rudely unawares.

The crooning came from the bathroom, where the crooner was relating his dear mother's injunction to Walk Tall. At its doorway Galina waited in tense attendance with a pink towel. Beyond her stood a bulky wardrobe and William was behind it in a single black-clad bound leaving Derek in the centre of the room. William then nodded to Derek. Derek nodded to Galina. Galina called, 'I have it ready for you, darling, all fluffy and warm.'

'Remarkably like you, my fine young filly!' came Lorcan's reply.

In other circumstances there might have been the hearty thwack of riding crop on thigh. Instead came the slap of soapy water on enamel and the squeak of bare feet on tiles.

Galina held the towel open. She clucked. 'Will you coming to me, Val Doonican?'

'Like a buck to his doe, my dearest; like a buck to his doe!'

He emerged from the bathroom nude but for his suds.

'Hello, Lorcan,' said Derek, grimly.

'What the . . . !' The buck grabbed at the pink towel. His antlers drooped. Derek wondered if any man had ever been caught quite so bare.

'Galina? Help!'

With the towel pressed against his privates Lorcan, irrationally, made as if to run away. William's large frame blocked his way.

'Agh!' Lorcan cried but only for half a second before William clamped his mouth with his left hand. His other hand snapped Lorcan into an arm-lock Superman might have struggled to break. The towel fell to the ground. Derek shut his eyes. As if being exposed to Grace and Favour's particulars wasn't enough.

'Bathrobe,' barked William, softly.

Galina reached one from a peg and tossed it on to the bed. William barked again – 'documents' – and Galina moved again, her movement followed by Lorcan's popping eyes. She reached behind a chair and pulled out a slim leather briefcase. From inside it she tugged a stack of cardboard files.

'Thank you,' said William, then spoke to Lorcan's right

ear. 'Are you going to keep quiet?' Lorcan nodded, convincingly. The foolish little pig had built his house of twigs and now the big, bad wolf had come to call. 'Then put the robe on and sit down.' Lorcan did as he was told. Derek could look again. William took the files from Galina and waved them under Lorcan's nose. 'You have read these, haven't you?'

Lorcan nodded. He perched meekly on the bed, swinging his legs.

William went on: 'And you do know what they mean, don't you?'

Lorcan nodded again.

'They contain the evidence against you; the evidence that has been gathered by the police and considered by the Crown Prosecution Service.'

Lorcan looked hopefully at Galina. She looked back at him, distressed. But she did not come to his aid. She turned to William instead, who took his cue.

'Yes, Galina knows all about it now. She and I spent several hours last night looking at another set of these documents, which I have managed to obtain; she and I and Derek, who may well qualify, albeit reluctantly, as the one friend you have in all the world. And yes, before you ask. They both know everything – *everything*.'

Lorcan stopped swinging his legs. It made it easier for him to stare at his feet.

'So let me spell it out for you ... *Lorcan*.' William uttered the name with sledgehammer irony. 'You. Are. Going. To. Jail.' Lorcan flinched. William went on: 'The best you can do now is try to go to jail for the shortest possible time. That means dispensing with your present fantasies of innocence and pleading guilty – doing the *honourable* thing. And if you do *that*, Derek here is once again prepared to help you in your dealings with the Law; though not, this time, by helping to get you off . . .'

William paused for breath. Derek recognised the same turmoil inside him he had seen when they'd met in Lorcan and Galina's garden. The voice stayed low, but the sheer weight of emotion made it break.

'All that money, tricked out of your so-called Aunt Mary as you claimed she was to your wife but who was, in fact, your own mother! Your *own mother* . . . !'

William closed his eyes. Lorcan found a whimper from somewhere. 'But it was my money, really, William. I was going to get it one day anyway.'

The reply came as from a wounded lion. 'Keep hiding from the truth if you have to. But please, from now on . . . please stop hiding from your own son.'


'Dad asked me to tell you he's not coming in today,' said Denise. 'He's gone to see Grandad Les and Granny Phyl.'

'OK,' said Charlotte.

'So I'll come in this evening too. I might bring Moz with me. Would that be nice?'

'Very nice.'

She looks better, thought Denise. 'How's the new breast pump?'

'Embarrassing and stupid. It's noisy and vibrates.'

'Is it working for you, though? Better than the other one?'

'I suppose so, yes.'

'And how's baby?'

'Better.'

'Weight?'

'Going up.'

'Did they say anything about feeding him yourself?'

'Maybe in a day or two. They're still worried about him coming out of the box.'

Denise had at least another dozen questions but fought the urge to ask them. Dr Coulton often came round about this time and she could pester him instead. Charlotte shifted and closed her eyes and Denise quietly checked that her grapes weren't decomposing, she wasn't out of sanitary pads and that the water in her plastic flask was fresh. It was a robotic process – she'd already done these things once – because her head was busy with quite different things. She'd driven down from Worcester that morning and come straight to the hospital without going home first. She didn't want to see Derek – it made it more difficult to think sensibly about him. Being with her father had been calming. She saw her situation more clearly. She knew what she had to do.

Charlotte was looking at her. Denise felt caught unawares.

'Mum, how is Scrag?'

'He's fat and lazy, darling. Are you pleased?'

'Oh yes.'

That's more like it, Denise thought. 'Charlotte?' she said with careful lightness. 'Dad had a call the other day from a woman called Elizabeth Ford. Do you know anything about her?'

'Hmmm . . .' Charlotte wrinkled her brow. 'No. Never heard of her.'

'OK. Just wondering.'

'She's probably his girlfriend.'

'I expect so, darling, yes.'

The Spitfire gained speed steadily and Derek was pleased after all that they'd left the roof down. Lester, typically, had checked the weather on Ceefax but when they'd left the bungalow the sky on the English side had been cloudy. Not so in Normandy. They'd rolled out of the tunnel into a late summer haze that seemed set to last throughout the afternoon.

Derek, cramped but uncomplaining in the tiny back seat where he'd insisted he should sit, looked fondly at his windblown parents in the front: Lester wearing his Graham Hill old smoothie cap, his right elbow resting casually on the door; Phyllis in her ear warmers, the long end of her flapper scarf fluttering at her throat. She looked over her shoulder at Derek and pointed at a sculpture on one of the bluffs supporting a traversing bridge. It was a footballer fashioned from metal scrolls. There was another sculpture on the other side, but the Spitfire was past it too quickly for Derek to see. Soon there were other bridges and other works of art on sporting themes: a rifle-shooter, a yachtsman, an athlete. He was a little boy again, going continental. This time, though, there would be no holiday.

At the outskirts of Paris they checked in to a small hotel where the reception staff greeted the older Hawkers like dear friends. From there the trio took a taxi to the nearest Métro station. It was seven in the evening when they came up from under ground into Pigalle.

'Well, son, here we are,' said Lester.

Derek felt humble. 'This is so good of you both.'

'Think nothing of it, Derek,' Phyllis said. She was rooting in her handbag. Out came a pocket street map. 'Here, you take it. We'll tag along. It's nostalgic for us, Lester, isn't it?'

Lester was grinning, hands on belted waist. 'They've cleaned it up a bit. Probably just as well.'

Derek took the street map and opened it at the page he'd marked. He checked his bearings and the three of them set off. Derek squinted at street signs. Lester provided a commentary. 'The aristocrats used to have their courtesans round here – so to speak. That's before they all had their heads chopped off, of course.' He chuckled gaily at the thought: one minute you're un-threading some mademoiselle's straining bodice, the next your head's over a basket. 'Then it was the cancan girls, of course. We saw them back in the Fifties, didn't we, Phyl?'

'We certainly did,' said Phyllis. 'Those were innocent days.'

'Before you had me,' said Derek, unable to shake free of childbirth thoughts. Doubt stalked him as they drew close to the right street. He'd let emotion get the better of judgement. He'd been mad to undertake this mission with his parents, sweetly supportive though they were. He'd been mad to undertake it at all. And how was he to put the last part of his plan into effect? Laurent might refuse to see him. He might not even be in.

At last the Hawkers came to the street where Laurent lived. It was narrow but lively with many shops and cafés along with a few remnants of the now besieged sex industry. Derek studied the bell panel by the ground level entrance door. At least this confirmed the identity of the resident of flat 4: *L. Fearnley*. Laurent had taken his English father's surname. Would he wish his own son to take it too? Would he wish to know that son at all?

'OK,' said Derek to a suddenly pensive Lester and Phyllis. 'Here goes.' He pressed button 4. He pressed again then a third time and waited fruitlessly. Shit: Laurent had definitely been in at lunchtime. Derek had rung him from a call box – the first time he'd used one of those in twenty years – after he and William had completed their exit from the Escape. Hearing the one word 'Allo' had been enough: the unmistakable vagueness, the distracted tone of voice. He'd hung up immediately, shaken William's hand through the window of the van they'd brought the ladder in, jumped into the Lexus and headed for the south coast. Of course, he'd recognised the risk that Laurent might have gone out by the time he arrived but in his adrenalised state he'd decided to take it. Well, it had seemed a good idea at the time.

Derek grinned at his mum and dad, embarrassed. 'Come on, let's have some coffee. How about that place over there?'

The café in question radiated orange light making it all the more inviting as darkness fell. Conscious that these days it was he who led the way – in this case disastrously – Derek pushed through the door then held it for his parents to follow. Lester and Phyllis picked a corner table and soon they were ordering sandwiches and cappuccinos. The setting was comforting. But the departure of the waiter left an impasse.

'I'm so sorry about this,' Derek said.

'It's all right, son,' said Lester. 'You're doing the right thing and we're happy to help you if we can.'

Phyllis nodded her agreement. 'He's bound to turn up sometime.'

'I know,' said Derek ruefully. 'But when?'

He needed a drink: a strong one. Excusing himself, he went up to the bar and was grateful the word 'whisky' was all he needed to say. He lacked the confidence to make use of his primitive French. He lacked confidence, full stop. Oh, and he'd need the *toilette* in a minute. He spotted it behind a solitary corner table at the back. And he spotted something else: a straw mop of hair; an unbuttoned trench coat; a shapeless canvas bag.

Derek forgot about the whisky. He advanced on the

corner table and when Laurent looked up and saw him his teeth stuck fast in the Brie baguette he was devouring as if it contained glue. His eyes stared out between the ridge of the crust and the flop of his fringe.

'Please, Laurent,' Derek said, 'don't look so scared. Just look surprised instead. Because, boy, do I have a surprise for you.'

# chapter 23

The following morning William and Galina sat together in the public gallery. Derek sat in the row behind them with a stray euro in his pocket, nerves fizzing, feeling tired. Next to Derek sat Duncan McBride while in the body of the court a twitchy-looking Crisp whispered with a barrister who fiddled with his wig. The jury took their seats. There was a sharp rap of knuckle on wood. An usher said, 'Court rise!' and everyone stood up. Behind the raised bench at one end of the room – Crown Court No. 2 – a door opened and the judge appeared. After tugging his robe around him he sat down rather wearily, and everyone else did the same. The judge then arranged his notes and located his spectacles. At last he cleared his throat.

'Well, I'm pleased to say we can continue, having digested this rather strange turn of events.' He opened his codfish mouth to take in air. 'Defendant stand please.'

Lorcan got to his feet. He wore a sober dark grey suit, a white shirt and what may or may not have been his old school tie. His hair was stiffly brushed and he stood erect in the dock with his hands clasped behind his back and his head held high.

'Now, to be quite clear . . .' the judge consulted a piece of paper and said, 'can you confirm your full and *true* name as Norris Norman Posselwit Flange-Boggin?'

'I can, your honour, yes.'

'Though also known as Sergio Xavier delMonte?'

'Yes.'

'Also known as Keplar Wim DeKlerk?'

'Yes.'

'Also known as Ronnie Grout?'

'Yes.'

'Also known as Dickie Lizzard?'

'Yes.'

'And also known – during the course of these proceedings, that is until now – as Lorcan St Patrick O'Neill.'

'Yes, your honour, that's correct.'

'Good,' said the judge with huge relief. 'You will now be read the charges. After each count you will be asked how you now plead: guilty or not guilty. Lord Flange-Boggin, are you quite sure you understand?'

'Yes, your honour, yes.'

To be sure, thought Derek sadly, to be sure.

The clerk got to his feet.

'Count One: Norris Norman Posselwit Flange-Boggin, you are charged with theft in that on the third of May 2002 you did dishonestly use the Coutts bank debit card of Baroness Eugenie Flange-Boggin to withdraw from her account by way of a cash dispenser the sum of three thousand pounds. Do you plead guilty or not guilty?'

'Guilty.'

He said it clearly and proudly. His voice was steady, his body still. The clerk continued.

'Count Two: You are charged with theft in that on eight occasions between the dates of 29 January 2001 and 14 June 2003 you did dishonestly use the National Westminster bank debit card of Baroness Eugenie Flange-Boggin to withdraw from her account by way of a cash dispenser sums amounting to £17,256. Do you plead guilty or not guilty?'

'Guilty.'

Derek passed Galina a hankie. Galina passed one to William. The clerk continued reading from the charge sheet until he had completed Count Twenty-nine and the court had heard the word 'guilty' twenty-nine times.

'Very well,' said the judge, 'very well. Now, Mr Davies, before we proceed to sentencing I believe you have some words to say in mitigation. And a character witness to call to that end. Am I correct?'

The wig-fiddling barrister who had been talking to Crisp jumped up. 'Yes, m'lud. I'll be brief.'

Davies's case for mercy hinged on the culprit's relationship with his victim. He acknowledged that it was unforgivable to trick an elderly widow with failing mental powers out of even one pound, let alone more than four hundred thousand. 'Moreover,' he elaborated, 'the fact that Lord Flange-Boggin did this to his own mother will make the crime appear still more heinous in some eyes.' But having conceded these points Davies went on to ask the judge to take into account the 'significant fact, accepted by both sides' that the stolen money was due to become his client's in any case upon Lady Flange-Boggin's death. And he remarked in passing that it was the solicitor who dealt with her estate who had noticed the abnormally high number of cash withdrawals from her numerous accounts and called in the police.

'I would therefore suggest to m'lud,' said Davies, 'that the character weakness that resulted in Lord Flange-Boggin's committing these offences was not so much heartless greed as uncontrollable impatience – that and a sadly ruinous capacity for self-delusion. His admission this morning on changing his plea to guilty that he has used an eclectic range of aliases in the past tends to confirm this unfortunate, ah, quirk, whose implications have become immensely damaging to him as well as to others around him. The psychiatric reports rather support this view. I submit, then, that no useful service to society will be served by giving Lord Flange-Boggin a lengthy custodial term.'

That ended Davies's remarks. Now it was Derek's turn. Called forward by the judge he stepped up to the witness stand plucking a stray hair from the lapel of his Paul Smith. It had stood the overnight Eurostar sprint back from Paris pretty well, but the crotch area was creased and the trousers were a bit tight round the waist. Derek took courage, though. He'd done the right thing by Laurent and hoped Laurent was now taking good care of his parents whom he had offered to reacquaint with Pigalle while trying to recover from his surprise. Now he had to do the right thing by Lorcan – as he would always think of him – and by Galina and William too.

'Your honour,' Derek began. 'I have known Lorcan O'Neill – Lord Flange-Boggin, that is – for only six months or so. During that time, however, I have discovered a great deal about him – and, as a result, about myself. I cannot pretend that the experience has all been beneficial. It has mostly been anything but. That said, I hope what I'm going to say will strengthen the case for his being treated as leniently as the Law allows.'

Derek drew breath: pitch your vision, Derek, he urged himself; make it live. 'My argument is very simple,' he said. 'Almost from the day I met him I've been trying to work out if Lorcan – if you'll allow me to call him that . . .'

The judge assented with a flap of one hand. Why not, he seemed to suggest. Call him Benny Hill if you prefer.

'I have been trying to work out,' resumed Derek, 'if Lorcan is an out and out villain or just a complete fool. I've now come to the conclusion he is neither. The truth is he is a mixture of Walter Mitty and Billy Liar. He is quite incapable of separating fantasy from fact. With your honour's leave I'd like to give an example of this.'

The judge perked up a bit. 'By all means, Mr Hawker,' he said.

'Earlier this year I was called as a defence witness on

Lorcan's behalf at another trial, one relating to a less serious matter. My evidence helped him to be acquitted. Yet even now I can't decide whether or not justice was done. It is possible that Lorcan was indeed a wholly innocent party to the rather torrid events from which the charges arose. It is possible that he was not. My main point, though, your honour, is that I honestly don't think Lorcan knows either. This is a man who can convince himself that day is night, night is day, and – as your honour may have gleaned – that he is not, in fact, a very, very eccentric English aristocrat but an expatriot Irish publican and loveable rogue.

'As with each of the personalities he has assumed over the years, he lives the part totally. The transformation may not be perfect but it is always wholehearted. My experience of Lorcan suggests strongly to me that the same character foible enabled him to fool himself into thinking it was probably all right to steal his mother's money. What is more, I truly believe that until yesterday, when his estranged son William and his long-suffering wife Galina forced him to look reality in the face, he thought a jury would find him innocent. I cannot imagine what his defence would have been. All I can be sure of is that Lorcan would have believed it. He is, in every way, an incredible man.'

Nice touch, that use of 'incredible', Derek thought; now to clinch the sale. 'There is one more point I'd like to make. It concerns Lorcan's – that is, Lord Flange-Boggin's – family life. I've learned recently that the previous Lord Flange-Boggin – Lorcan's father, as it were – died in a hunting accident when his son was a small boy. This trauma has, I suspect, had a profound effect. Lorcan has been married twice, the first time nearly thirty years ago when he was in his early twenties. The marriage was not a success. It produced one child – his son William – whom Lorcan lost all contact with soon after his divorce.

'His submersion in a string of alternative identities seems to have begun not long after and I've learned that each of these is inspired by his study of his genealogy. His Sergio delMonte phase, for example, seems to have been triggered by a distant ancestor on his father's side whose estate was famous for its vineyards. And so, for a while, Lorcan passed himself off as a Spanish wine importer. Similarly, the Flange line of the family can be traced back to the owner of a Transvaal diamond mine. So as Keplar DeKlerk, Lorcan ran a jewellery shop in Hassocks, but seems not to have made a convincing Boer. And Lorcan O'Neill too has an historic antecedent. The Flange-Boggin family became landowners in Ireland in the late seventeenth century in Kilkenny.'

The judge then intervened. 'If I could interrupt just for a moment . . .'

'I'm sorry, your honour,' said Derek, assuming he was going on too long. Maybe William had briefed him a bit too thoroughly.

'What about Ronnie Grout, then?' asked the judge. 'He sounds jolly interesting.'

'Oh, well . . . um . . . well, Grout is the exception. The

link there seems to have been with his grandmother's handyman, who was a bit of a local character, I hear.'

'Don't tell me,' said the judge. 'Let me guess. As Ronnie Grout he did bathroom tiling. Am I right?'

'I'm sorry to disappoint your honour,' Derek said. 'As Ronnie Grout, Lord Flange-Boggin was unemployed. He just lived with his mother and pretended he knew how to do odd jobs.'

'How sad,' said the judge.

'But not the saddest,' Derek said. 'That honour goes to the so-called Dickie Lizzard. This was a pen-name Lord Flange-Boggin assumed when he convinced himself he was a man of letters, as his great-uncle on his mother's side had been in a small way. As Lizzard he wrote – or attempted to write – a book about his failings as a father. In fact, I have read a few chapters from the manuscript. They were shown to me by its inspiration, his son William. Sadly, the material is mannered and self-serving with a rather snobbish tone. No publisher was interested, of course.'

'I can imagine,' said the judge. 'It doesn't sound much fun.'

'Anyway,' said Derek, 'the point of all this background information is to persuade your honour that Lorcan – Lord Flange-Boggin – is not an evil man, just a troubled, deluded one – as so many of us are from time to time. He has lost a great deal. His son William, who has only just reappeared in his life, has long used his mother's surname to avoid being associated with him. His second wife

Galina, who in his peculiar way he certainly adores, feels she has no choice but to divorce him. The part of his inheritance he stole from his ailing mother – she was either unwilling or too ill to give it to him – was used to finance his theme pub Doonican's, and then to impress Galina. After his mother died he was able to buy them the house opposite mine. He called it their dream home. Well, whatever dream he had is over now.'

With that, Derek stepped down. The judge thanked him, blew his nose, and before passing sentence made a few remarks. The gist of them was that Lorcan's crimes were very serious and yet he was persuaded that he hadn't meant any harm. Lorcan could have gone to jail for years. Instead, he was sentenced to just twelve months.

At roughly the same time as Derek was speaking, Denise was crawling along a kerb in her blue Impreza, reconnoitring uncertainly. She'd tracked the address through an online directory and driven over in a state of high anticipation – but anticipation of what? Could she really confront this woman on her own doorstep? What exactly was she planning to accuse her of? And what difference would it make anyway?

Denise had no ready answers to those questions. Yet some strange momentum seemed to propel her. More than any conscious, deliberate act of will it was this curious force that caused her to first park the Impreza in Kidley Road, Welwyn Garden City, then walk up to the door of number 7 and knock. It was opened by a woman whom Denise formed a first impression of quickly: petite, not bad-looking, pretty good body, brunette; early forties, maybe; red nail paint and lipstick; beguiling, certainly, but nothing Denise couldn't deal with.

'Are you Elizabeth Ford?' she said.

'Hello, Denise,' replied Libby. 'I've been expecting you.'

'I'm sorry. How . . .'

'And this is my partner, Jim.'

Jim had short brown hair and wore a Tottenham Hotspur shirt. He held out his hand and smiled. 'Nice meeting you, Denise.' Unlike Derek he looked as fit as a butcher's dog and can't have been much over thirty. Denise was reeling. Partner? What sort of partner?

Libby said to him, 'Jim, love, pop the kettle on, would you?' Jim said 'Sure' and went off down the hall. Then Libby said to Denise, 'If you'd like to come in . . . you're lucky to catch me, actually. I'm off to the shop soon.'

'The shop. I see,' said Denise, who didn't see at all.

'Don't worry, though,' said Libby. 'It'll still be there in an hour. I expect you'd like to know what I've been getting up to with your husband while you've been away.'

'I wouldn't mind,' Denise replied.

'Lovely. Then I'll show you. First, give me your coat. Then we go straight upstairs . . .'

Grace appeared at peace, content that all to the rear of her was proceeding as the Great Canine had planned. Favour humped serenely and when his work was done rolled over and lapped, as gentleman dogs will. A trio of humans looked on reflectively.

'How do you do that, William?' asked Sam.

'I'm afraid I've no idea. You're the yoga man, aren't you?'

Sam tutted forbearingly. 'You know what I mean. Get them to do whatever you command.'

'It's not a matter of commanding. I simply had to calm them down. My dog charming skills were half the solution . . .'

'Yeah, where did you learn those?'

'Can't divulge that, I'm afraid – Special Forces business. I'd be in breach of the Official Secrets Act.'

'OK. What was the other half?'

'Ending my father's bizarre practice of lacing their meals with Kilkenny Kicker. He seemed to think it was an aphrodisiac.'

Galina spoke for the first time. 'Didn't work for *him*, I am believing.'

'Yes, well,' said William. 'Didn't work for Grace and Favour either. Just made them hyperactive.'

'Everywhere but up,' confirmed Galina bleakly.

William looked grave. 'Terrible business. Anyway, fingers crossed, you may have some puppies before too long. Good homes only at eight hundred a time – that should help pay the bills.'

'Puppies will be good,' Galina said, though there was sadness in her face.

A fourth voice was then heard from behind a hedge. 'Can I come out yet?'

'Oh, sorry, Derek,' called Sam. 'The main event is over. Favour's just mopping up.'

'He's not using the curtains, is he?' Derek asked.

'Don't worry,' said William. 'I'll sort him out.'

Derek emerged from the foliage but kept his hand over his eyes. He heard William utter again that strange noise with which he'd wowed his father's garden party guests – that sad, persuasive howl – and squinted through his fingers at William's mystic hands wafting both shar-pei away. Only then did he join the group. 'I'm sorry,' he said. 'There are some things I will never get used to.'

'Don't worry about that, old chap,' said William. 'You've been a big hero today.'

'Not really,' said Derek. 'What do you think poor old Lorcan – sorry, Norris – is doing now?'

'Getting to know his cellmate, I expect,' William said. 'But he won't be there for long. He'll be in an open prison in a week. Thanks to your help, Derek – and the shrinks, of course – my errant father is effectively regarded as more crank than criminal.'

'That's fair enough, isn't it?' said Derek.

'I suppose so. He isn't guileless, exactly, but you said it yourself in court. He's basically a dreamer. Lives in his own wacky world. Unfortunately, other people sometimes get dragged into it too.'

There was a sober silence. None of the men said it, but Galina's plight was foremost in all their minds. Sam looked at his watch. 'It's three o'clock,' he said. 'I'd better go and get the kids. Are you coming to their swimming lessons, Derek? If you can't visit Charlotte you might as well come with me. Beats brooding around the house.'

'OK,' Derek said. 'I'll tag along.'

Libby held open the shop door. Denise thanked her and walked in. 'Now this is the legitimate side of my business empire,' Libby explained. 'And thanks to your husband it's going very well.'

The shop looked completely different from the day Derek first set foot in it. Instead of Kids Nite Out it was now called Kids Kaleidoscope, which Derek thought said 'colour and variety' more clearly. Libby had been keen to stick with the wide range of flashy party outfits she'd specialised in before, and Derek had encouraged this because it was her unique selling point. However, he'd advised a refit so the goods were better displayed. The result was more space, more light, and fewer toddler shoes knocked to the floor.

'It's *lovely*,' said Denise. 'Do you have anything for premature babies?'

'I knew you'd ask me that,' said Libby.

'How did you know?'

'Silly question,' Libby replied. They both laughed. 'Seriously, though,' said Libby, 'I did order some specially. They're over here.'

Libby headed towards the counter and Denise followed her, still gobsmacked by what she'd learned. 'So what you've just done for me you've been doing for Derek all this time?' she'd asked as they'd left Libby's house. 'Yes,'

Libby had said. 'Once a month since just before Easter. He liked the handwork best.' Denise had laughed. 'Typical man!' Libby had lowered her lashes. 'Ooh, you are rude!'

Now Denise was astonished again as Libby produced the premature baby clothes, a selection of doll-size vests and Babygros. 'They're so tiny, aren't they?' she said. 'It's frightening.'

Libby was sympathetic. 'Well, try not to be too frightened any more. As I told you at the house, I think things are looking up.'

Denise felt tearful suddenly. 'I hope you're right.'

Libby put a hand on her shoulder. 'Look, why don't you take all these to show Charlotte this afternoon? Worry about paying me later. In fact, why don't you just have them? To be honest, I think I'm still in Derek's debt.'

'No, really, I couldn't . . .'

'Yes you could! Let's bag them up and then pop out for a minute. June will hold the fort.'

They left the shop again and were soon huddled over lemon tea in Serenity, the café Libby and Derek had used before. 'Listen,' Libby said, 'I want to be honest with you about Derek and me.'

'I thought you had been,' said Denise.

'Oh, I have. What I mean is I sort of want to break a confidence. It's unprofessional really, but in these circumstances I think it's the right thing to do. To be completely frank, I think it would be good for your marriage.'

'OK,' said Denise. 'Impress me.'

'The thing is,' said Libby, 'I have quite a lot of gentlemen like Derek. Top men, executives, strong-willed, but they feel they've lost their way. They can't see the way forward any more. That's the real reason they come to me, I think. Oh, they get a kick out of what I do for them upstairs – it's a bit naughty, isn't it, a bit wild? But the true benefit for lots of them is having the chance to get things off their chest. They tell me all their worries, all their doubts, about their wives or their children or their careers. These are men who are used to feeling in charge of their destinies, and suddenly, for whatever, reason, they don't feel it any more. And that's where I come in.'

Denise looked at her closely. 'And that's how you see Derek?'

'Very much so, yes. Although I've a powerful feeling that now you're back he isn't going to need me any more.' She reached into her handbag. 'But just in case either of you do want to make use of me, here are a couple of my cards.' She handed them over. 'They're a new design – Derek's suggestion. Quite attractive, don't you think?'

'They're lovely,' agreed Denise. She read them appreciatively.

ELIZABETH FORD
palmistry – tarot – clairvoyance
premiere service – confidence guaranteed

There was a small viewing area beside the learning pool, mostly inhabited by mums. Derek felt conspicuous. Sam detected this. 'They probably think you're my boyfriend,' he said brightly. He offered Derek a sweet. 'Fancy a Starburst?' he said, thinking of Opal Fruits.

'Not before we're married,' said Derek, thinking of Geoff.

Norton was lined up with the other beginners at the water's edge. In the distance, Derek could see Nessie in her shocking pink costume and Day-Glo orange goggles duck-diving eagerly after a rubber brick. She was a born water baby. Her nervous little brother had a long way to catch up.

'I like his headgear,' Derek remarked. For once, Norton wasn't wearing the maths hat. Instead, he sported a bright red swimming cap.

'I did it with Tippex,' said Sam. 'It's quite water-resistant, but it does need touching up.'

Derek squinted. The M was still clear, as were the T and H. The S, though, was almost gone and the A had lost its legs. 'Behold the moth hat,' he said drily, but Sam wasn't listening. He bit on a finger anxiously as the young woman instructor coaxed the children in.

'He has to do his star float,' Sam said. 'He *has* to this time, God, please.'

'What's a star float?' Derek asked.

'It means floating on his front with his arms and legs spread out and his face down in the water. That's the part he can't do yet. It's the confidence problem. He's been stuck on it for months.'

Derek looked on, concerned. Norton was the last to wade into the water and even by his high standards he looked deeply serious. The instructor made the children frog-jump from one end of the pool to the other. Norton did this well enough, but held his head painfully high for fear of splashing. Then they did ring-a-ring-a-roses. All the other children ducked under the water when the rhyme reached 'all fall down' but Norton ducked no lower than his chin. 'Oh dear,' groaned Sam and bit harder on his finger. Norton looked scared, Derek thought. He'd never seen that before.

'Go on, Norton,' he said. 'You can do it.'

'And now let's try some star floats,' the instructor enthused. Derek was starting to bite on a finger too when his mobile bleeped in his pocket. He tugged it out and saw that Denise had sent a text.

Little lad much better. Charlotte holding him. Sends her love. xxx

Derek stared at the message and reread it several times. During the minute this took up, his senses shut out everything around him: the urging of Norton's instructor, the cries of the children, the whole damp steamy clamour of the pool. He might have stayed that way for ages had Sam not elbowed him.

'Sorry, what . . . ?' Derek said, then looked in the direction of Sam's nod. From the pool Norton was demanding his attention.

'Look, Derek,' he cried. 'Look!' And suddenly he was floating face down in the water with limbs stretching towards the corners of the pool, the world, the universe. He stayed down for one second, two seconds, three seconds, four, then flipped upright again, blinking and smiling and bouncing with delight.

Sam and Derek got to their feet. They raised their arms in the air. They faced each other, beaming. 'Yes!' they yelled in unison. 'Yes! Yes! Yes! Yes! YES!!!'

# chapter 24

'Hi Jade? It's Amber? You won't believe what I'm seeing? It's, like, *amazing . . . ?*'

It was well past Nessie's bedtime although as she'd said to Sam, this wasn't *egg-zackly* a normal Friday night. And she was eight now and had been in Year 3 for more than a half a term, so there. *And* she'd been allowed to hold Charlotte's baby now he was home from hospital and getting on for three months old. *And* like a proper pretend auntie she'd had lots of ideas for what to call him from Moz's little book called *A Treasury of Baby Names*. Tarquin was a good one, though Fernando was better. Charlotte had said she'd think about them, which was what Charlotte said about everything. She was thinking about her boyfriend, too; still trying to make her mind up about what to do with him. Boys, thought Nessie – who needs them?

It wasn't a bad question for a little girl to ask in the company she was keeping at the time. She and seven grown men were in the games room at her home watching Norton dance: more geometrically than rhythmically, maybe, but he was only following the dance mat's orders and the most impressive thing was that he wasn't wearing his maths hat.

'Go there, Norton!' shouted Sam, clapping in time. He looked the happiest man alive.

Matthew was capturing the scene on his camcorder. He'd attempted Disco Duck at level one and concluded that ESTJs just don't dance.

Geoff was resting in the corner. He'd selected Lady Marmalade but after rashly showing off his gitchy-ya-ya wiggle had decided to sit down. 'I say Geoff, don't overdo it,' he'd declared. 'Not in your condition, mate.'

Lester was waiting for Norton to finish so he could have another turn. He'd already hot-stepped to Manilow's Copacabana at level three and seemed hell bent on trying to beat the machine.

William and Duncan were entwining at Twister.

Derek was thinking about certain key decisions he had taken recently: keeping the snot-and-red-hair DNA test result secret; developing Nessie and Norton's idea; not divorcing Denise. Three good ones out of three. It was a Vision Thing, really. And on the subject of Denise, he wondered what the ladies were doing.

The ladies were sitting down to eat. They did not, though, include Grace who was feeding rather than being fed: six shar-pei puppies suckled at her side as she slept. Favour was down the garden taking pleasure in his own company (as gentlemen dogs will).

331

'Is ready, I believe,' said Galina, stirring a giant saucepan of Belarusan stew (adapted from an Irish recipe). The crockery was provided by Hayley who'd set six places with her hand-crafted plates, each one individually designed.

'My goodness,' marvelled Phyllis, 'I wish Lester could see this.'

'Maybe he will later,' said Denise.

'Are they flowers?' asked Boudica. 'Or butterflies, maybe?'

The other women chuckled fondly.

'I have heard them described that way,' said Moz.

'They're inspired by Judy Chicago,' said Hayley. 'Do you know her work? *The Dinner Party*? A triangle of dinner plates and embroidered settings, each representing a great woman from history?'

'I saw it when I was twenty,' Moz said. 'It changed my life. Well, my attitude to vaginas anyway.'

'Oh,' said Boudica, blushing. 'Silly me.'

Derek returned to Hawker House at midnight leaving Nessie and Norton to sleep and Sam and the others to misbehave in peace. He went quietly upstairs in order not to disturb Charlotte who had left Galina's early pleading young mother exhaustion and some business she had to do on the phone. She was still doing it. Derek could hear her through her bedroom door.

'Oh *please* come tomorrow! He's *so* adorable! You're going to love him, honestly you are . . .'

He tiptoed into his bedroom and to his surprise found Denise already there. She was sitting at her late mother's *nouveau* dressing table wearing some brand new frothy French underwear. She didn't speak at first. Neither did Derek. Instead he reclined suggestively on the marital bed and peeled off his socks. He glanced at Denise's bare shoulders and her face in the angled mirrors. He saw that little strings of lint were all over the powder blue carpet from the inside of the socks, which had been new on that evening. He decided not to trouble the Dyson. He'd sooner look at Denise.

'Derek?' she said at last. 'Are you getting ideas?'

'Yes I am getting ideas. Quite interesting ones, actually.'

'Well, stop having them this minute.'

Derek was crestfallen. 'Why?'

'Because I'm saving myself, aren't I? Like a good girl.'

Sitting at the water's edge the following afternoon Derek saw that a smear of posset had appeared on the left shoulder of his jacket – a Hugo Boss suit jacket in grey-green silk and virgin wool, fitting for a man of fifty-one who'd reached a crossroads in his life and knew which way to turn. He smiled at Charlotte and said softly, 'I've been puked on.'

'What, again? He obviously likes you.'

'I can't think of any other explanation.'

Derek shifted his tiny grandson to the crook of his left arm. Charlotte applied a baby wipe, first to her father's suit then to the damp chin of her child. It was the fourth time since lunch they had completed this manoeuvre. Still, thought Derek, better now than later.

He lifted up the baby and kissed him on the nose. The two of them gazed for a while into each other's faces, the infant intently and yet without expression, the grandfather with pure pleasure in his eyes. The older of the two was first to blink and shifted his focus to the tableau to his right. Derek knew every detail of the great structure, of course, although from this distance and angle it seemed less familiar, less like his . . . well, his baby.

'There's one,' Charlotte said. Derek followed her pointing finger as it emerged from the cuff of her newly bought best dress. He squinted at the water's surface and then saw it as it darted, wings whizzing, to its left then hovered for a second, then darted away again. They were in the most secluded part of the Organic Project, the section furthest from parked vehicles and from the avenues of Harboreta itself. Although it owed its existence to a complex compromise between Quintessential Futures, the planners and the conservation groups, it had already evolved a life force all its own. The fish and aquatic plants had been joined by other creatures, genuine wildlife that was native to the area: frogs, birds and now dragonflies that skimmed, zigged and zagged. Although earnestly seeking food they gave the appearance of acting purely on whim. Derek rather liked the idea.

Charlotte, of course, responded to the dragonfly completely differently. She'd disbelieved her father when he'd told her they'd be there but called up the website of the

British Dragonfly Society. In response to a query she'd had the following reply.

> It is quite possible to see some species of dragonfly as late as October, or even in November in some years. The most likely species to be seen that late in the season are Common Darters and Migrant Hawkers. Both these species are very late fliers.

'If you say "I told you so" I'll scream,' Charlotte said.

'OK. I won't say "I told you so",' Derek replied. 'What type is it?'

'A Migrant Hawker, I'd say.'

'How fitting.'

'That's what I thought.'

'I'd thought it already.'

'Hadn't.'

'Had.'

'Had not.'

'Had too.'

They sniggered, fairly fondly. Derek checked his Omega Constellation. It was almost ten to three. He said, 'Time to go in, I think,' then added, handing Charlotte the baby: 'Madam, is this yours?'

She took the little boy and placed him gently in his pram, a Silver Cross Balmoral that Derek had insisted was better than any buggys on the market having conducted exhaustive research. The child was still small, frighteningly so to Derek's eyes. It worried him that his daughter seemed so fearless with him, but it impressed him more. They set off towards the mall and were soon walking together down one of the tree-lined boulevards that cut between the ranks of the parked cars. Derek had been especially pleased with those. 'Gives it a continental flavour,' he'd explained to Amelia. He'd been thinking of his mum and dad, of course.

'*Aeshna mixta*,' Charlotte said.

'Pardon?'

'*Aeshna mixta*. It's Latin for Migrant Hawker.'

'Oh, really?'

Derek was too busy being the centre of attention. Passing shoppers kept beaming at them and trying to peek inside the pram.

'Aeshna would make a nice name,' Charlotte said.

'For what?'

'For the baby.'

'He's not an insect!'

'Aeshna. I like it.'

'You're mad.'

'Anything to make you happy, Dad.'

They were approaching the rear entrance. The volume of shoppers increased accordingly and Charlotte steered the pram between them with great care. Derek walked watchfully in front. The atrium at the entrance contained towering red hibiscuses around which artificial streams and waterfalls were furled. Once inside, Derek and Charlotte sat and rested against its glass. They contemplated Top Shop, Gadgetshop and Boots yet neither felt involved. It was soothing. Then Derek said, 'Well, he's got to have a name soon or else he'll be illegal. I don't know why you've been dithering so long.'

Charlotte sighed: 'I know, I know, I know.' She looked away from Derek and down at her precious cargo. 'The thing is, Dad, you see . . . I'm only just daring to believe he's still alive.'

A small crowd had gathered round the circular Water Nursery, intrigued by the activity. Some sat on the parapets of the perimeter fountains, others leaned against trestle shelves on which glorious flowering plants were arranged for sale.

Derek spotted Ronald first. He'd driven down that morning and was now spreading a heavy, gold-coloured cloth across a small rectangular table. Then, as Derek, Charlotte and Aeshna worked their way into the marble-tiled central circle Nessie and Norton ran up to them. Nessie wore a long, peach-coloured frock with matching sequinned shoes. Her curls were tied back in a bow.

'You look *gorgeous*,' Charlotte enthused.

'Double gorgeous,' added Derek.

'Egg-zackly,' Nessie said. 'And Jade thinks so too.'

Norton wore a black velvet suit whose top half had a body panel of reflective silver quilting. A white shirt, black patent shoes and black bow tie completed his ensemble. And still no maths hat.

'And *you* look very handsome,' Charlotte told him.

'Do you agree, Norton?' asked Derek, who had an

interest in the matter. He'd bought the rig-out for Norton at Kids Kaleidoscope.

Norton looked at him levelly. He tried and failed to suppress a smile. 'Ach-ully yes,' he said.

Derek looked around. He could see immediately that Amelia had ensured his instructions were followed perfectly. Two miniature white marquees stood slightly apart and angled towards the far side of the circle. A red carpet unrolled from each and met to form a V whose point lay directly in front of Ronald's table. Derek went over to Ronald, who was immaculate in a dark blue suit and spotted tie. They shook hands warmly.

'Where is everyone?' said Derek.

'In the little tents,' said Ronald. 'We're starting in a minute. You ought to be in one yourself.'

'You're quite right,' Derek said.

'And while you're at it,' Ronald added, 'can you throw some of the others out?'

Derek did as he was bid. After kissing Charlotte on the cheek and touching Aeshna's tiny hand, he disappeared into the marquee on the right. Shortly afterwards Sam, Lester and Geoff emerged from it. Then from the other marquee spilled Phyllis, Moz, Boudica and Galina. All were looking happy, all were dressed to impress and all converged on Charlotte to make fun of her for wearing a posh frock. All but Geoff, that was. He converged on Galina instead.

'I say you're a fine-looking woman,' he announced.

'And you are a bachelor, I am thinking!'

'I say not for long, I hope.'

'Do you like children, Geoffrey?'

'I especially like the ones I make myself.'

'It takes two, you know,' put in Moz.

'I can vouch for that,' added Sam.

Charlotte looked suspiciously at her neighbours. 'You're *not*!' she said.

'I am,' said Moz.

'Both of us are,' said Sam.

At three o'clock on the button Amelia arrived and picked up the public address microphone. 'Ladies, gentlemen and children,' she said, 'valued customers. What you are about to witness is not an official ceremony. However, it is an important trial run for what I hope and believe will be regular occasions at Harboreta. Before we get under way, I'd like to say something about the man whose enterprise it is.

'Derek Hawker has a special place in Harboreta history. Before striking out to start on ventures of his own he played a very special role – indeed, the visionary leadership role – in the creation of the magnificent leisure destination we are standing in now. Without Derek Hawker, I think it fair to say, Harboreta would not exist. And how typical of his broad mind and brilliant imagination that Derek dreamed up this event after seeing two small children – Natalie and Norton Blake, who are also here today – introduce just such a facility into the home-made model mall they had built themselves. Natalie, Norton, Derek – thank you for your inspiration.'

There was a small round of applause and Amelia handed the microphone to Ronald. Without further ado he said, 'Can the first couple please come forward?'

There was some rustling and laughter from inside the two marquees. Then from the right one emerged Matthew in a claret-coloured suit, matching tie and purple carnation buttonhole. From the left one came Hayley in a white lace dress and veil. They walked down their respective red carpets until they met in front of Ronald who got on with the job without delay.

'Do you, Matthew Derek Hawker ESTJ, take Hayley Veronica Oakley ESFP to be your unlawful wedded wife?'

'I do,' said Matthew gladly.

'And do you, Hayley Veronica Oakley ESFP, take Matthew Derek Hawker ESTJ to be your unlawful wedded husband?'

'I certainly do,' said Hayley. 'Who wouldn't?'

They kissed and rubbed noses – Bunny Love loved Big Bunny and Big Bunny loved Bunny Love – then moved to the left side of the table. Ronald looked up expectantly and from the men's marquee stepped William in full dress white navy uniform, complete with cap. The crowd went 'Wooh!' and then went 'Wooh' again as from the same marquee another strapping chap emerged. This one wore the dark blue formal attire of a ranking police officer. He skipped neatly across to the other red carpet and nodded smartly to William. The pair then headed to Ronald's golden table in marching time.

'Do you, Captain William Tristram Grainger, take

Detective Superintendent Duncan Fergus McBride to be your unlawful wedded partner?'

'I do.'

'And do you Detective Superintendent Duncan Fergus McBride take Captain William Tristram Grainger to be *your* unlawful wedded partner?'

'I do.'

The couple exchanged a kiss. The crowd went 'Woooh!' for a third time, though one or two of the men said 'Gordon Bennett' or 'Shouldn't be allowed' under their breaths. Nothing stronger, though – they didn't fancy being hurled into the middle of next week.

Duncan and William took their places to the right of the table. Ronald again looked up and two more people emerged from the marquees, one from either side. It was a moment that would always stay with Derek. As he looked to his left and saw Denise for the first time that day he felt something unusual for him – a warm rush of recollection for the past.

Their paths met at Ronald's table as the other couples' had. Ronald said, 'I really *am* having to improvise this one. Still, let's make the best of it . . .' He smiled at them and drew breath.

'Derek Lester Hawker and Denise Eliza Hawker. I cannot tell you how much happiness it gives me to see you together on this day, exactly twenty-five years after you were wed, so eager to renew your marriage vows.'

They kissed and Denise hugged Derek with such enthusiasm that she knocked off his long-sight glasses. It didn't matter, though. Even without them Derek Hawker could see much more clearly now.

Joy appeared unconfined. There was, though, one person who felt a little down. She kept looking around but couldn't see him anywhere. She picked her baby up and kissed his head. And suddenly, among the watchers, she spotted his mop of hair. She saw his trench coat hanging open. She saw his camera pointing their way.

'Aeshna,' Charlotte said. 'I don't want to worry you. But I think you are about to meet your dad.'

# DAVE HILL

# Dad's Life

'How does a man react to being dumped on a Monday lunchtime with no kitchen table and three small children to pick up at half past three?'

When Joseph Stone's long time partner Dilys walks out on him, he doesn't mope on the side-lines of single-parenthood. He knows where the Toilet Duck lives and how to knock up a storming chicken nugget and beans. He's sure he knows how to be a Mum as well as a Dad to his three energetic children Gloria, Jed and Billy. He even scores in his love life again. But after he and Dilys agree to share the care of the kids – one week at Mummy's home, one week at Daddy's – he begins to feel distinctly second best to Dilys's mysterious new man, Chris. What does she see in this computer nerd in bush shorts? What is a Manly Men convention and what does Chris get up to when he's at one? What drives Joseph to dress up as a moose? And why is there a dead cat in his sports bag?

*Dad's Life* is a wonderfully warm, witty and true novel about fatherhood when family values fall apart and you're left holding the babies in one hand and your sanity in the other.

0 7553 0189 7

review

You can buy any of these other **Review** titles from your bookshop or *direct from the publisher*.

FREE P&P AND UK DELIVERY
(Overseas and Ireland £3.50 per book)

| | | |
|---|---|---|
| Green Grass | Raffaella Barker | £6.99 |
| Cuban Heels | Emily Barr | £6.99 |
| Jaded | Lucy Hawking | £6.99 |
| Pure Fiction | Julie Highmore | £6.99 |
| The World Unseen | Sharwin Serrif | £6.99 |
| Blackthorn Winter | Sarah Challis | £6.99 |
| Spit Against the Wind | Anna Smith | £6.99 |
| Dancing In a Distant Place | Isla Dewar | £6.99 |
| Dad's Life | Dave Hill | £6.99 |
| Magpie Bridge | Liu Hong | £6.99 |
| My Lover's Lover | Maggie O'Farrell | £6.99 |
| Ghost Music | Candida Clark | £6.99 |
| The Water's Edge | Louise Tondeur | £6.99 |

TO ORDER SIMPLY CALL THIS NUMBER

**01235 400 414**

or visit our website: www.madaboutbooks.com

Prices and availability subject to change without notice.